Riddle in the Sand

JACKSON RIDDLE

This is a work of fiction. All of the characters, names, incidents, organizations, and dialogue in this novel are either the products of the author's imagination or are used fictitiously.

WestBow Press books may be ordered through booksellers or by contacting:

WestBow Press
A Division of Thomas Nelson & Zondervan
1663 Liberty Drive
Bloomington, IN 47403
www.westbowpress.com
844-714-3454

ISBN: 978-1-6642-1110-0 (sc)
ISBN: 978-1-6642-1111-7 (hc)
ISBN: 978-1-6642-1109-4 (e)

Library of Congress Control Number: 2020921677

Print information available on the last page.

WestBow Press rev. date: 11/30/2020

To the three J's.

"Look at the nations and watch –
and be utterly amazed.
For I am going to do something in your days
That you would not believe,
even if you were told."

Habakkuk 1:5 (NIV)

Prologue

Monday, July 21, 1986

Dallas, Texas

No matter which direction they looked, Maggie Stone and Jackson Riddle could not escape their reflections. The fluorescent lights humming above the building lobby illuminated them in the wall of windows separating the darkened city street behind. The polished marble floor below carried their shadows forward toward the mirrored elevator doors which captured their portrait. Even the slouching gaze of the night guard seated at the residents' concierge desk seemed to reveal them.

Maggie clutched the red leather purse strap stretched tightly across her chest, different in style and texture from her modest denim dress that hid her slender figure. Which was the guard studying? She wondered, and immediately looked the other way. Jackson, dressed in a starched white shirt and yellow silk tie pulled into a severe knot below his opened collar, didn't notice her flinch. His left hand gripped the brass handle of the burgundy leather briefcase at his side, dividing him from Maggie. His right arm, bent at a right angle, supported his folded pin-striped suit coat, which obscured a smaller case clutched in his right hand. He bent forward, extended a finger on that hand and pushed the already lighted button, impatiently, and then looked at his watch as he withdrew his hand. The hour and the minute hands pointed straight up. Instantly, a voice sang in his mind: 'It's midnight, and I'm not famous yet.' He suppressed a laugh as he studied Maggie in the mirror. Would she laugh with him if he explained the inspiration?

The question made him concentrate more on this young woman - almost still a girl - tall and thin, intriguing, but not mysterious. She looked as if she knew more than she should, or would, tell. Not intimidated by his gaze, Maggie leaned into Jackson and put her arm through his, but their bodies remained separated by the briefcase. He looked older, and not just because he wore the uniform of a professional. With dark brown hair and a matching brown beard trimmed close, he stood confidant and erect, as if perpetually ready to speak. They made an odd couple, Jackson thought, and then asked himself again whether he could really like her this much - even love her - after only two days. Now returning his gaze in the mirror as the elevator still did not come, Maggie broke into a mischievous grin that, to Jackson, first answered, "Of course!" and then asked, "Why shouldn't you?"

Feeling Maggie's dare, Jackson's breath caught as the light dawned, a bell dinged, and the mirrored glass and steel panels opened on their future.

Tuesday, August 1, 1989

Tarpon, Texas

I

"Are you *still* contemplating your navel?" Maggie said, not asked, as she walked out onto the condo balcony where Jackson was sitting.

"What do you mean?" he answered, in a tone that indicated he knew exactly what she meant, but felt obligated to defend himself.

"You know exactly what I mean," she answered. "Whenever you sit for hours stroking your beard and looking off into the distance, I know that you're thinking of something. In the mood you've been in lately, it is probably something like, 'why do I have any innie instead of an outie?'"

He feigned hurt.

"If I had known you could be so cruel, I never would have married you."

"You knew exactly who I was, and what I was capable of doing," Maggie said, "and that's why you proposed to me two days after we met."

Jackson smiled and put his arms around her as she came within his reach. It was true. He had discovered her temperament quickly in their relationship, and it had led him to ask her to marry him before he had even given the idea a moderate going-over in his mind. He believed that it was the only truly spontaneous moment in his life — excluding certain acts of yuppie consumerism that shouldn't count. What surprised him most about the experience, though, was not its occurrence, but its endurance - the fact that after three years he had not once had a second thought about it. He may not have planned it, but his marriage was certainly turning out right. It was the way most things in his life had occurred, falling into place without much direction on his part, despite his often excessive contemplation – a contradiction that was just beginning to dawn on him.

"OK," he responded finally, and then asked, "but do you still have to hold that one lie I told you against me, particularly in my most introspective – weakest - moments? I have told you – and shown you - that I learned my lesson."

"Well, I was thinking of your first proposal, not the second, but now that you mention it." She stepped out of his grasp, leaned against the balcony railing and looked across the port toward the Gulf of Mexico. "It is true you learned a lot about me because of that lie. I couldn't believe you were telling me she wanted to borrow soap when I had just heard you tell her to grab a beer and wait for you to get off the phone. Did you really think I couldn't hear you?" Jackson sighed, wanting to avoid this, but he knew he had to answer.

"I've told you I wasn't thinking anything at the time, except that I didn't want you to get the wrong idea. It was intended to be an innocent visit, but all the other girls I'd ever dated would never have believed me. They wanted to hear — and would believe — anything rather than having to summon the courage to accept the innocent truth. I had learned it was easier just to be evasive." He paused, and then grinned. "I admit, though, that even with the worst of them, I'd have been pushing it with my soap story." Maggie laughed.

"Fortunately for you, I was so mad I hung up. By the time you got me back on the phone, you had shifted to repentance. Of course, even more fortunate for you was the fact that I had known a lot of girls like the ones you used to date, and I understood exactly what you meant about it being easier to lie than take a week of grief from them. I did the same thing with most of the guys I used to date." She turned and put her arms around him again. He accepted her hug, smiling, and then spoke.

"So you don't mind that, although we sort of made up on the phone, and agreed that I would fly to Houston to see you the next morning, I still enjoyed the evening with my new neighbor?"

Maggie jumped back from their embrace.

"You better not have!"

"I'm joking," Jackson grinned, and tried to put his arms back around her. She resisted cautiously, but then went limp and allowed him to hug her. After a second, he added, "It's taken three years, but I think I finally figured out a way to get the last word in on this story. Maybe we can bury it now, okay?"

"Only if you're telling the truth," Maggie said.

"I am," Jackson reassured her, "You know I was not proud of my lifestyle, and that I wanted to change it. Why do you think I attribute my reaction to you to God's intervention? I want you to tell that story, if you have to tell it, because it shows how I realized that I love you, and couldn't live without you, rather than how I started our relationship with a lie. I don't want it to sound like I had to marry you to be forgiven."

"It wasn't the start of the relationship, remember?" Maggie said. "I had known you two months by then, and was pretty sure I loved you, even if I didn't know you." She took another step away from Jackson and looked directly into his eyes, as if still trying to get to know him. She continued her stare long enough to decide that Jackson was, apparently, now telling the truth.

"I was *kidding,"* he said.

"Okay, I believe you," she said, "but it would be just like you to tell me the truth like that, as a joke, to ease your conscience, but still keep yourself out of trouble."

"Wow," Jackson laughed, "could I be that deceitful *and* guilt-ridden?"

"Definitely guilt-ridden; I haven't decided about guilty," Maggie replied.

"Hey," Jackson said, "you were the one who hid the fact that you were practically engaged. How then can you fault me for wanting to experience my adolescence a little late?"

"Twenty-seven is more than a little late to be acting like you just discovered whiskey and women," Maggie said.

"Ok. Well, thirteen was a little young, too, don't you think?

Maggie started to protest, but paused, smiled and said, "I was fifteen and I was tall for my age. Besides, I knew what was right, and what was wrong, and I had already made a decision to change my lifestyle before we met. Maybe that is why God drew you to me."

"Obviously, He did just that, even before I realized what He was up to. I don't remember when I discovered women – or girls. You know, it's weird that there isn't another word for females that fits between girls and women. Neither of those words seems right for the ones I'm thinking of. 'Guys' works for us, but 'gals' doesn't for you." He shrugged. "Whatever those females were, it wasn't until the two years before we met that I learned they could be manipulated."

"Lied to, you mean."

"Again, I prefer my term," Jackson answered. "Either way, it's true; it just wasn't until I got out of law school and came down here where no one knew I used to let people call me 'Jackie' right up to the time I became valedictorian of my high school class, that I realized some important things about your sex. That doesn't sound right either. Gender, maybe? Anyway,

I guess I got an idea with some of the lies I told Laurel in law school."

"Don't even get me started on that topic! You know how I feel about her," Maggie interrupted him.

"I know you hate her, but she's an important part of my life. It wasn't until she followed me to Texas, and I got involved with the waitress, that I realized how easy women were to deal with. I mean, these were two intelligent, attractive women that *had* to know what was going on, but no, even after they both ended up in my apartment at the same time they didn't, or wouldn't, recognize the reality. So, I didn't volunteer it. It was a terrible way to be, and I knew it then just as much as I do now. I wish I had had the courage to admit it then."

Maggie looked at Jackson blankly, and he had to gesture to make her focus.

"What?" She asked. "You want credit for that? You used all of your credit with me to buy that box of soap." She paused, and then clearly made a decision to explain. "Here I was, a nearly-innocent twenty-two year old kindergarten teacher thinking I had met someone really different, and suddenly I'm hearing the dumbest lie anyone has ever tried on me. How do you think that felt? I don't know why I forgave you." She paused again. Jackson wisely remained silent, and this time she spoke with tolerance. "Maybe it was because I remembered what those days were like. Maybe I thought the fact you were just then going through them leveled the playing field - raising my teacher's stature and lowering yours as a lawyer, if that was necessary. And *no,* it had nothing to do with you being an attorney, or that you drove a red Italian convertible. I know that kills you, but your car meant nothing to me." Jackson gave her a disbelieving look, and Maggie returned the same, saying "I don't understand your need for the car to mean something. How can your self-worth be so tied to an object?"

Jackson looked at the diamond necklace dangling from Maggie's tanned, slender neck, where it had been for almost their entire marriage, and started to point to it. He shrugged, instead. If she noticed his glance, Maggie didn't acknowledge it, but after a noticeable relaxing of her shoulders, she continued quietly.

"You were some weird mix of charm, ambition and weakness. Fortunately, the charm and ambition came through clearer than your weaknesses, and they tended to round you out."

"I don't remember asking," Jackson said.

"Well, it seemed like a good time to tell you," Maggie said, "and I'm still trying to understand your contradictions - like the fact that your friends came from all over the country to be at our wedding, but then didn't spend any time with you. They must have found out before me that you're the best friend they'll never know."

"No, that's an overstatement," Jackson responded. "I think they all thought I was with someone else. Anyway, you know I was just as happy to be by myself on our wedding day. I spent the whole time thinking about you, and how excited I would be to see you walking down the aisle. You were, and always will be, my ultimate weakness."

"You see, there you go again. I'm trying to improve you, and you stop me by saying something wonderful. Well, it won't work!" she declared. "I remember your other weaknesses. I was just about to recall your explanation for not drinking until you got to college, and for having never tried drugs. I should have turned and walked away when you told me that the legal drinking age was nineteen and that drugs, marijuana included, have always been against the law." She paused, before adding, "I didn't actually think of walking away, but I almost laughed out loud. Then I realized you were serious, and I didn't know what to think. It was almost *too* much." Maggie shook her head, contemplating again something she could not comprehend.

"Is there a point?" Jackson asked.

"I don't know," Maggie replied, "maybe only that I must have forgiven you for the soap story because it seemed to make you less weak. I mean, even if you had missed out on a lot of things growing up, you were finally catching up to some of them."

"That's very kind of you to say, and reassuring," Jackson said. "I am weak, but you married me because I tried, unsuccessfully, to lie to you about a date with my new neighbor." Maggie's body tensed again, and she looked hard at Jackson. Again, Jackson shrugged without reply, and Maggie continued.

"I guess," she said slowly, "the fact that you were interested in her is important. Don't you see that? Or are you really still that weak?"

"Maybe and probably. All I really remember about that time was how easy it was to meet women – or girls, or gals, whatever."

"Waitresses," Maggie said.

"Those, too," Jackson smiled. "Did I ever tell you about how I got started as the new me you are grudgingly coming to admire?"

"No, but it has to be better than the soap story."

"I don't know. You can judge. As I said, I had had this revelation while driving here from Tennessee. No one knew anything about me in Texas. I could act like, *be,* anyone I wanted. You can guess who, or what, that person was. I was eating lunch the first day I was in town, and the waitress was pretty."

"Oh, please! I don't have to listen to this."

"Yes, you do. You started it by wanting some insight into my soul. And remember, you've already promised before God to love me 'for better, or worse.'" Maggie rolled her eyes, and Jackson continued. "I asked her, 'If I tell you something will you try to believe I am sincere?'" Maggie put her head in her hands. Jackson paused, and then continued. "I told her 'I think you are the most naturally beautiful girl' - I think I used 'girl' instead of 'woman' - 'that I have ever seen, and I know you must hear that sort of stuff from guys in here all the time, but I really mean it. You're beautiful, and you don't even look like you try.' I think I really did believe what I said, even if I wasn't saying it altruistically. She pretty much ignored me, but again, in my new persona, I kept trying. After about three more meals and one big tip, she said 'yes'." Maggie shrugged and held out her hands, palms up.

"So? Is there a point to *this* story?"

"Yes, as a matter of fact, there is. About two years later, I only had to ask *you* once."

"Oh, that is rich! Because you picked up some waitress in a bar, you became the man I couldn't live without?"

"The stories do have their similarities. That was in a bar. We met in a bar. She was naturally beautiful. You are the *most* naturally beautiful woman, ever. I was shy then. Well, it's not a perfect analogy."

"I'll say. You're not shy, or perfect. You just couldn't die without telling me that story. I'm really sick of this waitress. First you talked about her as your best friend. Then you admitted you had dated her; now I find out you picked her up in a bar, bought her actually. You just don't know when to stop, do you?"

"That's not true." Jackson said. "I always know when I've gone one step too far – like now. Someday, maybe, I'll be able to realize when I'm *about* to go too far, and learn to stop one-step short of that point. I know clients, and probably judges, would like for me to learn that. But look, I thought we were just trying to gain a little insight here. As painful, or just as annoying, as some of this information may be to you – and I'm sure you could give me some of the same medicine – the important thing is what we have become, regardless of what went on in our lives before that night in the bar." Maggie looked at Jackson for more than an instant without smiling, then finally spoke.

"*Bus.* We met on the bus, remember?"

"Yes, *I* remember, but you have always said that you don't remember being introduced on the bus. So, obviously, I fell in love with you first, because I remember clearly the first time I saw your face, leaning into the aisle of the charter bus when your brother introduced us. How many guys can say that about their wives? Do you know how special that is to me? You may think from all this stuff I'm telling you that I was just looking for my next step up the ladder of success – and maybe I was – but clearly there was something about you that demanded more of me. I certainly don't remember the first time I saw any other girl, woman, or anyone else in my life for that matter. And, I never seriously discussed marriage with anyone else, even though I dated some girls for several years. I was ready to marry you after two *days*. So, you had to be different, and frankly, I am proud that I noticed. I saw you as someone who was not just beautiful to me on the outside – which I realized when I first looked into your eyes – but then I learned that you were beautiful on the *inside,* after so many hours of talking to you in just two nights. We packed more discussion into those two nights and mornings than most couples do in months – or in my case – years! Miraculously, that contrast was not lost on me, and so, whether you like it or not, the experiences I had with other girls – and was still having when we met - somehow made me different at just the right moment. Sure, the soap story proves that I had a little more growing up to do, but I've explained that the episode – particularly your response - just shocked me into realizing that you were what, or rather who, I wanted and needed in my life. I'm sorry I didn't come to the realization in a more positive manner, but at least I got there, and have been trying to express my thanks to you ever since. That's worth something, right?" Jackson paused and tried to smile, hoping that Maggie would smile, too. After a moment, she did, and then spoke.

"Obviously, I found something in you that I liked, even if it didn't register quite as fast with me as it did with you. Of course, I did agree to go out with you the day after we met, so I wasn't exactly slow. I guess I didn't, and still don't, really care what you were like before we met."

"Including the soap story?"

"We're married, aren't we? I absolved you."

"Bless you, you truly beautiful woman," Jackson said, as he put his arms around her from behind and rested his chin on her shoulder.

"We are blessed, aren't we," she said, not as a question, but then asked, "so maybe that realization will snap you out of the funk you've been in lately?"

When Jackson did not answer, she pulled out of his embrace and turned back toward the open sliding glass door. "Then I'll leave you here with your fascinating thoughts, while I go make a pitcher of margaritas."

"Are you going to drink the whole pitcher like you did in the bar on the night we met?" Jackson called to her, but this time Maggie did not respond.

II

Jackson sat back down before the then calm, but soon to be troubled, waters of the Gulf of Mexico. He resumed the contemplation of his birth and near death, that had occupied his mind most of the afternoon. He reviewed again the familiar story as told by his mother. For as long as he could remember, she had told him, and anyone who would listen to her, that he should have died at birth - that the doctors had given him one chance in a thousand to live. She claims that she prayed to God to let him live, and promised that if He answered that prayer, she would raise Jackson right.

'Ha,' Jackson thought. Because he lived, his mother still insists that God has a special purpose for Jackson's life.

"Hmph!" Jackson expressed aloud this time, in apparent derision of both his mother and him. A seagull laughed aggressively on the dock one story below him, and Jackson wondered whether the bird shared his scorn at his mother's conviction, or rather expressed its own scornful view of Jackson. The gull took flight across the port, mocking him all the way with a fading call: "Jaaack, Jaacck, Jaaaacccck!"

Dusk began to settle on the water, and on the moored and moving boats visible in the port from the balcony. Now past 7 p.m., his mood brightened as the heat subsided with the lowering sun. Although only his third day on the island, early evening was already his favorite time in Tarpon, Texas.

Dusty sunlight, slanting from the west and broken by the building, created shadows on his balcony and provided some shelter from the insistent August heat. Boats returning from the day's activity in the Gulf seemed to glide by, satisfied with themselves. Gone was the noise and urgency of the morning's trek out of port that had awakened Jackson at 6 a.m. The voices on board were now muted, and Jackson noticed that even the boats' engines seemed to purr on the return to the dock, as if "Shhhh" had been added to the "No Wake" sign posted on the rock jetties. Co-workers and family members waited on the public dock with anticipation for the return of their fishermen. They all appeared content, rather than anxious, in the softening light. It was the time he had heard described as the "blue hour," and the royal blue and gold tints hovering over and reflecting off the water were almost enough to ease his problem out of mind.

He was just beginning to experience something in Tarpon that he could not yet articulate, but that felt familiar. From the books he had read before this trip, including one that lay under his chair at that moment, Jackson knew that Tarpon was a town — still a village, actually — that had outlived its namesake, even though it had been named for a fish rather than a person. Hunkered down on the northern tip of the gulf coast barrier islands at the entrance to Corpus Christi Bay, the sand had previously been home, in succession, to Indians, Spaniards, Mexicans, Texians, Americans, Confederates, Yankees, and then, Americans again, all who fought against invading forces to remain there.

Jackson wondered whether it was appropriate to distinguish Confederates from Americans, but he had been raised in "The South", and he knew that in a Southerner's mind the leaders of the Confederacy had intended to create a new America, one wholly distinct from the Northern America controlled by Yankee industrialists. Perhaps, Jackson thought, the designation should be Confederate Americans and Yankee Americans, like Central Americans. The continent's group designations were changing all the time – Indians had become Native Americans, and Blacks were now mostly African Americans. Why couldn't Southerners be Confederate Americans? They might like that, although he personally would not subscribe.

Whatever the diverse designations of the successive inhabitants of Tarpon, Jackson now observed before him the livelihood of almost all of them – fishing. At first, the inhabitants fished just to feed themselves and their families, but the plentiful catches soon enabled them to trade with others in a barter economy. Eventually, families began to focus on particular catches, and the shrimpers and bay fishermen began to earn hard currency by selling to restaurants. Later, coastal produce companies began to take the fruit of all of the day's labor from all of the boats. A community of fishermen began to assemble, but unlike the modern concrete and brick five-story building where Jackson was staying, these men lived spartanly, either on their boats or in loosely stacked driftwood shacks - dwellings that rested uneasily on the promontory just yards from the Gulf. These fishermen were unwilling to take refuge far from their boats.

Dug into the sand for both warmth and cooling, the driftwood gables barely reached above sea level. Any person approaching the island's point from the mainland glimpsed across the channel what appeared to be an armada of driftwood floating on the tide and guarding the entrance to the bay - as if flotsam had collected there after a storm. From his second-story condominium balcony, Jackson could see the very place where most of these fishermen once resided, and some fisherwomen, too. Within his narrow field of vision he could see commercial and pleasure fishing boats returning from the Gulf, cutting their motors in mid-channel at that very moment, as they made the sharp turn into the opening between the quarried rock jetties that now formed the port of Tarpon.

Although most of the old fishermen and these modern boatmen were likely ignorant of the fact, the soldiers of Cortez, Santa Ana, Sam Houston, R.E. Lee and U.S. Grant had all bivouacked in virtually the same spot, and fashion, for no real development came to Tarpon until after the wars had been fought. Once their nationality had been determined for good, though, the fishermen who founded the village to catch fish for themselves soon learned that a better living could be made by catching them for others. Some then discovered that an even better income was available by showing others where and how to catch the fish. The vocation of fish-guiding simply evolved when the stow-away on the commercial boat or the tag-along on the skiff either offered or was coerced into paying for the experience. Soon boats were hired for this purpose alone, first for one or two persons, and later for dozens at a time. The experience that most of them sought was to catch a tarpon.

Although he had been in Texas over five years now, Jackson had learned all of this only recently, following an unexpected invitation to fish the Gulf with one of his firm's clients. The impromptu offer had been made only three weeks before, in a 32nd floor conference room in a shimmering emerald glass skyscraper in Dallas, the exterior of which resembled the water in the marina immediately below his balcony. The blue had turned green in the shade from the sun, but retained its reflective quality, making it look even more like Jackson's office building.

He had never been off shore before, nor had he ever been to Tarpon. Although he was not totally committed to the fishing trip, he was intrigued by the promise of a week's rest on an island, even if it was just an extension of his adopted home state, and one that was perpetually in view of the mainland and often not actually distinguishable from it. Upon arriving two nights before, his ready acceptance of the invitation seemed validated by the feeling he had gotten as he crossed the channel at midnight on the brief ferry ride. There was something encouraging in the thick salt air, and even something intriguing about the dark water of the channel that stretched out toward the even darker Gulf. His uncertainty, however, about venturing out into the Gulf had undercut the freedom he had sensed in the salty air and gentle departure from the mainland.

Now Jackson forced a smile as he watched a commercial charter boat, the *Gulf Eagle*, chug through the channel with a dozen or so customers leaning on the rails, attempting to relive history. He reached under his chair and picked up the book, *Tarpon Quest*, by John Cole. Just that morning he had read the author's passionate description of the village's namesake - "an ancient and honored fish surviving from another geological epoch." The tarpon's reputation for valiant struggle had earned it the nickname "Silver Gladiator," and quickly made it the sport fisherman's obsession. Cole quoted a financier and fisherman named Anthony W. Dimock as declaring that "to one who has known the tarpon, the feeble efforts of the salmon to live up to its reputation is saddening...." Dimock further asserted that "the tarpon meets every demand the sport of fishing can make."

Such a challenge to the American spirit - and such an opportunity for commerce, Jackson thought - could lead only to the tarpon's demise, at least in a place so identified with it that it bore its name. Jackson paused at the thought that a creature's spirit, admired by all, would be the cause of its doom, and this brought him back to his mother's prophecy for his life, only from the opposite perspective.

Truthfully, he admitted only to himself, he had always felt special, like the most important person in any group - that his opinion was always right, and that everyone was always looking at him for the right answer to any question. Despite some actual experience to support his belief, he had never identified this as a direction from God. It felt, and occasionally sounded, like arrogance. But was it arrogance for a tarpon to refuse to acquiesce to the hook and line that tethered it to some unknown, but presumed tragic, destiny?

Only slightly bothered by the strained association, Jackson shook his head and tried to focus again on what confused him about his own story - how he could have been so close to death at his birth and yet have no disability, no scars and no memory of it. For a long time, he wasn't even sure that he believed it had been so. Although he did not yet have children, in his limited experience parents often exaggerated when talking about their children, and he had several other reasons to question his own mother's credibility.

Even so, several years before while he was in college, he had seen a television show about his disease. It reported that even then, in the late 1970's, almost half of the afflicted babies died from it. The show mentioned one of President Kennedy's children as perhaps the condition's most prominent victim. So, assuming his mother was telling the truth and he had had the disease, its seriousness could not be doubted. He wondered if his medical records were still available, but then frowned again. What would actual medical evidence prove? His being alive confirmed his recovery. What he wanted to know was what effect this experience had had on his life. Was it the reason he thought so often of death now? Perhaps having escaped it once, he was doomed to succumb in his next serious encounter.

'Just my luck,' he thought, and even wanted to mutter aloud, thinking of having exhausted his allotted supply of grace as an infant when he didn't understand or fear death. Now, as an adult (at least, at 30, he guessed he was an adult), he still did not understand death, but certainly feared it.

A sleek and beautiful sport fishing boat, over forty feet in length he guessed, sauntered by the balcony to the rear of the port, with two equally sleek, beautiful women showcasing themselves on deck. Their glances toward his balcony caused Jackson to look down and open the book, intimidated even from a distance of perhaps thirty yards. He focused on the book's back flyleaf, and then flipped back a few pages from the end, scanning the conclusion. "As for the tarpon, no one knew exactly when the end came, or even whether the fishermen had won. Suddenly, one day, someone realized that no one had caught a tarpon in Tarpon for a while; and then, no one ever did."

The realization of the tarpon's demise was delayed because other fish remained, and the fishermen kept coming — both for a living and for sport. Lodgings and restaurants were built, often together. The early ones appeared in a fashion only slightly advanced beyond the original driftwood shelters. Some were more civilized. The earliest and most enduring one was named simply, the Tarpon Inn. It stood barely one hundred yards from where Jackson sat, but was obscured from his view by the bricks and concrete of his condo building, which as a sign of "progress" had been built actually *in* the port on reclaimed wetlands. The mere names alone – "condo" and "inn" – struck Jackson as telling distinctions between the eras.

The inn was a long, barracks-style wooden structure built a few hundred yards back from the channel, just beyond where the original driftwood huts had crouched. Only two-stories high, but raised six feet off the ground to protect against a storm surge, it presented a full-length porch on the first floor and a matching balcony on the second, complete with white posts and picket railings, and white rocking chairs before each room's matching window. Its length (twelve rooms' worth) in proportion to its depth (a single room's worth) suggested a movie-set construction, just like the two-dimensional, sepia-toned historic pictures prominently featured in all the visitors' guides. The Inn had, in fact, appeared in several movies filmed on the island, both fictional and documentary, and boasted that the famous actress Hedy Lamarr had once stayed there. It was a building that evidenced a sense of purpose, one that spoke to anyone who looked at her, saying *I know why I am here.* As Jackson and Maggie discovered it on their first night's walking tour of the island, she had commented on how "authentic" the building was. Recognizing its sense of history, Jackson instead heard a challenge: *why are you here?*

Understanding that one has a purpose in life does not, of course, resolve the more important question: what is it? Jackson had concluded repeatedly that he could never discern his purpose from his disease because he never felt a part of the experience. Indeed, for him, it was no experience at all. He was struck by the thought that infant trauma is actually an experience for the adults, rather than the stricken child. The parents feel the pain as palpably as the child, and if the child dies the parents must live with the loss – although he believed that his parents did not live so well with his recovery. He hypothesized that the child who never lives at all suffers no loss, and he was unconvinced that an infant could really experience pain since it is forgotten as soon as it goes away, like in a dog. Is pain really in the moment or in the past? Or is it in anticipation - before the moment and the past? What was it Solomon had written about a dying infant? *Though it never saw the sun or knew anything, it has more rest than does a man even if he lives a thousand years....* Jackson's own case was evidence of that. He had nearly died at birth, and he couldn't remember anything about it – couldn't even prove that it was so. Now, as an adult, he craved knowledge about it, and from it.

Now, he thought again of the self-assurance and definite sense of belonging expressed by the Inn, and shrugged at being mocked by a building. *First a seagull, and now a motel,* he thought. Yet, architecture can be a powerful force, he knew, and this really wasn't just any motel, he rationalized. The location, the look and its length of operation (since 1886) were perhaps distinguishing enough characteristics, but, like all established landmarks, the Tarpon Inn had a further story to tell, a specific claim to fame.

Entering the office that first night through a French door on the far right of the first floor, Jackson had been startled by the dingy, peeling wallpaper. He was inclined to turn and walk out, satisfied that the façade that had arrested him was a fraud (and hadn't that word come to mean just that?) But before he could flee, Maggie had plunged forward and begun her typically curious evaluation of the matter. Upon closer examination, she discovered that the walls were not peeling, but rather *scaling.* They were covered from shoe-molding to crown-molding with individual tarpon scales, over 7000, they learned, and each one bore a handwritten record of the date its body was caught, its total weight upon arriving back at the dock, and the signature of the conquering angler. Gazing around the room at the thousands of catches recorded there, the story of the tarpon's demise in Tarpon was written on the motel's walls – or tacked there.

The sight had fascinated and repulsed Jackson. On the one hand, it was an enduring memorial to the tarpon, and a fitting public record of the village's popularity with fishermen. On the other, it was more sad evidence of the insatiable obsession of men (and women) to subdue the earth and its creatures, as if to prove forever they have dominion over both. Jackson had wandered around the room for several minutes reading various scales and wondering about the events recorded by them. Were there twin scales nailed to walls in paneled rooms all around the country, or pressed between the leaves of books and wedged on overcrowded shelves, perhaps never to be seen again by the owner, or anyone? Was this the purpose of these valiant fish – to placate the desires of conquering humans, or to provide a seedy authenticity not only to this room, but to the village as a whole?

Jackson was jolted out of his reflection of the inside of the fish, back into the twilight of his balcony, by a blast from the jetty boat's horn as it launched, carrying the fishermen to be transported across the channel and deposited on an adjoining island for the night. He marveled at the passion, and then scoffed at the folly, of fishing all night on an otherwise uninhabited island when the same catches would be available at several restaurants and even the local grocery store tomorrow. Clearly, these fishermen – and women, too, he noted - had developed their sense of purpose.

Such assurance caused Jackson to turn his thoughts toward a broader consideration - instances in history of lives lived with a clear sense purpose, even destiny. From his morning's reading, the name Saul came into his mind. Not the one who was chosen the first king of Israel, although he was some evidence of destiny as one hand-picked by God from all the men of the nation, but Jackson was not even a member, much less the tallest or the most handsome of God's chosen people. He thought rather of another Saul – one of shorter stature and, by his own admission, much poorer features. This Saul was also chosen by God in miraculous fashion, but for religious slavery rather than royalty. His servitude included a new name, and recognition that he had been set apart from birth to accomplish a mission established by another. That seemed proof, to Jackson, that one can have a purpose, even from infancy. Saul lived by the conviction that he had been so wrong in his persecution of Christians that Jesus personally had intervened from Heaven to blind him, rename him Paul, and send him into the desert for three years of instruction on "all that he must suffer for My name's sake."

I don't think I want that much direction, Jackson thought, *even if it means having the certainty of knowing it comes directly from God.* Suddenly, he heard a different voice, that of his wife, calling from the kitchen.

"Tequila!"

He stood quickly, as if compelled, and his head rushed. He leaned forward and grabbed the railing with both hands - the night falling over the water briefly fell also over his sight and mind. The sensation passed and he stood up straight, and then looked directly out across the port. At that moment, a silver ribbon fish jumped and reflected the first visible rays of the security light from the jetties.

Would you give up your life to be famous? He asked the fish, thoughtfully. Jackson wondered if the last scale that he had viewed at the Inn was the answer to that question. As he had finally turned to leave the motel office, he had paused at the door beside the check-in counter, where one more scale caught his eye. There, under the glass top of the desk, beneath an old ledger-book, laid another historic record — an archive, even - a small crinkling tarpon scale inscribed with these numbers: *5/9/37, 77 lbs., 8 oz.* Below the shakily written numbers was an even shakier, but legible, signature: *Franklin D. Roosevelt*. Even the Nation's president had been drawn to Tarpon by tarpon during the worst period of the Great Depression, perhaps to show the country that he (and they) could overcome something, or anything. Jackson's initial reaction was to be impressed, and he had even called Maggie over to show it to her. Now, however, the thought of a crippled U.S. president being lowered into a boat in his wheel chair to hasten the tarpon's demise depressed him mightily. Did the tarpon die for its country, or did the country just destroy it? And should the village of Tarpon be praised or razed as a consequence? How would the apostle Paul answer that question?

Now Jackson was staring into the water searching for an answer as Maggie returned to the balcony and handed him a margarita made as he liked it – on-the-rocks, with salt. He took a sip, and tasted first the salt, and then the liquor, feeling relief. He raised his glass to Maggie, who returned the salute with her own. Jackson then reached out and touched "play" on the portable cassette player balanced on the railing between him and the port. The machine clicked and growled and broke into the gathering silence with words from quite a different prophet than Paul — one Jackson quoted more often, and perhaps valued more highly, and certainly consulted more often. Jimmy Buffett prophesied or philosophized in a high-spirited wail:

"Salt air it ain't thin. It'll stick right to your skin and make you feel fine.

And I want to be there, I want to go back down and die beside the sea there,

With a tin cup for a chalice, filled up with good red wine."

Wine or tequila, it didn't matter. Jackson breathed deeply, as if inhaling the sentiment of the song. The words were more cheerful than those that had stuck in his head earlier:

"Spinning around in circles, living it day to day.

But still twenty-four hours, maybe sixty good years, it's really not that long a stay."

Shaking his head at the thought that he was already

half-way through his good years, Jackson concluded, as he always did, that it is tragic to be born with a sense of purpose, but no proof or understanding of it.

He raised his glass to Maggie again, and then took another, longer drink. He felt some relief, even if momentarily, from his search for meaning, but he knew that he would have to live with the burden until he either figured out his purpose, or simply accepted that he had already failed it. Either way, he was certain that she believed he had already overthought it.

III

George Waters had planned their fishing trip for Wednesday. It was intended as the highlight of the vacation, and was the actual basis of the invitation Jackson had received. Jackson had told everyone in his office that they were going fishing off-shore, as if that was the sole purpose of the trip. It sounded to him more exciting than admitting that they would mostly just be sitting by a swimming pool in a condo complex by the Gulf, which, of course, wasn't even a real ocean. Despite his expressed excitement, Jackson was actually dreading the fishing trip. Neither he nor Maggie had ever been out to sea, and their discussions of the trip were always burdened by an unspoken fear. It wasn't so much a fear of the sea, as it was a terror of seasickness. They anticipated it so clearly that the experience loomed before them like a surgery, and this was even before they heard the stories about George, or learned about the hurricane.

Later Tuesday evening they wandered the island looking for a place to eat. It's commercial establishments crouched at the sides of less than a mile of two main roads, one extending about a half mile east from the ferry landing to the only traffic light, and the other running perpendicular to the right for another half mile to the beginning of the state road. They had walked to one end and back, investigating the many run-down buildings trying to pass as inviting restaurants, when they finally decided on a low cinder-block bunker painted white with ocean blue trim. It was next to their condo, and would have been their first stop had they turned right rather than left coming out of the complex. The name "Island Cafe" was painted in ocean blue block letters above the door, but a former name, "Jacque's," was still visible through the painted white background. Beside the door stood a newspaper box shaped like a television set on a pedestal. The screen flashed this warning: "COAST BRACES FOR HURRICANE CHANTAL."

"Look at this!" Jackson said, with concern, as he turned to Maggie who had been walking behind him. Reading the headline, Maggie responded in her own excited voice.

"Where is it?"

"I don't know," Jackson answered, and then added, "Unusual name, though."

They fed three quarters into the upper-right corner of the box, extracted a copy of the paper, and took it into the cafe. Ignoring a weathered waitress, they studied the weather map which showed in a four-color swirl a cloud mass like a galaxy invading the Gulf of Mexico, heading directly for the Texas coast. This was news to them.

In planning the vacation, Jackson had agreed to abandon his usual devotion to the news. On a normal day, he would wake up at 6:30 a.m., to the morning news program on public radio and listen through at least two cycles of news reports, which were repeated on the half-hour. At his office by 7:30, he would spend at least thirty minutes scanning the New York *Times*, which repeated most of the news reports he had just heard on the radio. *Which reported it first, he wondered?* Surely, the *Times*. Later, at 4:00 p.m., he would turn on a radio he kept in his office for ninety more minutes of news and information on the public station's afternoon program.

His dedication to this schedule was almost an obsession, and it had irritated Maggie when they had first met. But soon, Maggie found herself adhering to his schedule, even if he wasn't around, and it became a source of conversation for them.

One of their agreements for this vacation, however, was that they would break out of their routine, and go without news. It helped that there was no television or radio in George's condo. Consequently, word of the hurricane, such as it was prior to the newspaper account, had escaped them. Now, they learned that during the previous night the then tropical storm had accelerated in strength and shifted direction, so that it appeared to be headed straight for their island as a full-fledged hurricane, with a name neither Jackson nor Maggie were familiar with. Strangely, its appearance seemed to brighten their spirits about the fishing trip, rather than heighten their fears. Perhaps it was because they now had some justification for their dread, but more likely by the possibility that the trip could be canceled due to an act of God.

"Wow! It knocked over an oil rig," Jackson said. "Ten men are missing."

"Where was that?" Maggie asked, concerned for the men principally, but also for herself.

"About forty miles off the coast of New Orleans," Jackson read from one of the multi-colored illustrations that accompanied the brief text.

"That sounds pretty far out for an oil platform," Maggie observed.

"It sounds pretty close to here, especially for people who are about to go on their first deep-sea fishing trip in the same Gulf," Jackson answered, but then added quickly, "not to be unconcerned about the missing men."

"Well," Maggie said, "we can't do anything about them,

but we can watch out for ourselves. You should check with George. It doesn't sound like we should be going out there tomorrow."

"We can call him after we eat," Jackson decided. "He said he'd be at his shop late tonight." Jackson completed his review of the front page, and flipped through the sections of the paper like a roll-a-dex, glancing quickly at the headlines in "Business" and "Sports." When he reached the section named "Entertainment!" - punctuated with bright red ink and an exclamation point - he instinctively pulled it from the pack and handed it across the table to Maggie.

"Thanks," she said. "I could use some good gossip from Hollywood."

"Fine with me," Jackson said, pulling out the Business and Sports sections for himself, and dropping the rest of the paper on the floor beside their table, "just keep it to yourself." They read quietly for several minutes, interrupted only by the waitress, who handed them greasy, laminated menus.

"Wow!" Jackson said again, as the waitress walked away from the table and toward the open counter separating the kitchen from the dining area. Maggie looked up, thinking that he was referring to the waitress, but his head was still in the paper. "Look at this," he continued, showing her a picture of a very large oil tanker listing badly and being pushed into a harbor by several tug boats. "It's the Exxon *Valdez* coming into the San Diego harbor for repair," Jackson explained.

"How could it make it all the way from Alaska to San Diego with a hole in its hull big enough to spill millions of gallons of oil?" Maggie asked, glancing inattentively at the photo.

"Good question," Jackson admitted. "Better ask your brother the oil-company engineer, not your husband the English major turned bankruptcy lawyer." Maggie didn't respond, but rather went back to her section of the paper, and read for a few more minutes in between bites of a wheat cracker.

"Okay," she said suddenly, "you've got to listen to at least one hard news story from me." Jackson didn't look up from the Sports page, but Maggie continued. "That actor avoided prosecution for videotaping a sex act with a 16 year-old."

"What? Did they decide she entrapped him?" Jackson looked up, and asked.

"I'm sure he just talked his way out of it somehow."

"I'm sure she told him she was at least 19," Jackson offered. "A clear case of entrapment, if not false imprisonment. Kind of like us."

"Yeah, right." Maggie folded the paper as the waitress brought the dinners they had ordered. She was having a salad, and Jackson a cheeseburger with fries. After only a few bites, Maggie put down her fork. "There is so much dressing on this salad I might as well have had a cheeseburger like you. It would stay with me longer, and be about the same calories."

"You can order one if you want," Jackson suggested, "or you can have mine. I'm losing my appetite anyway."

"Why?" Maggie asked. Jackson folded his section of the paper and handed it over to her. She took it from him and looked at a picture of an old woman in a heavy coat and scarf, looking at empty shelves. Maggie read the caption to herself: 'There are increasing food shortages in Poland as the Communist government tries to hold on to power by implementing some Western reforms. One of those is removing price controls, which causes food shortages.'

"I'm a few years removed from Economics class," Jackson observed, after the moment he assumed was long enough for Maggie to absorb the report, "but I think I understand the connection." Maggie unfolded the paper and started to read the text of the story. She stopped after a few lines, and handed the paper back to Jackson.

"Then, that would make one of us. We didn't even cover *Home* Economics in my education classes."

"No macroeconomics?" Jackson kidded her. "How about world affairs?" Maggie shook her head when it wasn't necessary. Jackson continued, "Well, if you look at the bottom of that page, you'll learn that Vietnam has labeled the Khmer Rouge 'the most barbarous regime in history' in the talks over Cambodia. There has to be a lot of competition for that title," he observed. "And, no one knows how many students were killed in Tiananmen Square, not even the Chinese government." He looked back down at his plate. "Kind of reminds me of my childhood - watching Walter Cronkite's reports about Vietnam while we were eating dinner. It wasn't very good for my digestion. Let's not do that to our children, okay? Assuming we ever have children."

"Hey, of course we'll have children," Maggie responded, sounding surprised.

"Okay," Jackson conceded, "I just don't want them to associate family dinners with world politics and man's inhumanity to man. Starving children in Africa, perhaps, as a reminder of our blessings, but mass murder and questionable wars, definitely not."

"Okay," Maggie answered emphatically, "we agreed, no news this week, so we should practice what you're preaching." She started to drop her section of the paper on top of the pile on the floor, but stopped and skimmed a short story. "This probably won't help your appetite, but the Bee Gees are starting their first U.S. tour in several years, and are hoping for a little respect from the American music critics."

"You're right. That didn't help my appetite," Jackson said, as he pushed back from the table. "Let's go get a local weather report from George." They stood up to go as the waitress was bringing the check. Jackson had picked up the paper and started to fold it under his arm, but instead handed it to the waitress in exchange for the check. "Maybe one of your local customers will be more interested in this," he said.

"Oh, did you read about the TED's?" She asked in an excited tone.

"Ted Kennedy?" Jackson asked.

"No, no," the waitress laughed, laying the paper open on the table and searching for a story. "T.E.D.'s! Turtle Exclusion Devices. The government is trying to make the shrimpers use them to avoid trapping the turtles in their nets. It's all the environmentalists' doing, and the shrimpers are pretty mad about it. Here it is." She picked up a page from the paper and handed it back to Jackson, who read the headline aloud:

"'Federal judge threatens to order shrimpers to use T-E-D's.'" Jackson spelled out the acronym. "The dateline is Aransas Pass." Jackson added, referring to a larger village across the channel on the mainland.

"Sure," the waitress replied, "they've got the largest private shrimp fleet in the world over there, and like I said, they're not happy about this. Several of them were in here earlier, since they couldn't go out in the storm, and said that they are not going to accept this without a fight."

"Well, I guess they've got good lawyers," Jackson observed, skimming the rest of the article as if looking for his own name.

"What?" the waitress exclaimed with a partial laugh, "they aren't going to let the lawyers decide this dispute."

"So what will they do?" Maggie asked, interested. The waitress turned to her for the first time.

"I don't know, but it won't be in a courtroom, I'm sure of that."

"Don't they care about the turtles?" Maggie asked, more interested.

"They care about eating," the waitress answered flatly, "and that comes first. Same with me, I better get back to work."

Jackson and Maggie left the café and walked to the convenience store located at the intersection of the village's two main streets, Cotter and Alister. Jackson was digging in his pocket for a quarter for the pay phone when he stopped and looked at Maggie.

"Need change?" she asked, and started to open her purse.

"No," Jackson said quickly, as he drew a quarter out of his pocket and showed it to her. "I just realized that the waitress said the shrimpers were not going out in the storm." He gave her a look of dread. For once, she seemed to agree with him.

"You need to ask George about that!" She said emphatically.

He deposited the coin and slowly dialed the number of his client and host. George owned the condo only twenty minutes from his home on the mainland, so he had not installed a phone. He had bought the unit mainly for the boat slip. Jackson was picturing the smallish boat moaning among large waves when an almost as annoying recorded voice sounded in his ear – "the number you are dialing is a long-distance call, please deposit an additional $1.25 for three minutes." He slammed down the receiver and went into the convenience store for more change.

Jackson had met George Waters only twice when he accepted the invitation to be his guest on the island. George was the grandson of a wealthy south Texas oil man and had utilized the good fortune of his birth to live his life as he wanted, pursuing what would otherwise be considered risky ventures but for his advantages, such as automobile restoration and boat building. Presently he was producing shallow-bottom bass boats by hand at the rate of a few dozen per year. Sales were good, but not very profitable. Also, the family fortune was feeling the strain of its volatile oil foundation. Indeed, it was due to trouble in the family business that George had sought legal counsel.

George had made several trips to Dallas to meet with the partners in Jackson's firm, one of whom had recently asked for Jackson's help on the case. During a break in one meeting Jackson had asked about the boats George made. George eagerly launched into an exposition of his craft and within minutes had invited Jackson and Maggie down for a fishing trip. Uncharacteristically, Jackson had accepted immediately. The spontaneous response was uncharacteristic because it would require that he be away from the office for several days in succession, something Jackson had not done since his honeymoon with Maggie three years before. However, fewer than three weeks later they were standing outside the island's only convenience store trying to call George for a weather and wave report. With one hand full of quarters and the other griping the payphone receiver, Jackson finally reached George at the warehouse in Corpus Christi where he and a partner built the boats.

"George, this is Jackson Riddle," Jackson said explanatorily. Jackson always introduced himself with his full name. It was part of his professional formality, but also protected him from his inner fear that others did not routinely remember him.

"Jackie!" George replied in an excited, teasing manner. "I was expecting your call."

"Well," Jackson said uncertainly, "how does it look?"

"It's looking goood, reeaall gooood," George answered, drawing his words out in a dastardly manner. Jackson pictured George, who by his appearance seemed to be about fifteen years older than Jackson. He had a dark, wind-blown complexion, with wiry jet-black hair that was accented by its repeated appearance in a fantastic mustache. At first impression, Jackson couldn't decide if he thought George looked more like Leroy Neiman or the Frito Bandito, or if there was a difference between the three. Now, George's speech made him seem more like the bandito.

"That's great," Jackson said, his tone suggesting the opposite was true. He had liked George from the first, but now he was unsure whether he was being teased. He decided to investigate. "We were a little concerned, what with the hurricane in the Gulf." George responded immediately with his same tone.

"Ha! That thing's just gonna make the fishing better. She's blowing pretty good, but I don't think you should worry about it. You've been out in rough water before, haven't you?" he asked, sounding a bit more serious.

"Well, no, neither of us have *ever* been out before," Jackson reported immediately. "Didn't I tell you?"

"Maybe you did," George said, now in a normal tone, which Jackson took as a sign of concern. "I tell you what, I'll check with some of my buddies that do charters and see what they think. Don't worry, it's gonna be greeeaaaat!" George said, returning to his earlier manner. "I'll call you back later," he added, and promptly hung up before Jackson could explain about the shrimpers.

He hung up his receiver in a deeper state of dread than he could remember. Maggie had sensed this as soon as she had heard him remind George that they had never been out to sea. She tried to confront their fear.

"He thinks it is still OK?" she said, half questioning, half asserting.

"Yes," Jackson answered, "he said he'd double check with his friends that do charters, and call us back."

"How can he call us back on this pay phone?" Maggie questioned, slightly annoyed.

"Oh yeah, I didn't think about that," Jackson answered, revealing the obvious. As if just seeing her, or perhaps just to forget his fear, he smiled and asked, "How did you get so beautiful *and* smart?"

IV

Magnolia Rivers Stone Riddle was not a beautiful woman - not yet, anyway. In fact, Jackson found it difficult to even think of her as a woman. She seemed more girl than woman to him, but truly she oscillated between girlhood and womanhood, right before his eyes. Either way, her appeal for now was in her wholesomeness. Her bright freckled cheeks and steely blue eyes spoke both "youthful" and "mischievous" – in equal tones. This appearance was actually magnified by an independent air. She appeared to Jackson to have no concern for what he or anyone else in the world thought of her. As he was the exact opposite personality, he had been drawn to her immediately. And besides, he thought, her youthful looks would likely mature into beauty.

Not then being recognized as a beautiful woman – at least as the world would define the title – did not mean that Maggie's appearance was not striking. At 5'11" and under 130 pounds, her natural appearance could require notice, but on the rare occasion when she actually wore make-up and made an attempt to look glamorous, she came closer to success than most women who made a daily effort. Proof of this occurred when she was recruited by a Houston modeling agency while simply shopping at a boutique near her parents' home. Although Maggie didn't stick with modeling long, she gained more assurance in herself. She had swiftly lost interest in being a model when she realized that becoming one would require a change in even more than her cosmetics. The modeling environment, and the people inhabiting it, were not like her or for her. From Maggie's description, Jackson figured them to be the female equivalent of boxing promoters, hair and all, and she had dropped out of the ring after only a couple of undercard events.

In Jackson's opinion, though, the experience was priceless for one selfish reason - her portfolio pictures. For Maggie's only time before a camera, he felt hers were remarkable. The addition of layers of make-up and a professional hair styling gave her a true "cover girl" appearance. One shot in particular almost convinced her to stay with it longer, and made Jackson encourage her. It was in one of those unnatural positions that only good models can pull off. Maggie's right shoulder was hunched and pointed toward the camera and her head was cocked slightly to the right, as if in response to the photographer's call she had done a half turn with her body and a full turn with her head. Her hair, dry and wavy from aggressive preparation, was parted on the left and tossed across her face, falling down off the hunched shoulder. Her upper lip was curled straight back creating a full smile aimed directly at the camera, which surprisingly did not reveal the imperfection in her teeth. Her make-up, surprisingly not overdone, highlighted the softness of her checks without altering the natural look of her skin. She was wearing a rough weave olive green turtleneck sweater, and the dull color and high neck kept all the attention on Maggie's face and, particularly, her eyes. Although they were in reality between blue and gray, the green of the sweater and perhaps the camera's filter and the lights of the studio turned Maggie's eyes into glistening emeralds. They were the eyes that Jackson had first noticed when they had met, and which had unnerved him on their first date. They provided the magic that made the good picture a great one.

Jackson was so proud of this vision of his wife that he kept a 5 x 7 copy of the picture on his nightstand at home and an 8 x 10 on credenza at his office. He was delighted by the reaction to it of those who happened to see it. Almost everyone, men and women, commented on it, mostly asking if she was his wife, and then remarking on her beauty. A few even replied, only half-jokingly, that the picture was so perfect they thought it was the advertising photo that came with the frame. He liked that; he liked even better, however, the look of confusion on the faces of those who had already met Maggie, most likely in her normal state - without make-up, hair in a ponytail and wearing teacher's clothes or a jogging suit. Jackson was certain from their befuddled expressions that these people, particularly the men, could not believe that the worldly-woman in the picture was the same local girl they had met.

Jackson knew that, in a sense, these doubts were well-founded. Maggie rarely appeared as the woman in the picture. This was not to say that she was not attractive to him, which she almost always was, but mostly in her warm and wholesome way that was quite different from the glitzy sex-appeal radiating from the picture. He thought, perhaps, that she might look that way again in the future as her features matured, and if she changed to a career in which make-up and designer clothes were valued, but that was not important to Jackson. He held onto the portrait as proof of what he had seen the first time he had met her. He considered the Maggie of the picture and the Maggie of everyday life to be a representation of his transition from the old, insecure Jackie, to the new, confidant – or, at least, less uncertain - Jackson. He got from Maggie everyday what he had miraculously come to understand was most important in a marriage:

trustworthiness and devotion. He got from the woman in the picture what he once thought was important, but still considered welcome: the satisfaction of having captured an object of some envy among his fellow men.

Maggie, on the other hand, looked at the portrait with detachment. To her it really was a store-bought photograph, because she could not see it without recalling the process by, and atmosphere in which, it had been created. In the studio, the girls were assaulted by make-up and hair experts, and appeared before the camera as if they were swimming against a raging current, driven by a primordial force. When directed, each in turn would dart forward before the camera, swim to the right, then drift to the left, and then pause briefly before circling back home, a school of one. Maggie's own session was such a blur to her that it very well could have taken place under water. The vagueness of her recollection added to her detachment from the photograph, which was anything but vague. She was glad Jackson was proud of her picture, and she was too, but she was more thankful that he did not expect or even seem to want her to look like that every day. Despite the visual proof before her, she knew she couldn't repeat that look often, if at all. She preferred not to try, but rather to let Jackson keep the portrait prominently displayed like a gold medal from her one-time, personal-best performance.

V

To lift their spirits, or divert their attention, they decided to walk to the beach. It was about a half-mile walk from the convenience store through a winding gravel and sand road lined alternately with high dunes and old cottages. Both were covered with vines, and the houses were at least partially hidden by overgrown palm trees and other tropical foliage. It was a dark, moonless night and the dense foliage created even darker shadows from the few lights along the road. Jackson and Maggie could hear the sound of the waves well before the coast came into view. As they rounded the last and highest dune, the wind and sand buffeted them hard.

"Wow," Jackson said, for the third time that evening, grabbing the bill of his baseball cap and pulling it down lower on his head. Maggie turned sideways to let her hair fly free, and then pulled it quickly up under her own cap with a deft twist of her wrist.

"I'd say Chantal is coming our way," she said. "Do you want to turn back, or keep walking?"

"I'm okay if you are," Jackson answered, still leaning into the wind and sand.

"Sure," Maggie said, as she turned to her right and started down the beach. "I'm just glad I didn't put my contacts in." Impulsively, she shielded her eyes with one hand. She took

Jackson's hand with the other. As they reached the softer sand of the beach, she led him down to the edge of the surf where the water and waves had packed the sand harder. The waves were breaking about a hundred yards away, and were higher than they had seen before. They were still not very high, Maggie thought, considering that they were being driven by a storm strong enough to cause an oil rig to collapse. "You know," she said aloud as they continued walking down the beach, stepping around seaweed and a few dead jelly fish, "I love the water, but I hate the beach. I would much rather stay over on George's balcony and watch the port than be over here right on the beach, with all this sand and salt and junk."

"I don't mind it that much," Jackson answered, "but I agree that I'd rather be on the port. Much more tranquil, and interesting there, if that makes sense."

"I know what you mean," she said. "The port is mostly peaceful, giving you time to think as much as you like, but it also has all the activity in the morning and evenings, kind of like rush hour. It is a combination, kind of like White Rock Lake on our first night. The water was nice and peaceful, but it was made so much more exciting by the neon Dallas skyline in the background." Maggie finished with an excitement in her voice.

"And I thought I was the exciting part," Jackson said. Maggie squeezed his hand, but didn't answer. "So what were you thinking when I chose that spot to park?" Jackson asked. "Weren't you a little concerned about my intentions?"

"Hey, it was my idea to find another place to go after the bar closed at 2, remember? I didn't want you to take me home because I was having a good time," Maggie said, this time pulling him closer to her by wrapping both of her arms around his left arm.

"I guess that's true," Jackson acknowledged. "I can't

imagine being bold enough to keep you out that late if you weren't having fun, or at least acting like you were."

"Really? But I thought you were the new Casanova?" Maggie teased.

"I was working on it, I guess. I just remember not wanting the night to end. I wanted to be with you from the moment I met you on the bus."

"You've got me there," Maggie interrupted him. "Obviously, we met some time during the evening, but mostly what I remember is a bunch of lawyers and several pitchers of margaritas. Obviously you didn't make a bad impression, or I wouldn't have agreed to go out with you the next night, and I certainly was having a good time then, or I wouldn't have agreed to stay out till 6 am, even with the Dallas skyline as a backdrop." They had reached the pier that formed the south boundary of the village beach, having walked away from the jetties marking the north end of the beach and the south side of the ship channel. A pier extended about fifty yards into the surf, about a quarter of the length of the jetties. The waves were breaking violently against the pilings now, creating foam and surf like a blender.

"Want to go out on the pier?" Jackson asked. Maggie stood for a moment, looking into the bubbling foam and feeling the spray and sand hit her face.

"No, I don't think so." She turned and walked away from the water toward a path leading through the dunes.

"Ok," Jackson followed her. As they moved in among the dunes again, the wind was blocked and the sound of the waves muffled. Jackson returned to their conversation. "You didn't tell me what you were thinking when we parked at White Rock."

"I don't remember," Maggie said, emphatically. "I don't have your lawyerly recall or your sense of nostalgia, wherever that comes from. I was just having fun, and probably thinking that I'd never see you again, so whatever...."

"'Whatever, what?" Jackson asked quickly. "Whatever, let's go to bed together?' or 'Whatever, let's talk about something totally off-the-wall, like religion'?"

"You know the answer to that, because all we did was talk about religion."

"Yeah, that's my point." Jackson said seriously. "I'm not faulting you for the first, I'm just trying to figure out where you got the idea for the second. Was asking guys about God your usual way of keeping your distance on first dates – even on ones that last all night?" Maggie shrugged and sighed.

"I've told you before, I don't know where that came from. No, it was not a topic I usually brought up with guys – whether it was a first date, last date or anywhere in between." She paused and was surprised when Jackson didn't respond, so she continued. "There was something about you that was different – and, no, it wasn't your car." She stopped walking for a moment as a gust of wind almost took her cap away. She pulled it down tighter on her head, and again took Jackson's arm as they continued walking back toward the main street, away from the Gulf. "I liked the things you said, but I can't remember what they were, so don't ask," she said. "I don't know, you just felt right, but where I came up with the question about going to church is a mystery to me – at least it was at the time." She paused again as they reached Alister Street and turned north back toward the port. Jackson still didn't speak as she let go of his hand again, and they walked side-by-side down the sidewalk. "I just don't know," she continued. "There must have been some promise there, or I wouldn't have cared about whether you went to church. Up to that moment, I didn't care if *I* went to church. Something, or someone, put the thought in my head - not just about your life, but about mine, too." She paused again, and this time Jackson interrupted her.

"And, by inference, of course, about our life together," he said.

"It certainly seems that way now. I don't remember if I realized it at that moment, though."

"I do," Jackson said, "and I did then, although I couldn't believe that you were thinking about our future together only 24 hours after we met. I was imagining it for myself, but I was amazed that you could be, too. I was even more amazed that it didn't scare me. I had dated several girls for years without thinking about marriage."

"Can we leave them out of this discussion?' Maggie interrupted him.

"Sure," Jackson corrected himself quickly, "because they *were* out of it. I was totally focused on you from that moment on."

"Except for the moment that you gave me the soap story," Maggie reminded him.

"Oh, yeah." Jackson stopped walking at the corner where Alister Street crossed Cotter. "Can we leave that out, too? It comes up a little later, remember. We're focusing now on the moment I fell in love with you, not the moment I knew I couldn't live without you." They turned left, and then started across the street holding hands again. The condo building was in front of them about two hundred yards away.

"Nice recovery," Maggie said.

"It's the kind of quick thinking I get paid for," Jackson said.

"You mean your ability to divert attention from the truth?" She said.

"No, I mean my ability to keep the judge – that's you, in this case - focused on the events that truly matter. I won't say, 'just on what's relevant', because it's almost all relevant, but some events are dispositive, and others aren't."

"Whatever that means," Maggie shrugged again.

"You might not find it in an ordinary dictionary, but it's a legal term used to describe something that finally resolves a matter. In our case, it means that I loved you from the minute I laid eyes on you, but that it took a little testing for me to understand what to do with my love. Anyway, you're pretty good at diverting attention yourself. We were talking about where you got the idea to ask me about church."

"I told you, I don't know," Maggie answered. "I guess the devil made me do it."

"That could have been true," Jackson said, without laughing, "except that I clearly got the impression that you wanted me to say 'yes' about church. I never really thought about the possibility that you wanted me to say 'no.' I certainly wasn't bothered by you wanting me to be interested in church. I don't know what I would have thought if it had been the other way around." Jackson looked down at his feet as they walked, as if looking for guidance, Maggie thought.

"That's what's so bizarre about the whole thing." Maggie decided to take up the question. "I had never been interested in church myself, but for some reason I wanted you to be. Then you explained that you had been to church your whole childhood, but were rebelling against it. Neither of us were looking for a long-term relationship – at least with each other – and here we found ourselves having a spiritual revival, and an immediate emotional attachment, at 4 in the morning, sitting in an Italian convertible at White Rock Lake, looking at the Dallas skyline."

"Kind of a bad plot line, I'd say," Jackson offered.

"Unlikely, that's for sure, but someone dreamed it up," Maggie concluded, as they reached the gate to the complex.

"I'd like to take credit for it, but I don't think it was me, or you," Jackson said. "I'm just glad we both got the picture."

They went upstairs to George's unit and went to bed without further discussion or contemplation. For once, there was interaction between them that required neither talk nor thought.

Wednesday, August 2, 1989

VI

The next morning they both woke late, dressed in their swim suits, and took up residence at the pool on the dock by the port. Maggie swam a few laps while Jackson sat on the step and cooled off in waist-deep water. It was 9:30 a.m., and the temperature matched the clock, 93°. They both then laid out on lounge chairs, and soon Maggie could tell that Jackson had returned to sleep. She tried to read, but could not keep her mind off the previous night's discussion.

She was surprised that, after three years and numerous times telling their story, she had never actually pondered where her question about church had come from. After they had talked for at least an hour about her close family ties, with Jackson quizzing her about what that meant and how it worked, Maggie had felt it was her turn. Whether her chosen topic was compelled by the perceived need to be as serious as Jackson, or whether she was truly interested in the subject, she had never really known. But whatever the reason – Divine intervention again, perhaps – she had chosen to ask him about God. She wasn't conscious of considering the angles of approach to this unusual first-date topic. If she had been, she probably would have realized why she didn't begin with the typical (and inflammatory) question (accusation?) *Are you a Christian?* If she had thought about it, she might have concluded that she wasn't even sure she was – at least not one with a sense of the true meaning of the title. No, that was too specific a question. Neither did she go for the general, almost philosophical inquiry: *Do you believe in God?* Again, had she thought about it consciously, she would likely have concluded that she did not want to even imagine being this interested in someone about whom she couldn't assume even that level of spirituality. Yet, truthfully, she had rarely considered even her own level of spirituality. God, for her, was bound up in the mechanics of religion. So, she asked the only question that made sense to her, subconsciously, or otherwise, one that presumed a certain level of spirituality, and yet also could be considered non-threatening.

"Do you go to church?" She had asked, in the moment when Jackson had asserted that she was mistaken about the closeness of her family. To Jackson's credit, she thought, his answer seemed honest, and even open.

"I used to," he answered, without hesitation. Maggie had been encouraged by the answer. It gave her several directions to go, and provided her the opportunity she wanted to turn the conversation away from her family. There wasn't much to say about their church-going. She chose to follow-up in a manner that could have seemed provocative to Jackson, joining the topic of religion with what she felt could be happening between them.

"Do you ever plan on going back?" She asked, also without hesitation. Jackson had not been offended. Again, she felt he answered with honesty, keeping the discussion focused on religion alone, rather than turning it prematurely toward their future. He explained how he had attended church regularly - three times a week – for most of his first 18 years. He had learned much about the Bible, all of the stories, and promises and the threats, and had been "saved" when he was 8. At least, he understood that to be the result of his profession of faith and baptism before his church congregation. However, the constant admonition to "do good" – and the consequences of failing this command – began to weigh him down, even in adolescence. Of course, he could not always do good. Total abstention from alcohol and drugs, even pot, still left a few vices under the Biblical standard. Even so, this inner conflict had been kept relatively in check while he was in his father's household and under the constraints of general parental supervision – not to mention church attendance three times each week. The tension, of course, between who he thought he should be and who he knew he actually was, only increased when he left home to attend a large state university. In a snap of independence first, then guilt, the matter was decided. More conduct brought more guilt, and eventually Jackson concluded he could not face God to receive the consequences of his actions. So, he stopped going where he assumed God was. Of course, the guilt had not been left there. It remained with him, bothering him still, even stifling his pleasure in the condemning conduct. And that is where Maggie found him – physically and emotionally separated from God – at least in *his* mind - and with an expectation of a future encounter he was convinced would result in permanent separation.

"If damnation is the result of my actions, and I can't or won't control those actions, then what can I do but just give up and enjoy my sins until judgment day?" Jackson had asked with resignation. Not having attended church much herself (her parents simply had not made her go), and never inclined to Bible study inside or out of the church, Maggie could not respond to Jackson on a theological level. However, the dilemma he described sounded familiar to her.

"Are you Catholic?" She had asked him, innocently. Jackson understood her analysis better than she did, and had actually laughed.

"No, but it does sound like it, doesn't it?" Then they laughed together. The laughter helped them both. It was a grown-up recognition, and it somehow validated the conversation they each wanted to have. Jackson went on to explain that his "church" had been called simply the "Christian Church." He had never been taught exactly why they weren't Methodist or Presbyterian or some other Protestant adjective. Of course, he had fully comprehended that they weren't Catholic. Now that he was older, he understood that others would call his church "fundamentalist." He was now aware that this was a pejorative and presumed a lack of intelligence. It wasn't the first obstacle to his return to church, but it was one. Finally, after nearly an hour of discussing her initial question, he had answered just as she had hoped he would.

"I *could* go back. In fact, I want to; but I need encouragement." He had paused and then added, challenging her, perhaps, "What about you?"

This was the moment she remembered most from their beginning. Not the first introduction, or even Jackson's nearly immediate inquiry (suggestion?) 'Have you ever thought about moving to Dallas?' She remembered the moment that something awakened in her, something to which Jackson immediately attached himself. Perhaps he had awakened it, but whatever the cause, she knew at that moment that she could help Jackson in his relationship with God, and in doing so, he would help her. It made no sense, and yet it was perfectly clear to her. Jackson had the knowledge; she had the understanding. She had never struggled with her religious beliefs or her conscience; he always had. Neither were a strong factor in her life, but they weren't absent. She simply believed there was a time for everything. The fact that love and faith would enter her life at the same time surprised her only a little, and pleased her a lot. It was just so, and she did not hesitate to admit it.

"I want you to," had been her emphatic answer to him. Although Jackson had been fully focused on her, these words caught him unprepared. He looked down at his feet, calculating. Before he could complete the equation, she added, "I encourage you to go back." He had looked back at her quickly, beginning to understand. Somehow, she thought, he looked relieved. Presumably, it would be easier for him to deal with in the short term, than in the long run.

"I just might," he had said, after the first awkward moment they had had all night.

Laying in the sun beside Maggie, Jackson also continued their previous night's reminiscence, only as in a half-dream which the sun's heat made even more intense. He remembered waking in the recliner in his apartment two days later, still wearing the slacks and starched dress shirt that he had worn to the office the previous morning. He looked at his watch - 6:45 a.m. He realized that he had been asleep for less than an hour, but still felt refreshed. The excitement he had felt as he tried to sleep had not left him. A quick shower and a short walk from his downtown apartment had brought him to his high rise office building before 8 a.m. Stepping off the elevator at the 20th floor, he glanced at the bold brass letters, set like a crown above the solid oak doors, Wunder & Parrish.

After an hour at his desk, he was surprised to find himself alert and not preoccupied, or asleep. He leaned back thoughtfully in his chair, and looked out the window at the Dallas skyline, now illuminated by the sunrise rather than neon lights. He tried to grasp the bankruptcy issues confronting a real estate partnership, but instead thought constantly of Maggie. He stared at his office door, as if expecting her to appear, but instead was startled by the somewhat annoyed appearance of her brother. Jackson instantly thought he looked like the one who had stayed out all night, and braced himself for a lecture, or perhaps even a fight. He was pleased to hear a note of caution in her brother's voice, when he spoke.

"I got up at 4:00 this morning, and Mag wasn't home yet," he said.

"Don't worry, she was in good hands," Jackson said, expressing more than he had intended.

"Right," her brother responded, still being cautious, "she says nothing happened, and I believe her, but I want you to watch it; she's my little sister."

"I was good," Jackson said, intending to be sincere, but missing the mark again. Her brother had just turned and walked away.

Despite this caution, Jackson and Maggie went out to dinner that night, and then went to his apartment and talked all night. He took her home after sunrise again, and this time her brother didn't wait to reproach Jackson. As soon as she entered his home, he demanded that Maggie act properly so long as she was a guest in his house. Maggie, however, was unrepentant. Something amazing, but nothing improper, had happened. Lying beside her on the balcony of his twenty-first floor downtown apartment, looking up at the neon-framed buildings of Dallas, one of which was topped with an electric-red Pegasus, Jackson had tried to be philosophical.

If I believed that some people are absolutely meant for one another, no matter how long they've known each other, or how little they've been through together - which I don't, or didn't - I think I would say that we were meant for each other, and ought to just go ahead and get married.

Maggie hadn't answered directly; which he took as a positive response.

"You know, I was sort of named for that," she said, pointing to the winged horse astride an oil derrick rotating in a neon-red glow atop the building across the street.

"Pegasus?" Jackson asked, uncertainly.

"Yes, and no." Maggie answered, standing up and leaning against the railing. "That's the symbol for the old Magnolia Oil Company. My dad, being an engineer in Houston, thought Magnolia was a good name for his Texas daughter." Jackson stood up, too, but stayed back from the rail.

"Your name is 'Magnolia'? Wow, that's cool," Jackson had responded immediately. When Maggie frowned slightly, he turned his attention back to the building and the art work. "I knew that was called the Magnolia Building, but I didn't know it was an old oil company. Of course, I've seen Pegasus on the signs at gas stations, so I guess they must have bought Magnolia. I never put the two together. That's a neat story, though – that you're named after it. He, or she, has been watching over me here for three years," he said, as he inched closer to Maggie and the railing.

"It's a better story than a name. I'm glad I can go by Maggie," she said, leaning back toward Jackson.

"Funny," he said. "You're still taking refuge in your nickname, and I couldn't wait to take refuge *from* mine." It was then that Maggie stepped back from the railing and faced Jackson. The intensity of the look in her eyes was as hot as the coastal sun, as he recalled her words.

"I think we could take refuge in each other, but it's going to be complicated," she had said.

Jackson shifted in the chair, as he kept his eyes closed and tried not to show a lingering shock to the Maggie sitting next to him, just as he had shuffled his feet, and shrank from the gaze at her words that evening. He hadn't known what she had meant, but like all guys, he refused to admit it.

"Yeah, I know," he had said.

"You know about Davis?" Maggie asked, sharply, and stepped back away from him to lean against the railing.

Jackson's stomach had jumped, both at the question, and at his fear that Maggie would fall backward over the railing.

"Davis who?" He asked, in a forced voice as he reached out to take her hands.

"Davis, my boyfriend?" Maggie had answered meekly, a tone she had never shown to him before, and with a slight cringe as she avoided Jackson's reach. She had turned away from him and looked up at her namesake, as if seeking the means for a quick exit. A winged horse could come in handy when trapped on the 21st floor of an apartment building. Jackson lurched again in his chair, as he recalled the hammer that had hit his chest and kept him from speaking, which may have been a good thing. He had stepped backward, hitting the sliding glass door of the apartment, and chose his words carefully when he finally could speak.

"Oh, *that* Davis." He then forced himself to step forward beside her and lean against the railing. He looked down. Maggie wasn't sure this was a good sign, since he had admitted earlier that he was bothered by heights. She moved closer to steady him physically and emotionally.

"I've been trying to find a time to tell you since about midnight Saturday. It's over." She paused, as if recognizing that this was not technically true. "Actually, it's not exactly over. We've been dating for two years. I need to get back to Houston to end it." Jackson finally turned to face her, relieved to no longer be looking down the twenty-one stories to Commerce Street.

"You've been dating him for two years?" Jackson maintained his calm voice, but his tone was accusatory.

"Yes, but..." she stopped, not sure how to explain or whether she should even try. Jackson turned away from her and glared at Pegasus, as if she had been unfaithful. "Look," Maggie continued after a longer pause, "I was going to break it off, anyway. Now that I've met you, I really will. I just haven't been home to do it."

Jackson shifted again in his musing, remembering how uncomfortable it had felt to be shocked and embarrassed over this news only two days into a relationship. Yet, he had remained uncharacteristically calm. He was unsure where it would lead them, and he was trying, to the extent possible under the circumstances, to plan ahead for it. Strangely, Maggie worried more about her boyfriend. She hadn't adequately explained him to Jackson, and she wasn't sure she could. They had dated for two years, and he wanted to get married. She had been hesitant, and she couldn't explain why, until now. Now she knew what it felt like to know, but could she convey that convincingly to Jackson? She spent the next three days trying.

When Maggie left to return to Houston on Friday, she promised she would end her old relationship right away. Jackson thought that this meant the night she returned, even on the way home from the airport. He was shocked by the further realization that there was even someone to play the role of collecting her at the airport. When she didn't call all that evening, he finally called her at 2:00 a.m. She was apologetic, but not repentant. Yes, they had gone out. No, she hadn't told Davis about him.

"What? You didn't even tell him I exist?" Old feelings of jealousy and mistrust flamed in Jackson, as they once had in the old Jackie. Could he have been wrong in his conviction that Maggie was different? That their instant relationship was different? An hour of predictable argument over the phone brought no answer to his question, but he felt better. He had been in her position before, and had balked at conveying the plain truth to the other party in the relationship. His soap-story had been a variation on this theme. Although he still wondered whether Maggie deserved the absolute trust he had credited her with from the start, an extraordinary coincidence helped calm his fear. Maggie had described going to an outdoor cafe in Houston with her boyfriend directly from the airport. As they sat and she avoided explaining what had happened to her in Dallas, an Italian car identical to Jackson's parallel parked outside the railing immediately beside their table. Maggie said it was like further Divine intervention, or at least supernatural - Divine or not. She still didn't tell her boyfriend about Jackson, but she felt he was there the entire time. Jackson was cheered by the story – "You know I love that car!" he had said to her.

In his mind, he sat in the car watching them through the iron balusters of the fence surrounding the restaurant's patio, their profiles facing each other across the table, their heads and shoulders visible above the boxwood hedge. Davis was looking at her; she was looking down – at the menu? at her plate? At a ring on her finger? Jackson strained to hear, but the scene was on mute. Now suddenly she raised her head and turned toward Jackson. He flinched like a baseball fan behind the screen, ducking a foul ball. He knew he wasn't visible, just as a fan knows he can't be hit by the ball, but flinching is involuntary. She did not smile or otherwise acknowledge his presence. Instead, she turned back to look across the table. She leaned back as her boyfriend leaned forward. The sound came on.

"What do you mean you were in no hurry to get back? Didn't you miss me?" His voice sounded very uncertain. She paused, making him wait and wonder, Jackson thought.

"Sure," she finally exhaled, "but I was enjoying Dallas with my sister-in-law. You know how she is."

"Yes, you always seem to have more fun with her than with me."

"That's not true. You're just pouting." She felt guilty about teasing him, but still couldn't find the right opening to tell him the truth about Jackson. "I may go back next weekend," she said, thinking that this might lead her to disclose why.

"You just got home," Davis protested. "Why do you have to go back? I'll come with you," he added, without waiting for an explanation.

"No," she said, firmly. "There's no place for you to stay."

"There isn't a place only if you don't want there to be," he answered.

"What is that supposed to mean?" She asked.

"I mean, I could stay with you if you wanted me to. Your brother wouldn't care."

"Oh, yes he would," she shot back, "he just said...," she stopped suddenly.

"Said what?" He asked, shrinking back in his chair.

He knows he's losing her, Jackson thought. He's not very strong. She should just tell him!

"Look," she said, ignoring his question. "I want to go back and have some fun before school starts again. I won't have time to leave Houston after that. We'll have time together then."

Jackson's body tensed, and his face frowned. What is she saying?

"Okay," her boyfriend leaned forward again, and put out his hand. "You can go back to Dallas, but take this with you." Jackson saw him reach across and place a small box on her plate. His mouth formed a word, and he was trying to scream it, when he awoke with a jerk. A strong gust of wind off the port blew over a chair next to him. He squinted in the graying light, now diffused with cloud cover, but bright nonetheless. His eyes focused on Maggie, who was still sitting beside him. Even half-awake and mired in the memory of her old boyfriend, he understood from her expression that a different crisis was on her mind.

"Do you think we should just tell him we don't want to go out?" She asked.

"I don't know," Jackson replied, still struggling to shake himself out of his half-dream, but understanding enough to be thankful that she was referring to George rather than Davis. Maggie was annoyed, though she wasn't sure at what.

"What did he say exactly?" She asked, referring to George. Then not waiting for a reply, she added, "I mean he's not going to take us out if it's really dangerous, is he?

Jackson shrugged, but didn't answer her. He was still trying to separate Davis and George, and the pain of potentially losing Maggie versus the danger of an on-coming hurricane. Each had seemed terrifying to him, but with Maggie in full view he could concentrate on the hurricane. He was able to recall that he didn't really know George, and how the other owners in the complex had smiled and said "Good luck" when he had said that George was taking them fishing. One of them had volunteered the observation: "He may be eccentric, but George knows the Gulf better than anybody." Jackson sat up straighter in the lounge chair and looked down the dock to where George's boat swayed and bobbed in the surf. The boat was like the others in the dock, perhaps smaller than most, but for the twin 225 horsepower outboard motors mounted at her stern. He recalled George telling him she would do fifty miles per hour. Jackson had smiled and shook his head, wanting to look impressed, but was actually wondering if George had really said "miles per hour" instead of "knots", and trying to recall the difference. Then, realizing he hadn't answered Maggie's question, he spoke quickly, though trying to sound calm and relaxed.

"I told you. He's going to call his buddies who take commercial charters, and see what they're doing." Trying to convince himself, he added, "It'll be OK." Maggie smiled too, as if to acknowledge that they were being childish.

"OK," she said, "I'm getting in the hot tub to steam my troubles away." Jackson went inside and opened two bottles of Mexican beer and picked up the tape player. "Thanks," Maggie said as he returned and handed her one of the bottles of beer. Then, pointing down to the player, she added emphatically, "But no Jimmy Buffett."

"All right," Jackson responded, without protest, "you pick."

Maggie opened the tape box and quickly selected a recording by a new Canadian group led by a deep-voiced female singer. Her rendition of "I'm So Lonesome I Could Cry" was sung with such passion, and at such a tantalizingly slow tempo, that it would have made Hank Williams feel even more lonesome. In the hot tub, which like the pool was built over the water, Jackson and Maggie's crisis seemed to evaporate along with the rising steam. Then, as they took in the music, beer and serenity, they caught the stiff salt breeze as it snapped the riggings and further declared the hurricane's approach. Before they could resume their deliberations about the trip, they heard the phone in the complex office ringing. The office was located beside the pool and was unmanned, but the door remained open. Jackson struggled out of the water and ran, dripping, to the phone to which he had been summoned by clients four times already since their arrival.

"Hello?" He said, as his ear flushed water into the black handset he had grabbed off the rotary base.

"Jackie?" George's voice came clearly and excitedly through the wet plastic. "Is that you?"

"Yes, George," Jackson answered, surprised. "How did you know to call me here?"

"Mary told me you were poolside," George replied, referring to the manager. "She told me to try you on this line. I hear you've been doing more work in that office than she has."

"Well, you know I've been practicing just long enough

to get all the responsibility, but none of the profits," Jackson replied.

"Then you'll be happy to hear that they're not making any money off me," George quipped back.

"That's great," Jackson said, "they'll probably try to charge me for using your condo under some kind of subrogation principle. They're very creative at collecting fees."

"Don't worry," George said, "I'll cover you."

"Thanks," Jackson said, and then returned to the main topic, "What's the story with the storm?"

"Weeellll," George drew out his words again, "she's blowing real good out in the Gulf." He paused, and Jackson wasn't sure whether that meant they were going or not going. Finally, George continued, "I may have jumped the gun a little in predicting good fishing. My commercial buddies didn't go out today, and aren't planning on going out tomorrow. Maybe we ought to wait another day, if you have the time."

Relieved, Jackson immediately agreed. "OK; we weren't planning on leaving 'til Saturday. So, why don't we try it Friday?"

"OK," George assented, "call me tomorrow afternoon."

"I will," Jackson concluded, and breathed a sigh of commutation as he hung up the phone. Returning to the hot tub, he didn't conceal his relief.

"We live another day," he said.

"What do you mean? We aren't going?" Maggie asked. She had pulled herself out of the steaming water and was sitting on the tiled ledge with her feet swishing.

"Not until Friday, at least," Jackson answered, trying now to sound as if he was fearful that the adventure would not happen at all, but Maggie knew better.

"You bankruptcy lawyers," she laughed, "your cases never go to trial." She laughed again as she splashed water in his face with her feet.

VII

As they were on their second walking circuit around the island that evening, looking for a good dinner spot, Jackson was passing through distraction and entering irritation. Maggie had rejected seafood ("we've had it three times already," "We *are* on an island." Jackson had responded); Italian ("too heavy"); pizza ("we have that all the time"); Mexican ("the place looks filthy"); and finally even the Island Café ("my stomach – and my lungs – can't take many more meals there").

So, they were walking for the second time down Alister Street, away from the port and toward the state highway and undeveloped area of the island. Maggie kept looking around, as if she expected some new possibility to present itself magically. Perhaps through magic - or at least her imagination – one did.

It had been sunset when they first left the condo, but was fully dark now. The darkness behind them, however, was overcome by a haze of light ahead of them. As they approached, they could see that the light drifted down from five tall towers standing in a semi-circle around a poorly manicured public ball field. The lights were not bright, and their effect was obscured by swarms of bugs in the hot gulf air. Maggie had not noticed it the first time past – probably because it had been daylight then, and no one had been playing - but now a vague glow hung over the near-dead grass and brick red clay, attracting her attention, and Jackson's. The drab earthly colors contrasted with the bright red shirts and quick movements around the field of the members of the team from Half-Fast Boat Repair. Jackson was the first to notice the team name as he steered Maggie off the sidewalk and up to the backstop, hoping she would take an interest in the game, eventually, as he had instantly. Following Jackson's pointing finger, Maggie read the team name on the back of the catcher's red shirt, just above the number "5" in white. She smiled.

"A good number for a catcher," he said. "Johnny Bench. Right color of uniforms, too." Maggie rolled her eyes, and let her smile go. She turned as if to go with it when a sharp ping rang out, and a loud yell went up from the dugout of the team batting. Yankee's Yankees – Jackson recognized the name and logo from one of the restaurants Maggie had rejected - wore white numbers on dark navy shirts, of course (although Jackson always thought the real Yankees should just admit that they wear black). The batter for these Yankees, a slender male with boyish, too-long hair and faded jeans, was by then rounding second and straining for third as the throw came in from right field, missing the cut-off man. The runner slid awkwardly into the bag as the third baseman for Half-Fast (a woman) stepped out of the way and shuffled down the line toward home, trying to catch the errant throw. It bounced past her and into the cyclone fence. The runner scrambled to his feet and started toward home, but the pitcher – a man who had been trying to get the woman out of the way to make the play at third base – quickly scooped up the ball and chased the runner back to the bag.

The entire sequence had taken fewer than thirty seconds, and Maggie had only watched part of it, but she could see that Jackson was already fully engaged. She thought about just walking on without him, or grabbing his arm and dragging him away. She had already spent too much of their brief marriage fighting baseball for his attention – even his affection. She did not want a night of their vacation to be spent sharing him with two co-ed softball teams. She paused, trying to decide how to react, and looked across the street at the grocery store that was still quite busy even though it was approaching 9 p.m. She wasn't sure why or how, perhaps by force of Jackson's will, but an idea came into her mind. She turned back to him and spoke in her most affectionate voice.

"You stay here and watch the game. I'll be back in a minute." She could see Jackson start to question her, but then stop when he recognized her tone. The surprise of hearing her sound happy at his interest in the game left him speechless. She started across the street toward the grocery and did not look back until she was about to pass through the double glass doors that had parted automatically at her approach. She paused long enough to locate Jackson on the top row of the bleachers, on the Half-Fast side (3rd base, she thought, incorrectly). He was applauding some action in the game she had not seen and wouldn't have understood anyway. He was still applauding about twenty minutes later, she presumed for some other action, when she returned with a large paper sack. She held it out in front of her for balance as she climbed the bleachers, weaving through eight or ten fans clumped alternately on the lower rows. Jackson looked surprised, but she could see that he was hopeful. He would not have expected to get to watch the game, and he certainly could not have expected her to join him.

"Hungry?" She asked. Jackson nodded with the same look of surprise, as she sat down several feet from him. She placed the sack on the foot rail below them, and quickly laid out a checkered red dish towel on the bleacher between them. The tag was still stapled to the corner of the towel, but it looked nice against the curved aluminum. "Ready for a picnic at the ball park," she added, knowing it did not need to be in the form of a question.

"Always," Jackson answered, anyway. Maggie smiled at his truthfulness, and then pulled from the sack a large summer sausage, a box of crackers, a block of cheese, a small paring knife and a large strand of red grapes. "Amazing." Jackson beamed at her.

"I got some wine, but I forgot to get an opener. Guess I'll have to settle for some of your beer. It matches the surroundings better, anyway." She saw Jackson look hesitant as she put her index finger through the aluminum ring and started to pull the tab on a can of beer. "What? Think it won't taste good with your dinner?" She asked.

"Well," he hesitated again. "It's a public park."

"Right!" Maggie nodded sharply. "We'd better not offend these fine citizens with our public consumption of alcohol." She spoke in a light tone, but loud enough that a couple two rows in front turned to look at them. Jackson diverted their attention by applauding some movement on the field. Maggie shrugged, put down the unopened beer and cut Jackson a slice of cheese and summer sausage. He took both with a cracker, but stopped before putting them in his mouth.

"I remember the first time you fed me this stuff," he said.

"Me, too." Maggie answered. "Only then it was because we didn't want to leave the apartment, and this was all you had in the fridge." She glanced out to the field with a look of mock disgust.

"This is a distant second," Jackson offered. Unconvincingly, Maggie thought.

"Sometimes you make me feel like a distant second, you know," she replied, realizing too late that she had not tried hard enough to hide her conviction about the statement.

Jackson heard her clearly, but paused, not sure how he should respond, she thought. "It's okay," Maggie excused him. "I know you're trying." She meant that, too. It had seemed incredible to her at first, but gradually during the first two years of marriage she realized that baseball was a true rival for Jackson's affection – not just his attention. She had reacted badly at first, unwilling to accept any explanation for such an insult. When even that had not broken its attraction, she nearly panicked. After all, the same response in connection with another woman had jolted Jackson into a proposal. This rival had, however, proven much harder to vanquish. Noticing Maggie's contemplation, and thinking of her encouragement – first at simply deciding they should have a picnic at this game, and then at even his failures of the past – Jackson found the confidence to try to explain himself again. His earlier efforts had been quite unsuccessful, but that was before he realized that Maggie viewed his relationship with baseball as infidelity. She seemed less judgmental at the moment, and he took a chance.

"What do you see out there on the field?" He asked, in a tone that was clearly a preface. Maggie looked up casually as she finished chewing a large bite of cheese, and spoke carelessly as she swallowed.

"Five guys and five girls."

"True enough," Jackson admitted, "but that's not everything." He paused, but Maggie did not offer any further observations. She knew he was ready to give his, and she didn't mind. "I see a poorly coached team," Jackson observed. Maggie looked again at the players, and then back to Jackson, as if giving him the sign to continue. "You see, they've got a girl catching. That's the first mistake. In softball, as in baseball and any sport, really, you need to place your best players where most of the action will be. Now, assuming that all five of your male players are better than all five of your females (which is not always true, I'll admit), I think you should put a guy at catcher, shortstop, first base and left field. Catcher because covering home plate is the object of the game. Most people think a guy playing infield can cover home, but I like to see the catcher control every pitch like they do in real baseball. You need a guy at shortstop because that's where most of the hard ground balls are hit, and he can cover second base and, possibly, even third, on put-outs. The first baseman is obviously important to get outs on ground balls and throws over there. You need a good left fielder because most batters are right handed, and most pull the ball in slow pitch." He paused just as a batter for the Yankees lined a pitch sharply, but foul, just outside the third base line. Maggie didn't connect the event and his comment. She was trying to decide whether or not to listen to his commentary, whether it was *worth* listening to. This was her husband talking, teaching actually, about a subject that he knew well and cared for deeply – too deeply she thought. She neither knew the subject nor cared for it, but she loved him. Did that require her attention? She was still trying to decide, when Jackson continued his lecture. She cut herself another piece of cheese and summer sausage. It was, at least, a lovely night for a picnic. It hadn't registered with either of them that the wind had calmed.

"That leaves pitcher or centerfield to cover with your fifth guy," Jackson continued. It's really helpful if you have a woman who can pitch strikes. There is no real strategy in slow-pitch pitching – just try to get it over the plate and make them put the ball in play. If you've got a girl who can do that, you can put your fastest guy in centerfield. He can cover two-thirds of the outfield and even back up the shortstop at second base." He paused again, as the Yankees made the third out in an inning, and the players hustled out to their positions. They had scored five runs and were in good spirits as they exchanged high-fives with their teammates. Some took gloves from the Half-Fast players who were coming off the field.

"They used to do that even in the major leagues – share gloves," Jackson said, as he nodded toward the field. "It wasn't until late in the 19th century when Spalding Sporting Goods was started by a former player that gloves became readily available and most players got one. Spalding had played for the Chicago White Stockings, now the White Sox. He was a pitcher, and they finish their delivery only about 55 feet from home plate – the rubber on the major league mound is 60 feet, six inches from home plate, compared to the forty-two feet of this softball diamond. The ball can come off the bat of a major leaguer at more than one hundred miles per hour, so you can imagine why pitchers would be the first players to want to have a glove. I guess Spalding was the first one to do something about it, even though I think he waited until after he had quit playing." Jackson paused, and Maggie thought about what to do with all this new information.

"I like that they share," she said, ignoring most of what he had said. She had noticed two girls in particular, who she imagined were sisters, but were on opposing teams. They had stopped behind second base to talk for more than a minute between innings. The one who was playing for the red team was now batting.

"C'mon! Hit the ball, Sherry!" Her counterpart called from her ready-stance at second base. Sherry did her best to comply and swung at the first pitch, but missed.

"You don't see that kind of fraternizing and cooperation any more in the major leagues. It all ended with a guy named Ty Cobb." As Jackson was speaking, the girl named Sherry had taken the next two pitches, one for a ball and one for strike two.

"C'mon, Sherry! It just takes one!" The girl at second base called out to her again.

"She better be swinging now," Jackson said, and then added under his breath, "not that it will make much difference." Maggie was turning to reprimand him for insulting Sherry when again she heard the ping of the aluminum bat – not as loud this time, but still firm. She turned back to the field in time to see the ball floating over the head of the girl at second base. It landed softly in the grass and took two hops before it was picked up by the centerfielder, who had raced over to jump in front of the woman playing right field. Another yell came up, louder than before, because this time everyone – so it seemed to Maggie – was yelling. The red team in their dugout, the black team on the field, and the fans in the bleachers on both the first and third base sides, all were cheering in unison. Sherry had run unsteadily to first, and was now standing with both feet on the bag and both hands over her mouth. Maggie could still see the smile in her eyes.

"My first one!" Sherry called out as she raised her arms and then screamed, finally clasping her hands above her head as if in triumph. Maggie started to applaud now, too, as she noticed that Jackson was already.

"Probably her first hit ever," he said.

Jackson, Maggie and the rest of the fans sat back down after a moment, and the game continued at its friendly pace for another thirty minutes until the Yankees batted around and scored six runs in the bottom of the sixth, making the score 12-2.

"Ready to go?" Jackson asked, as Maggie gathered up all the wrappers from their dinner. They had eaten everything except a small piece of the summer sausage. As they were stepping carefully down the bleachers, she asked the woman on the first row if she could give the meat to her dog, a chocolate lab that had been stretched out quietly through most of the game, save only for a few barks in honor of Sherry's base hit.

"Oh, sure, go ahead," the woman replied, and Maggie dropped the meat in front of the dog's nose that lay flat on the grass. Like a crocodile, he snapped it up with his mouth without lifting his jaw off the grass. As they walked back toward the dimly lit port, with the black water of the ship channel acting like a darkened stage in front of them, Jackson put his arm around Maggie's shoulder.

"Thanks for the concession," he said.

"Maybe I should open a stand at the ballpark in Dallas," she replied.

"I was referring to your willingness to watch the ballgame, but I like your interpretation even better."

"It wasn't so awful," Maggie replied. "They were fun to watch playing," she admitted.

"It was as good as a major league game for me. You just never know what's going to happen at a ballpark." He paused, and Maggie knew that he wanted to say more.

"Is that why you love it so much?" She decided to ask.

"I think that's a big part of it. Every pitch holds the possibility of a lifetime's achievement. From Sherry's first hit to Hank Aaron's 715th home run. It can even *be* a lifetime. A player named Ray Chapman took a fast ball in the head and never got up. That was in 1920, before batters wore helmets." Maggie looked up at him, surprised that Jackson could actually prove that, on at least one occasion, baseball had truly been a matter of life and death.

"I've never heard that before," she said.

"It's not one of the statistics you hear quoted a lot – one fatality – but it's part of the history of the game." For the first time that he could recall, he thought about the fact that the fatality had been a batter, rather than a pitcher, and wondered whether Spalding had then invented batting helmets. His voice quickened again. "Look, they've been playing hundreds, thousands, of games each year for the past 150 years, and still things happen all the time that have *never* happened before. How many games have been invented that have that many possibilities? None. With baseball the possibilities are apparently endless."

"Well, I can agree with you that it feels endless sometimes," Maggie joked, but she took his arm as they turned through the opening in the walls forming the gate to their complex. "It's okay," she added, as Jackson was trying unsuccessfully to frown. "I had a good time, and whenever I can say that after a trip to the ballpark, any ballpark, you should just declare victory and leave the field." She smiled, and she looked to Jackson as fresh and beautiful as baseball.

He saluted her.

Thursday, August 3, 1989

VIII

Jackson woke on Thursday morning with an awareness of both light and heat. The punishing Texas light in August pierced the dark tint of the sliding glass doors facing due east, its warmth radiating through as well. Maggie lay sleeping with her arm across her face, and he quietly slid off the bed without waking her. Slowly pulling open the door, he was momentarily blinded by the shock of the light's true brightness against the tenderness of his retinas, which were not fully ready for the new day. Although he was usually an early riser, he could tell by the angle and seeming velocity of the rays that he had slept later than usual - -probably, he thought, due to the events of the day and night before. He turned toward the bathroom and on his way picked up his watch which read 9:14. Without the morning paper he usually had at home and the office, he finished quickly in the bathroom and returned to the bed to verify that Maggie was still alive. From their first nights together in their apartment in Dallas, Jackson had been amazed at her capacity to sleep. Even then, when their lives were being lived in the hours usually reserved for sleep, she got the most out of the time that was given her. She was neither a light, nor a short, sleeper.

She still did not wake as he dressed while sitting on the

bed. "Dressing" during this week meant stepping into his only pair of swimming trunks, making a selection from his collection of Jimmy Buffett concert t-shirts, and then pulling on tube socks and his tennis shoes. This done, Jackson rolled to his left and let his chest meet the bed as his knees hit the floor, his face falling near the jumble of pillows and sheet and hair covering Maggie's face. "Hey," he said in a normal tone, "wake up; it wasn't that good."

"Huh?" came her reply, muffled by the pillows, sheet and hair. Jackson helped her flailing hand clear the debris from around her face and repeated himself.

"I said 'wake up.' It's almost ten o'clock." He exaggerated his tone and the time.

"Oh," Maggie snapped, half responding to Jackson and half complaining as she blinked her eyes against the light from the open glass door. "It's so bright."

"It's already 90 degrees," Jackson announced, "it's gonna get really hot today, so if we want to get our sun bathing in, we'd better do it early. Come on, let's get some breakfast at the cafe first."

Fully awake now, Maggie sat up in bed and let the sheet fall forward, exposing her chest. Jackson noticed, but did nothing for once. She recovered herself and said, "I'm not hungry, but I'll go with you," as she turned to the bed side looking for her clothes."

Jackson resisted the urge to snatch the covers away. Instead, he said, "Well, you ought to eat something with all this sun we're getting. They probably have bran muffins or something healthy."

"Not likely. I'll be surprised if I can find something light I like," Maggie answered.

"I know what I'm having, and it isn't light," Jackson asserted. The fact that the Island Cafe stopped serving breakfast at 11 a.m., was a strike against it in his personal travel guide. He didn't want the waitress to be impatient with them again, and he didn't want to miss the ocean-blue-plate special: "two-eggs, any style, hash browns made from whole potatoes, three pieces of bacon or link sausage, toast, juice and coffee -- $2.95." Breakfast had always been his favorite meal, and this was a story line from his childhood. He hadn't ordered juice and meat with his breakfast since he entered college, when he first had to pay his own tab, so outrageous were the additional charges for these "extras." He had continued this practice on principle, even now that he could not legitimately be concerned about a relatively small additional expense. Shortly after waking, he had remembered his discovery and was now doubly anxious to experience his favorite meal at this more than favorable price.

It was 10:30 by the time he guided Maggie down the steps, across the parking lot, and around the privacy fence separating the complex from the cafe. There were more cars in front this morning than the day before, and Jackson had to step over a curb and then lean against the tailgate of a pick-up in order to feed more money into the TV-shaped newspaper stand and obtain Wednesday's multi-colored report on world events. They debated briefly about avoiding the day's news, but decided they had to have the weather report. Before they seated themselves on the same side of a table for four, Jackson discovered that the hurricane was no longer front page news. In fact, there was no mention of it anywhere, including on the weather map. It continued to show a cloud mass in the Gulf, but one which now was nameless and much smaller than yesterday's depiction.

As they ordered, they discussed what this meant for them, and the fishing trip. Maggie settled for a grapefruit, which she was surprised to find on the menu. Either the hurricane had come ashore somewhere else, or had gone back out to sea and become a dud. Or, Jackson thought, perhaps the editors of the paper felt that yesterday's coverage had fulfilled their responsibility to readers, and they had decided to go on to other paper-selling dangers. In any event, Jackson and Maggie concluded, quite bravely they thought, their future was still in George's hands, and they wouldn't learn it until they called him later. So, as they waited for his decision and their breakfasts, they divided the paper again - business and sports sections to Jackson, front page and entertainment sections to Maggie. They took turns repeating to one another the significant stories in their respective sections, Jackson starting.

"President Bush is considering sending the Marines to try to rescue the soldier kidnapped in Beirut."

"*Lonesome Dove* and your hero, Gus McRae, got 18 Emmy nominations!" Maggie replied.

"Wow! That gives me new respect for the TV critics," Jackson quipped. "Which is more than I can say for the Rangers. They lost again. They had a two-run lead in the ninth and McMurtry gave up a three-run homer. I'm glad I wasn't home to listen to it," he said, with sporting disgust.

"So am I, but I guess President Bush's son doesn't share your disgust. He announced that he's not running for governor because he can't take time away from running the baseball team." Maggie chuckled at the thought.

"That makes sense," Jackson answered, in all seriousness. "Fixing the Rangers is probably a bigger task than running the state."

"Little Friskies is looking for another Morris," Maggie reported. "It seems that the replacement for the original isn't selling as well. Speaking of which, you need to call to check on Mickey and Misty."

Jackson pushed back from the table and asked the waitress if he could use the phone, not wanting to have to return to the pay phone at the convenience store. The waitress gave her permission, and Jackson went to the wall behind the cash register, in front of the counter on which orders were placed and served, where a phone hung at eye level with a serpentine stretch cord that reached all the way to the floor. He picked up the handset and balanced it between his shoulder and head as he reached for his wallet. Through the open rectangle formed by the raised counter and lowered ceiling, he could see the staff at work in the kitchen as he dialed. He had always liked the precision and utility of a short order kitchen and observed the staff before him carefully. Everything he saw impressed him, including the realization that there were only women workers at the Island Café. After consulting his calling card from his wallet, he dialed the 9-digit phone number on the touchtone pad, and then entered his 12-digit calling card number. The phone at the other end of his line rang several times before it was answered. He recognized the voice of one of their neighbors' four boys, all of whom were under the age of 12.

"Jácob?" Jackson guessed.

"No, this is Peter," came the reply from the oldest son, trying to sound insulted, Jackson thought. Jackson ignored this and explained, "This is Jackson Riddle. We wanted to check on our cats. Is Jacob or your mom there?"

"No," Peter answered, "they're out, but I don't think they've seen your cat since you left."

"Which one - Mickey?" Jackson asked, surprised at the concern in his voice.

"I don't know; the one that goes outside," Peter said, again trying to sound annoyed.

"Where have they looked?" Jackson insisted, beginning to be annoyed himself.

"I don't know, all over," came the contradictory reply, "you'll have to ask them." Accepting the obvious, Jackson concluded the discussion.

"OK, tell your mom we'll call back later. When will she be home?"

"I don't know," Peter concluded for himself.

"OK, fine," Jackson said, and hung up the phone, too forcefully, he knew.

"What's wrong," Maggie asked, before he could finish crossing the twenty feet of dirty tile floor between the phone and their table. How did I get put in this role of the bringer of news? Jackson thought, and then wondered, too, whether Maggie always watched him when he was away from her and, therefore, could tell from his actions what he should be telling her upon his return. He decided to answer her directly.

"They can't find Mickey."

"Since when?" Maggie spit out the question as if she had already formed the words before he had spoken.

"Apparently since we left," Jackson reported, and then tried to clarify, "I don't know, though; I talked to Peter, and he didn't really know what was going on. He's probably still mad that we pay Jacob to look after them instead of him, as the oldest. I told him to tell Mary we would call her later."

"Well, I hope he's all right," Maggie expressed her concern. Mickey was her five year old orange fat cat whose laconic personality was Morris-like. Maggie had gotten him while she was in college, before she knew Jackson or practically everyone else now in her life, and she wanted him to be around for a lot longer. Jackson, too, had taken to him and her other cat, Misty, who was all white with blue eyes, and was stone deaf. The four of them usually went everywhere together, but Jackson had feared it was too presumptuous to accept George's hospitality on their own behalf, and that of their cats. Now, he wished he had been just so presumptuous. Maggie called him back from his reappraisal. "I was just talking to these women about their cats."

Jackson turned to look at the table directly behind him

where three women had seated themselves, and were drinking coffee. They must have arrived while he was on the phone, because he didn't recall seeing them before, and he was sure he would have remembered them. They were dressed alike in cotton jump suits, the kind that industrial workers wear over their regular clothes. The suits were a steel-blue color and each had a red and white patch on their left shoulder. There were three walkie-talkies standing at attention in the middle of the table.

"They're paramedics," Maggie explained. This fact registered with Jackson, and he shook his head, nodding in their direction. It went with what he had first thought about their appearance. They all had short hair and wore no makeup. Through the outline of the jump suits, Jackson could see that they each had developed muscles like a body-builder. Jackson knew it was wrong, but he couldn't help drawing certain conclusions about such women who obviously felt that they had to look unfeminine to prove that women can do a job that they believe is wrongfully considered a man's work. Was this the expression of their feminism or his sexism? Again interrupting his thoughts, Maggie continued, "I overheard them talking about somebody getting bitten by a rattle snake, and I was concerned. When I heard they took him to a vet, I had to ask about it, and they told me it was only a cat."

"There are rattlesnakes on this island?" Jackson asked, alarmed, ignoring the crisis at hand and projecting himself into a future one.

"Oh yes," one of the women answered, joining their conversation, "they're everywhere." Jackson turned all the way in his seat and looked at the woman speaking.

"Don't go walking in the dunes at night, whether you're on the beach or away from it," she advised them, "that's what happened to the cat we took in last night." Still thinking about her warning and remembering his evening walks with Maggie, Jackson responded to her other statement which confused him.

"Someone called the paramedics for a cat?"

"Well," the same woman answered, as the other two laughed, "yes and no."

"It's my cat," said another of the women, the one with her back to Jackson, who then turned completely as she spoke. She was the stoutest of the three, and seemed to pull herself up larger as she talked of her cat. "He likes to hunt them, but last night he must have met his match."

"I started to tell you," Maggie said, "listen to this." The woman with the wounded cat repeated her description of his battle tactics.

"Well, he finds a snake and then circles around till it raises up or at least coils to where he has a target. Then he swipes at it with his paw and just slices it open with his claws. I don't know how he does it, but I've seen the results." She shook her head, and the other women joined in unison. Maggie shook her head, too, and commented further to Jackson.

"I told them about Mickey getting bitten in the Hill Country, and how he survived it. They don't know if hers is going to make it, though."

"Well," Jackson said, taking in all the information given to him from both sides, "I hope he does make it, and that we find Mickey." He looked back at Maggie hopefully.

"Oh, is your cat missing?" The first woman that had spoken asked.

"Well," Jackson explained again, "we're not sure we're getting accurate information from...." Before he had finished his sentence, all three walkie-talkies on the women's table squawked and reported in stereo that they were needed at the university microbiology lab. As two of the women turned off their radios and rose from the table, the third reported into hers that they were on their way. Then, as the first two went out the door, the third woman stopped at Jackson and Maggie's table, and said goodbye.

"Good luck with your cat," Maggie said to her.

"You too," she replied, "and don't forget what I said about watching out for snakes."

Good grief! Jackson thought to himself. Around here, it's not safe on sea or land.

IX

By noon, Jackson and Maggie had returned to the swimming pool with books, tapes and suntan lotion. Neither of them sun-burned easily, but now in their fourth consecutive day in the sun, their skin was in need of moisturizing. Jackson usually disliked reading in the sun, and preferred listening to music. Here, however, the sea breeze made the heat bearable, enabling him to concentrate to the extent his choice of reading required.

Jackson had always enjoyed reading, from as far back as he could remember, but he had generally done it for credit, whether in grade school, his undergraduate literature classes, or in law school. He had gone many years without reading much for "pleasure" until a couple years after law school when he had finally regained the desire to read, having lost it due to the nature and amount of reading required in studying and practicing law. He remembered that he was a literature snob, having only read those works that his classes had required or that were publicly known to be "classics." Of course, this precluded him from reading practically everything written in his lifetime. Recognizing his narrow-mindedness, Jackson had decided to read only contemporary books for as long as it took him to understand modern themes, or the modern treatment of classical ones. He was now in the third year of this study.

Conversely, Maggie had never been a reader before she married Jackson. She had always preferred spending her time with other people, and in less cerebral entertainment, such partying or just watching television. As she put it, she had studied popular fiction in the romance genre. At the time she married Jackson, she had given little time and no thought to literary fiction. It was only through observing Jackson's habit of not only reading, but contemplating and discussing the books he read, that she discovered there was more to reading than just scanning the words. She had begun asking him for book recommendations, and had even selected some from his shelves on her own. In preparation for this trip, she had gone to the library and checked out four books. Jackson had bought three for the trip. He always bought the books he read, and did not even own a library card. By Thursday, they had each finished two books, and had begun a third.

Jackson first read a book about an Iowa farmer who heard a voice in a cornfield telling him that if he built a baseball diamond on his farm, "he" would come. The farmer accepts the voice's proposition and ballplayers magically appear from an apparent baseball purgatory. They had recently seen the movie based on the book, and Jackson had liked it very much, as its subject was baseball. Before finishing the book, however, he had decided it was one of those rare instances when Hollywood had done a better job. While reading, he noticed several passages that he believed needed a strong editor.

Next, Jackson had gone to a well-established writer, although he was reading his first book. The author, a Texan, who was now middle-aged and had achieved enormous success in the late '60's when this first book and then a subsequent one about small town life were made into popular movies, one starring a young Paul Newman and the other making a star of an unknown actress named Cybil Shepard. Jackson had not read any of his works until the mid '80's when he published *Lonesome Dove*, an epic western centered on a cattle drive from the Texas-Mexico border to the unsettled region of Montana. The book was wildly successful and won a Pulitzer Prize. After hearing rave reviews about the story in his adopted Texas home, Jackson had picked up the Western out of curiosity. He was very surprised to find that he loved it. He believed the main character, Gus, was the best drawn figure in American literature since Holden Caulfield, and certainly more likeable. Now, the TV critics apparently agreed, giving the mini-series adaptation of the book eighteen Emmy nominations.

Having proclaimed the work "great" literature, Jackson figured he needed to give the writer's work a deeper review. He had selected his debut novel because he liked the title, taken from the poet W. B. Yeats. Jackson liked the fact that he knew it was from Yeats, and that it was inscribed on Yeats' tombstone, knowledge that he shared with Maggie. The early work was on as small a scale as the Western was grand. Jackson liked it, but he did not feel for the characters as he had in *Lonesome Dove*, particularly Gus. This wasn't the writer's fault though, Jackson thought, just evidence that he had grown as a writer.

Jackson was starting on another writer's prize-winning book, one about racial tension in a small town in Georgia that had been compared in subject and style to Faulkner. Jackson was skeptical of such a comparison, since he believed Faulkner to be America's - if not mankind's - greatest writer, but he was anxious to see what type of writing the supposed experts considered comparable. Now, he sat in the bright sun facing the Gulf, with his back to the pool and the horseshoe-shaped complex, and tried to keep his arms off his sides and his hands holding the book resting on the fabric of his swimming trunks. He knew that such care was necessary to ensure full exposure of his body to the sun. He had hoped that this week would give him the first real tan he had had since passing the bar exam five years earlier, and his wish was coming true.

Maggie sat next to him in last year's bikini. She had not found one this year that she liked; so, she had bought a new one-piece and continued to wear her old two-piece. She was thinking about her body and its appearance in what she considered old clothes. This was brought on by her reflection on the book she had just finished, a gothic-like romance about a family estate and the apparent super-natural effects of a tree planted by one of the family members several generations past. It was trivial she knew, particularly by Jackson's standards, but she had wanted to start the vacation with something similar to the almost mythical nature Jackson attributed to the island. She thought she had succeeded, and was excited. She was trying to draw Jackson into a discussion of the book when a woman they had seen briefly every day at the complex came out to the pool in her bathing suit, with a towel and a book in her hands. She was older, early forties or perhaps later, Maggie thought, but was trim and still had long blonde hair. Her skin was dark brown, which seemed to say that she had been there all summer, if not all her life. She smiled at Jackson and Maggie, but said nothing as she took a chair near them. In the stillness of the port at mid-day, and the solitude of their dock, the woman's arrival seemed to Maggie like a home invader, and she broke off her conversation with Jackson. She turned instead to her next book, a collection of short stories by a little old lady from Mississippi - the "female Faulkner" Jackson had said. After only a few moments of getting settled in her chair, the woman turned to Maggie and spoke in a raspy, twangy voice that seemed to Jackson at least partly affected.

"I just have to know what you kids are reading. You all have had your noses in those books all week, and last night I came out onto the balcony and said, 'Bob!' He's my husband. 'Come out here. Those kids are reading in the dark!'" She paused, taking what Jackson believed to be her first breath since she had begun speaking. Before he could finish the thought, however, she continued, leaning up in the lounge chair and turning sideways toward them. "Then this morning I saw you down here again, and I said to Bob, 'I'm going to the library and get me some books. Those kids are making me feel ashamed.'" She paused again, and Jackson thought perhaps it was his turn to speak. Smiling at what he took to be a compliment, he responded.

"Thanks; I'm glad we inspired you."

"You won't want to read any of the stuff he's reading though," Maggie broke in, wrinkling her nose.

"Oh?" the woman started up again, understanding the insinuation. "I don't know about that. I used to read a lot, and of course at finishing school we had to read all the classics." As she talked, she casually pulled a gold case from beneath her towel, opened it, extracted a cigarette and then lit it, all in three short, graceful movements. Jackson observed this while trying to remember when, if ever, he had heard the term "finishing school" used in conversation. He glanced quickly at Maggie as she was looking at him, and their stares were a mixture of mocking and intimidation.

"My name's Bette. Where're you all from?" the woman said, and asked in the same tone.

"I'm Maggie, and this is my husband, Jackson," Maggie answered.

"We're from Dallas," Jackson added

"Really!" Bette shrieked. "I *love* Dallas, That's where I went to finishing school."

"Let me guess," Jackson said, and named the exclusive girls' school that trained all of Dallas' elite daughters.

"Why, of course," Bette replied, "but it's not like it used to be. Bob and I went up there last month for a summer fund-raiser, and this little doll, a staff-member, I guess, met us at the gate sitting in a convertible Mercedes. She got out wearing this low-cut silk blouse and pencil skirt and tip-toed up to the driver's side window. She leaned in to welcome us and give directions. Then she sauntered back to the car, giving Bob ample time to study her outline. I thought he was going to have a heart attack, or worse, that he'd give them all our money. Honey, when I went to school there, the only thing we could wear that tight were white dinner gloves." She paused long enough to shake her head and exhale smoke, which Jackson thought she must have been swallowing. As far as he could tell, this was her only exhale after several draws on the cigarette. "Things sure have changed," Bette continued, leaning her head back in her chair and closing her eyes for an instant, as if recalling things as they used to be. Her reflection was only momentary. "Did you grow up in Dallas?" she asked, opening her eyes, and turning her head toward them again.

"No," Jackson answered quickly, then paused, before adding, "I'm from Tennessee, and Maggie is from Houston."

"Oh, well that's a coincidence. One of the books I checked out this morning is Sam Houston's biography. He was from Tennessee, you know." She reached under her chair and picked up a heavy, cloth-bound book with clear plastic wrapping around its dust jacket. "I like biographies," she added. Jackson nodded vaguely before speaking.

"I'm into fiction, but with realism," he said, remembering the genesis of their conversation.

"Yes, I *must* know what you've been reading," Bette replied. Jackson showed her the book in his hands, and Bette shook her head unknowingly. He then mentioned the Western, and she slapped her thigh.

"I just finished that one. It is wonderful! I picked it up after seeing the mini-series. I just loved Gus. You know he was from Tennessee, too."

Jackson smiled, glancing at Maggie as if to say 'See!' "Yes," he said instead to Bette, "it says in the book that if he hadn't come to Texas to be a Ranger Gus probably would have stayed in Tennessee to be lawyer. I like to think I've combined the two," he said proudly. Bette nodded vaguely this time, before speaking.

"I liked the way he remembered his days in Tennessee," she said, "the misty mornings and the green mountains. I've been there and it's really like that." Suddenly, her voice had taken on a faraway tone. Jackson leaned forward, surprised.

"You really did read that book. I guess I've discussed it with fifty people, and you're the first to mention that part. I thought it was just nostalgia for home that made me notice it."

"Child, nostalgia becomes part of your breath when you get to be my age. But those mountains aren't in your head, they're real. You ought to know better than me." An uneasy silence formed as Bette concluded. She looked into the water, and Jackson thought about what she had said. Maggie looked up at the blue sky and circling gulls, thinking she'd like to be feeding them.

"Well," Jackson said finally, as the moment passed, "I guess I'm a Texan now, anyway. I wouldn't move back. I like the wide open spaces too much. When I go back to Tennessee now, I get claustrophobic. Everything seems so small and closed in, trees and kudzu grow right out to the roads, and the hills crowd in on each other, and crowd out the sky." Jackson paused, looking as if he felt surrounded.

"And don't forget the winding back roads that make me throw up," Maggie interjected.

"Yeah, that, too," Jackson said. He looked over at Bette. "She hated it when my family insisted on taking us for a ride in the country." Patting Maggie's leg, he added, "She turned white as a wedding dress."

"Hey, it wasn't just a ride in the country," Maggie insisted, "and it was you, not your family. You had to show me where all your old flames lived." Jackson rolled his eyes.

"Let's don't go there again," he said.

"That's exactly what I said," Maggie replied, emphatically, then smiled at Bette and added, "and my wedding dress was actually off-white, for the record."

"Ok, you two," Bette interrupted. "We were talking about geography and statehood, not matrimony.

"Right," Jackson said, more to Maggie than Bette. Then he looked past her, to Bette. "And as you pointed out, Tennesseans had a lot to do with Texas's statehood, or at least independence. Sam Houston was one. Davy Crockett was another, and there were many others. There are more Tennessee flags in the Alamo memorial than any other state – thirty-three, I think."

"Well," Bette remarked, "I don't need to plow through the biography of Sam Houston, I can just sit here and listen to you." Jackson shrunk back a bit, if not visibly, at least audibly.

"No," he said in a quieter tone. "That's about all I know about it, but I have been aware of the connection between Tennessee and Texas. I feel it, somehow, but I can't explain it exactly. I like being *from* Tennessee, but I like living in Texas more, even the uglier parts like Dallas. Now, where I would really like to live is the Texas Hill Country. I'd take that over Dallas, or Tennessee, anytime."

"Really?" Bette asked. "I'm surprised. The Hill Country is nice, but I can't see it being more attractive than the Smoky

Mountains – real mountains and trees, with fantastic colors in the fall, not just hills and scrub oaks and cedar."

"Most people say that, and maybe they're right." Jackson said. "But, I fell in love with the Hill Country the first time I saw it. When Maggie took me to Hunt to meet her parents a few years ago, I couldn't believe how beautiful it is. Sure the hills are low, and so are the trees, but it has such an unspoiled feel to it – like Africa. The air is clear, and so is the river. It just felt like home – not that I should ever feel at home in a place called Hunt." Jackson smiled to himself, and shook his head slightly. Maggie and Bette were looking at him, Bette with her own slight smile and Maggie with a slight frown.

"What?" he asked Maggie, "you think I *should* be from Hunt?"

"I don't know where you're from," Maggie said, rolling her eyes toward Bette.

"Just hush!" Bette told her. "He could be from wherever he's thinking about at the moment, and I like that. I can tell he's a thinker, just like Gus." She smiled at Jackson, as Maggie rolled her eyes again, this time back toward Jackson.

"I'll take that," Jackson said. "You can associate me with Gus in any way that you want. And, despite what he says in the book, I think Texas was just as attractive to Gus as the Smoky Mountains. He stayed at least, and I think I will, too."

"That's good to hear," Maggie broke in, "since I refuse to move to Tennessee."

"But you just married me so you could get out of Houston," Jackson joked.

"Don't whine, you get something out of it," Maggie shot back.

"Be careful. Maybe I'll make you live in Hunt someday, or worse, the Panhandle where Gus's creator is from," Jackson tried to answer her.

"You kids," Bette laughed, returning to her girlish pitch,

as she sat back and opened her book. "All I'll say is that Texas certainly is an interesting place. I saw in the paper this morning that they were holding a casting call for another movie version of one of this guy's books, and somebody robbed the post office while no one was paying attention." She reached under her chaise and exchanged the book for a newspaper folded in quarters. She opened it fully, and held the pages in her outstretched hands, like a conductor calling his orchestra to attention. She gestured through several bars, before stopping with both arms, as if holding a crescendo.

"Here it is. 'The robbers forced their way into the Archer City post office, bound two female employees, and took $40 and some blank money orders from the safe, authorities said.'" She lowered the paper to her lap and looked at Jackson. "Kind of makes you want to know more. Were the robbers from the town, or part of the production crew? Maybe they were just passing through the Panhandle and saw a commotion they could take advantage of. Hard to say. You don't know exactly what commentary is being made about American society – or, at least, about which part." Maggie and Jackson looked at each other yet again, this time in acknowledgement of their new friend.

"A good observation, I'd say," Jackson spoke for both of them. "We," he nodded at Maggie, "are coming to the conclusion that the newspapers and other media never tell us enough about the stories they cover to do us any good – to really form responsible opinions."

"I don't know if I'd go that far," Bette responded, "but, I see your point." She orchestrated the refolding of the paper to its delivered state. "Like this," she pointed sharply to the front page headline. 'Pro-Iranians in Beirut Claim to Hang U.S. Hostage.' Do they have to put that in the headline?" Her posture stiffened as she turned more toward Jackson and Maggie. "First, it's just a claim, not proven yet. And second, if it is a fact, shouldn't they focus on what President Bush is going to do about it?" She stopped, without looking directly at either of them. When she didn't continue, Jackson answered.

"Not really much he can do, I don't think. He could send the Marines to Beirut, but that didn't work very well for President Reagan, or even President Carter before that."

"He could invade Lebanon with the entire U.S. army!" Bette shot back, surprising them all with her emphasis.

"Do you risk thousands of American lives because one has been taken – or just might have been?" Jackson asked, trying to sound dispassionate. Maggie cleared her throat.

"Okay, now you two, stop it," she said sternly. "We just met. It bored me to hear you talk about literature, but it's scaring me when you get into politics."

"Oh, don't worry, honey," Bette softened her tone, and relaxed back in her chaise. "I just get a little worked up sometime. The sisters said I had a spirit like a demon."

"That's not necessarily a bad thing," Jackson volunteered.

"You couldn't tell them that," Bette laughed now. "They were probably right, though. If I can't control myself, I ought to stay out of matters I can't do anything about. I'm just wasting my energy." She lifted the paper off her lap, and flipped it over to the lower half of the front page. "Now, here's something I could be passionate about, and maybe have an impact on. Those jokers in Austin are talking about making the wealthy school districts give money to the poor school districts – calling it the 'Robin Hood' plan!" She folded the paper again with scorn. "What do you think about that?" She looked at Jackson with the same emotion.

"I'd say calling in 'robbin' would be pretty accurate," Jackson said. Bette gave him a collusive smile, "It sounds good in principle," he added, "but probably bad in practical results." Bette nodded, still smiling wryly, as she shoved the paper back under her chair and picked up the library book.

"That sounds like Sam Houston's view of secession, and he was right that it wouldn't work," she said.

"I don't think I can agree that secession was all right in principle," Jackson said. Bette shot a sharp look at Jackson and started to speak, but was stopped by Maggie's hand held up between them.

"Don't even start on the Civil War," Maggie insisted.

"You mean the War of Northern Aggression," Bette said, grinning, but then held her tongue.

"Grant called it the Rebellion in his memoirs," Jackson slipped in, before Maggie could glare at him. He refrained from any further comment when she did.

The three of them read quietly for nearly an hour, with only Jackson stirring to cool off in the pool. After his second dip, he went to the office by the pool to call George. The intervention of the hurricane had come so swiftly and, they thought, providentially, that neither Jackson nor Maggie still felt the fear or loathing that had gripped them earlier. Their resolve to let George decide their fate had not melted. Even now, as he dialed George's number for the verdict, Jackson was not concerned. Perhaps it was because he knew that even though the conditions on the island were fine, the Gulf must certainly still be feeling Chantal's effect. Three boats had left the dock since he had risen that morning, and all three were now again securely lashed in their slips. Even as a newcomer to the port, Jackson surmised that this meant the weather had forced them to return. His hypothesis was confirmed when he reached George at the warehouse.

"Weeeelll, Jackie," George began, "the first lesson a fisherman learns about hurricanes is that it's not just the storm, but also its aftermath that upsets the fish. The reason your paper didn't mention it today is because it hit Galveston and Houston last night and broke up. It didn't do anything there, but we've got some five foot swells in the Gulf. It will probably still be pretty choppy out there tomorrow and that may discourage the fish from feeding."

"I understand," Jackson replied, confident and agreeable.

"But a little extra challenge won't bother you, will it?" George changed his tone and surprised Jackson with the challenge.

"Uh, whatever you think," Jackson stammered, not being able to think fast enough to say 'yes, it will'. He hung up the phone feeling as if he had been outsmarted by opposing counsel, or blind-sided by a judge. When he returned to the pool, Bette and Maggie were again engaged in conversation, but Maggie had gathered her things.

"Poseidon is still restless," he said, and then, realizing that Maggie did not understand the reference, added, "it's still rough, but George wants to try it tomorrow anyway."

"And you agreed?" Maggie answered, accusingly.

"That's what we came for, isn't it?" Jackson snapped back, hearing the annoyance in his voice, but unable to control it, even if he was actually annoyed with himself.

"We came for relaxation," Maggie scoffed, trying to sound offended.

"Well," Jackson said, "I didn't tell him we would definitely go, but I couldn't think of a good reason why we wouldn't. I would like a better excuse than that we're just chicken."

"You're right," Maggie conceded, with resignation in her voice. "Of course, we'll go."

"What are you all deciding about?" Bette asked, finally.

"Whether we should put our lives in George Water's hands," Jackson answered quickly.

"Oh, are you going fishing with him?" Bette asked, without a trace of inference Jackson thought.

"We were," he replied, hoping to draw an opinion, "but the storm has delayed us."

"Well," Bette answered in her calmest tone yet, "nobody

in this place knows fishing the Gulf better than George Waters."

"Really?" Maggie asked, sincerely. "I've never met him, but he sounds a bit – eccentric."

"Oh, honey," Bette laughed, "George is way more than a bit eccentric, but that doesn't change the fact that he knows how to fish the Gulf." Maggie considered this for a moment, perhaps thinking that Bette would expand on her views. She didn't. Maggie stood, as Jackson gathered his things.

"I guess we'll find out soon enough," was all that Maggie could think to say, and Bette just smiled in return. She was intently reading the book on Sam Houston when Maggie glanced over her shoulder, as she and Jackson climbed the stairs at the end of the building to George's unit. Instead of searching the refrigerator for a late lunch, they both went straight to bed and fell quickly to sleep, sapped of strength by the sun's seemingly magnetic force.

Now it was Maggie's turn to dream. She was in her parents' kitchen in Hunt. 'Yes, Mom, I know I just met him, but I love him. No, I don't know why, I just know I do.' She was surprised to hear herself talking this way to her mother. They had never had such direct conversations before. ("You aren't *really* close," Jackson had asserted that first night.) Why start now? Had she been chastised for seeing Jackson so much, for spending so much time in Dallas with him? Maggie shifted on the bed next to the motionless Jackson. She was straining to see her mother, but couldn't. Where did she go? Who was I just talking to?

'From what I hear, he's not like anyone else you've ever dated,' a voice said to her.

'No, he's not,' she started to reply, thinking that it was her mother's voice. She also thought she understood the comment, but then hesitated. 'How exactly do you mean that?' No reply. This made Maggie uncomfortable. She felt she needed to defend Jackson, and her feelings.

'He's....' she stopped, not knowing exactly how to describe him, or her feelings for him, 'different,' she finally continued.

'Is that the best you can come up with?' the voice asked, almost taunting her. It was not her mother's voice, she was sure now. It was familiar, though. Maggie wanted to be angry, but wasn't.

'What more do you want?'

'Meet me in Memphis. That's where I'll be,' the voice replied in rhythm, almost like singing. Now Maggie recognized the voice, but why was he in Memphis? She was about to call out a name when she woke with the sound of the jetty boat's 7 pm departure-whistle screaming across the port. When it stopped, and Maggie came fully awake, the familiar voice continued singing: "*Meet me in Memphis. My wild days are through. Still nothing replaces, me next to you.*" Jackson was singing along with Jimmy Buffett.

X

The early evening's calm light glided through the slightly open glass door. Maggie raised her head and saw Jackson through the tinted glass, sitting in what now seemed like his director's chair, looking out to their port. She heard the too-familiar voice of Jimmy Buffett coming from the tape player perched on the railing, and the constant duet that played in their home and car, when Jackson sang along. She laid her head back on the pillow, and the first complete thought she grasped was a question: what should she do about Jackson? For weeks she had noticed an increase in his moodiness. He had never been one to talk about the office, but lately she felt he was talking much less about anything, and for him that meant something. And when he sang Jimmy Buffett songs, she knew he was thinking deeply about something.

Although she had been married to him for over two years now, they had known each other for barely three. That was not really long enough to know someone well, even if you loved him. She wondered at the fact that she could be so certain that she loved Jackson, even as she reminded herself that she didn't truly know him. She was not able to read his thoughts, or even his moods. This was true despite the manner in which he had stormed into her life and dominated its course since she had admitted on their first date that, yes, she could see herself moving to Dallas. He had a way, which she did not fully understand, of vividly expressing his personality traits without clearly revealing himself, other than that he loved Jimmy Buffett and William Faulkner. After one date, she had learned more about what he thought than she knew of any of the boyfriends she had had, but even today she did not feel like she knew him. From the start, she had presumed that he was a success as a lawyer. Apart from the superficial signs in his lifestyle – fancy car, high-rise apartment and travel - there was his professional self-assurance and the respect he was shown by his superiors. She was surprised that he showed little tension from the practice of law in a major American law firm, except that he insisted on being at the office every day of the week. It was something of a miracle when he came home and told her they were coming to this island for a week. He hadn't been away from the office for more than three days since their honeymoon, and that included weekends. He had actually gone to the office directly from the airport upon their return from their honeymoon. Even a commute from Europe was apparently not too much for him.

Though he rarely discussed his day, through careful observation Maggie had discerned a difference which she believed signaled its events. If he came home and talked of other things, (he never talked of his cases), all was well. However, on days when nothing could engage him in conversation, she guessed that things at work were compelling him to silence. A marked increase in these latter days had Maggie searching for a way to be the support she believed a wife should be. But how, exactly, was she supposed to support him? Nothing had presented itself yet, and she didn't think there was cause to panic. After all, very little if anything had changed in Jackson's behavior toward her. He still brought her flowers every Friday. He still told her he loved her at least five times a day, and he still found her desirable. Obviously, his work was of no concern for their marriage. Perhaps, she thought, their marriage was creating concern for his work. Morning after morning he turned to wave to Maggie as she drove away from the plaza of his office building. To spend more time together after they had bought a house away from downtown, she had started driving him to work in the morning and returning downtown in the evening to meet him at the gym. Recently, in the mornings, however, his appearance in her rear view mirror had reminded Maggie of her kindergarteners as they said good-bye to their parents the first few days of school. This same look of resignation, even pain, often occupied his face, even when he sang Jimmy Buffett songs. Now, as she got up from the bed and walked through the sliding-glass door and onto the balcony, she recognized the look as she listened to him sing.

The light was brighter here than in the bedroom, but still soft, and it set a mood calmer than her thoughts. Being careful not to conflict with it, she remained silent as she put her arms around Jackson's neck and bent her head to his shoulder.

"Hi," Jackson said softly. "I didn't hear you get up."

"That's because you're on some other island with Jimmy Buffett," she said, also softly, as she stood back upright and reached over to lower the volume of a song she recognized. The recording had been released at about the time they had met, and it was her introduction to Buffett's music and Jackson's obsession with it. At first she was annoyed by the constant replaying of the same tape as they drove in his car, or sat on the balcony of his high-rise apartment. Later, she had learned that Jackson always did this with Buffett's new releases, and she had grown to tolerate it. Now she even liked most of the songs, but still didn't like hearing them over and over.

"Thinking about Buffett's music again?" She asked, deciding to pry.

"Sort of, I guess," he answered. "Yes," he then admitted, and continued. "I listen to these songs and get this incredible feeling that I can't explain, and then I wonder, 'Am I the only person who thinks this is great, painful stuff?'" Maggie didn't answer him, and wasn't sure she could treat it as a serious question. He didn't notice. "Then I think, 'Would he appreciate how seriously I listen to his music, or would he laugh at me?'"

"Well, yes," she felt obligated to respond, "you probably are the only person who listens to this music like it is a sacred Mass, but I'm sure he wouldn't laugh at you," Maggie said. "He'd probably be grateful to know someone takes him this seriously." Jackson smiled, as if trying to diffuse the emotional pitch he now realized he had set.

"Not likely, if it was just coming from me. Fortunately, we'll never know."

"Ok," she said, "it's good to know that you aren't going to abandon me for some crusade to confront your idol," Maggie said.

"Of course, I won't," Jackson said. "I'll just stick around and drive you nuts worshipping him through his music. But, I won't go looking for him, because I don't want to discuss it with him."

"You mean if you met Jimmy Buffett you wouldn't try to talk to him about how much you get from his songs?" Maggie asked.

"Of course not," Jackson said, his voice rising, "Do you think I could get him to understand my feelings? I can't even explain them to you, and you married me. He'd think I am an idiot, and he would probably be right."

"Well," Maggie answered, backing down, "I guess it would be hard to describe, no matter how much time you spend thinking about it." Sensing some sympathy, however, Jackson quickly decided to test his ability to describe it.

"When we first met, and were dancing around in your brother's front yard to Buffett's music playing on my car stereo, did you have any idea what he was singing about?" Jackson let the question hang in the air as Maggie stepped back from his chair, a little startled.

"I don't know," she said. "I don't remember thinking about it."

"Would you be surprised if it was about betrayal in his personal relationships, and depression about his future?"

"Of course, I'd be surprised," Maggie answered sharply. "No one thinks Buffett sings about those things."

"Well, you just weren't listening, then," Jackson said, "and it wasn't the first time he wrote about loneliness and betrayal. He wrote a whole album about the apparent failure of his second marriage." Maggie was skeptical.

"You're telling me," she asked, critically, "that Jimmy Buffett writes love songs about the break-up of his marriage?"

"Absolutely, I am. It's one of my favorite albums – 'Riddles in the Sand.' The tempo is typical, light and upbeat, but the words are really powerful. If he is dealing with his relationship with his wife, which seems obvious once you listen to the songs and see that he dedicates them to her - he even calls her the 'ultimate riddle in the sand' - it is remarkable how willing he is to lay himself bare and express the pain they have caused each other. You can get the picture with just the titles." Jackson reached down and picked up his ever-present cassette case from beside his chair. He opened it, revealing two rows fully occupied with tapes. Maggie could see, and knew from experience, that Jimmy Buffett recordings represented more than half of the twenty-four selections.

"I remember the first time I saw you carry that case,"

she said, leaning into him, smiling. "We were walking down the hall to your apartment the first time. You had your brief case in one hand and were carrying your suit coat over your other arm, and this cassette case was just a bulge under it. When I asked what it was, you showed me, and said it was for your 'small cases.'"

"And you laughed out loud," Jackson grinned. "I remember, because I loved your laugh," he said, pausing to look intently at her. "And, because it was only about an hour later that I decided I loved you, too. And then, another hour or so after that, I told you we were going to get married." He looked out at the water, and then back to her quickly, as if he had just realized something. "You know, I think that was happiest night of my life."

"It probably was for me, too," Maggie said, "because that was before I knew how much competition I had from Jimmy Buffett - that you would always be holding me with one arm and him with the other. See what I mean?" She pointed to his right hand, as he had taken his gaze off of her and begun to review the tapes in the case.

"Come on, I know *you're* not that sensitive." Jackson ran his finger down the row and pulled a cassette from its slot with his thumb and forefinger. "But, I hope we've reached a point in our marriage where you can handle, or more importantly, will take seriously, what I am trying to explain here about his music. It's really important to me." He paused, but Maggie didn't reply.

He ignored her silence and held the single cassette up to his eyes in the dim light to read from the cover. "Listen to these titles - '*Who's the Blonde Stranger?*' '*When the wild life betrays me.*' '*Love in Decline.*' '*She's going out of my mind,*' *Bigger than the both of us.*' That ought to tell you something, but the lyrics are even more pointed – even poignant. Listen to this." Getting excited, he quickly pressed a button on the tape player; the cartridge opened and he replaced the existing tape with the new one. After a couple of mechanical clicks and a pause, Buffett's familiar voice came through the small speakers singing solo about a trip to Texas. It took Maggie a few lines to concentrate, but when he sang the chorus, she began to understand:

Who's the blonde stranger out there with my wife?
What were they doing in the moonlight?
This side of Texas is all new to me
Who are these strangers who live by the sea?

A small fish jumped in the empty dock slip directly below them, and Jackson leaned forward to see. Buffett continued to sing.

We talk in our sleep and then the next morning
I ask her who's Dan and she says who's Marie?

The chorus began again, and Jackson turned down the volume slowly. As the music faded, Maggie looked at him and nodded.

"It does seem to suggest a little problem in their relationship, or whoever he is talking about," she said.

"I agree," Jackson said, leaning over to turn the volume back up. "Now listen to this." Again, Buffett's lone voice came through the machine, but seemed closer to them with the slower tempo in the diminishing light:

I see a trembling hand
And a gold wedding band
Wonder where do I stand?

When the wild life betrays me
And I'm too far from home
Will you be there to save me?
Will you shelter my heart till I'm strong?
Or will you just hang up the phone?"

Maggie shook her head in agreement when it was quiet again, but she didn't speak. Jackson pressed the 'fast forward' button on the player and then looked up at Maggie.

"Sound like a more serious subject matter than you'd expect from one of his songs?" He pushed the 'stop' and 'play' buttons, and then the 'forward' button, again, when the song he heard was not the one he was seeking.

"It is different than what I would expect, if I ever actually listened to the words," Maggie admitted. "It sounds pretty personal."

"Yes, but also universal." Jackson stopped and started the tape again. He let it play this time, but turned down the volume in the middle of a song. "I could have used that last line on you after the soap story." Maggie stared without responding. "Fortunately," Jackson continued as he turned the volume up once more, "I saw the light in time and, apparently, so did Jimmy." Buffett's spirited voice returned:

This comes from deep in my soul
Your sweet love has taken control
I'll swim across the ocean if you tell me so
I'll take you to the jump-up if you want to go
It never is too late to make a brand new start

I'm down on the knees of my heart
Down here on the knees of my heart.

Once again he lowered the volume, and waited for Maggie to speak. She hesitated and looked out to the port that was now in darkness, broken only by sabers of light striking out across the water from the light posts on the dock. After another moment, she turned to him with a warm smile.

"I hear what you're saying, but it's a good thing that you waited three years to explain it. I don't know if it would have made as much sense if you had tried to get me back by singing Jimmy Buffett songs."

"Fair enough," Jackson nodded, "but wait, there's a little more to explain." Once again he raised the volume, and then punched the forward button briefly. When he released it, Buffett was in full voice.

Feel it all with a willing heart
Every stop is a place to start
If you know how to play the part with feeling
I play with feelings.

"That's it," Jackson said quietly, but emphatically, as he pressed the 'stop' button. "He plays with feelings! He may live the dancing life, but it's not unexamined. And even that line has an ambiguity. In the liner notes the lyric reads "I play with feeling," but listen to this." He punched the button marked "rewind" and then quickly punched "stop" and then "play." Buffett's voice rang out again. "....know how to play the part with feeling. I play with feelings.' Jackson jammed his finger down on 'stop' again, and turned sharply to Maggie. "Did you hear that? He said *feelings*, plural. Maybe he means the same thing as if he had said *feeling*, sincerity, but he could just as easily be confessing that he's played with *her* feelings – her emotions, her trust. That's what I think it means, and that's what he does with me, his music, I mean. It plays with my emotion, although it usually puts me in this kind of introspective mood, even with a song titled 'La Vie Dansante.' That's 'The Dancing Life.'" Maggie almost laughed, but managed to stifle it into a smirk, as she looked up to the sky and saw the night's first stars appearing.

"That's good," she grinned, "because I was hoping that you weren't going to quit being a lawyer and take up dancing under the stars, or become a music critic. Neither would be a good career choice, from what I've seen."

"The 'dancing life' he refers to is a metaphor," Jackson responded with his own smirk. "I probably can't do it, whether it is actual or theoretical, but I'm certainly drawn to the idea. Of course, I don't intend to have the same kind of troubles with you that Buffett's apparently singing about." Maggie came back to his side, and put her arm around his shoulder.

"I'm all for that," she said, and leaned her head down against Jackson's. "There's a lot of weird stuff going on in there," she bumped her head against his, "but it doesn't have to lead you away from me."

"I'm all for that," Jackson agreed. "Of course, commitment and happiness in our relationship will likely prevent me from ever being an artist. I think it takes this kind of pain to write anything good. That's the reason why I never wrote you any other letters while we were dating, you know. I was just too happy."

"Well, that doesn't make any sense to me," Maggie said, straightening up and releasing his shoulder, "but if it *keeps* you happy, I'm fine with it. I'd rather have you, than all of those letters that you said you wrote to Spider Woman. She must have made you really miserable, which makes me happy."

"Ok, Ok, like you said before, let's don't go there." He stood up and stretched, and then turned to put his arms around Maggie. "I am happy," he said, "and I'm glad I got a chance to show you a little of what I hear in Buffett's music. And all this is from *one* album, and we didn't even cover all of it. You really need to listen to it from beginning to end to understand how good it is – what a trial and redemption in his life it represents."

"Whatever you say," Maggie chuckled completely this time. She had not seen everything that Jackson described, but she couldn't miss the seriousness and appreciation in his description. She heard it again now in his voice, and wanted to respond. "But, I hope you won't have to try as hard to keep me," she said.

"Oh, I'm going to try much harder," Jackson answered, smiling, "whatever it takes to stay out of the problems they had, even if it does cost me some literary experiences."

"I'll make a deal with you," Maggie said. "I will let you keep on looking to Buffett for your emotional outlet, if you don't follow in his footsteps."

"Well, there's more, you know, than just this emotional connection. He's got songs about writers I love – Faulkner, Twain, Marquez." When Jackson started to explain, Maggie quickly moved in close to him and put both of her hands over Jackson's mouth.

"Enough for tonight!" She whispered through smiling lips. "You've got years to show me all of the facets of Buffett's brilliance, and yours."

XI

Maggie held her body against Jackson for a moment. He started to protest, but then accepted and returned her hug. He was still squeezing when she jumped backwards.

"What we need is some *fun*, Buffett style!" She almost shouted as she turned to the tape player and quickly ejected the tape, and then replaced it with another. In an instant Buffett was jamming with his band and singing about cheeseburgers. Maggie sang with him, and Jackson could not avoid joining them. The music and their voices echoed around the three wings of the complex and perhaps even across the port.

"If you've got to listen to him while I'm around, I want the party stuff. You can get all philosophical with Bette or anyone else who will listen." Then she added as she danced around the balcony laughing, but serious, "But I will make you a drink in his honor!" She laughed again and dashed into the kitchen. Jackson could hear cabinet doors slamming over the sound of her continued singing, and then she yelled out, instead of singing – "George left us an extra bottle of tequila! Gold! Remind me to kiss him tomorrow. After this stuff, I might not remember." The next sound Jackson heard was the whirl of the blender and then the grinding of ice being crushed. In minutes, Maggie was back on the balcony with blue frozen margaritas.

"He even had *blue* triple sec. George does have a certain style," she said with feeling, and smiled as she handed Jackson a large glass with salt around the rim. He took it and smiled broadly back at her. "Here's to George, not to mention Jimmy and his 'dancing life,' although I prefer 'wasting away'," Maggie said. Jackson took a deep drink, licked his lips and exhaled.

"It kind of puts meaning behind the phrase, doesn't it?" He grinned, which Maggie took for an improvement over simply a smile. They both sipped quietly for about five minutes as their mood, Jackson's particularly, mellowed. He looked at his watch, and then back at the gold light slanting across the port, turning the water from green to royal blue. He did not know why, but the light turned his mellow feeling to melancholy. He also did not know why he liked that, although he continued to ask himself the question.

"Ready for that cheeseburger?" He finally asked Maggie, getting up from his chair and taking her empty glass from her hand. She noticed his was still almost half-full. She always drank faster than Jackson, and usually in greater quantity.

"I guess it won't hurt to keep the mood going. How about Tortuga's?" She named a restaurant and bar right on the port, in an area called "The Flats." Ten minutes later they were standing at the hostess stand waiting to be seated. The tables inside were only about half-full, but the two-tiered outside seating was fully occupied. Since the sun had set and a good breeze was blowing, they decided to wait for an outdoor table. They both looked around the room, a long bar across the entire wall on the right and two rows of tables on the left, with an isle down the middle leading to the outdoor deck. The stained wood floor and the photograph-covered walls gave the room a dark, intimate feel, even though the entire back wall facing the port was made of glass. Maggie realized that a heavy tint had been placed on the windows, reducing the natural light coming through.

The hostess re-entered through the patio door, revealing the true light, and approached them at her stand. Before she could speak to them, Jackson pointed to a picture hanging just behind where the hostess normally stood. It was an aerial view of a boat at full throttle in the Gulf, a large wake cascading behind the outboard motors. The captain was on the fly bridge holding the wheel with both hands, but looking directly at the aerial camera and smiling a familiar smile.

"Maggie," Jackson said, "that's George," pointing to the picture. As she leaned over the stand to get a closer look, the hostess arrived and picked up two menus from the table just below the picture. She responded to Jackson.

"Oh, do you all know George?" She asked.

"Yes and no," Maggie answered as a joke, intending to explain. Before she could, the girl replied.

"Oh, that's what everyone says about George. We all know him, but we aren't sure we want to admit it." She laughed, and Jackson could see that she was young, probably not even through college, if she was attending college. Maggie looked at Jackson, and he gave her a look that attempted to say 'Drop it,' but Maggie did not catch it.

"So, you know him well?" she asked the hostess, sounding serious.

"Sure. He's good friends with my Dad," the girl answered with another smile. "George told my Dad that he put this picture here so he could keep an eye on me, but he told me that he just wanted to keep his eyes on my backside. I'm not supposed to let Dad hear me say that," she added, with a giggle. Jackson looked again at Maggie and then back at the girl, as she started toward the outdoors table. Glancing at her as she walked, Jackson thought about saying 'I can see why George is still smiling,' but caught himself.

"We won't tell," he called to her, trying to sound indifferent. She escorted them outside and seated them at a table on the upper level. They enjoyed the beautiful sunset and another round of margaritas. The cheeseburgers weren't as pleasant.

"These aren't quite as good as the song makes you expect," Maggie said as she was wiping the grease from her hands with a fourth napkin.

"Or too much of a good thing..." Jackson observed, starting his own cleaning action. "We ought to walk it off." He paid the bill, and they left the restaurant, pausing on the landing to listen to the sounds of the band coming through the open doors and closed windows of the club across the parking lot. A large billboard over the door was illuminated by spotlights. *Barracuda's* was written in aggressive blue and silver script, and a huge rubber fish hung below it from poles on either side, like a hammock.

"Feel like dancing?" Maggie asked, hopeful.

"I said walk it off, not dance it off," Jackson protested.

"Oh, you never take me dancing. Can't we? Just this once? Weren't you just talking about *La Vie Dansante*?" She grabbed both of his hands in hers and started to lead him across the lot. When he resisted, she let go of his arms, but turned to look again at the club. Neon lights flashed in the windows announcing several beer and recreation choices. "Oh! They have foosball! C'mon, we can play instead of dance." She went ahead of him this time, not trying to lead. She didn't even turn to make sure he was following. She was looking through the windows beside the door when Jackson got to the top of the steps and reached for his wallet. The woman at the door waved at him.

"You kids just go on in," she said. Maggie giggled as if to confirm the description. The bar was immediately in front of them as they entered. The dance floor was to the right and the games to the left – foosball, pool and video games. The two foosball tables were occupied, but Maggie went straight over to watch. Jackson caught up to her and yelled into her ear above the electric bass of the recorded music.

"Want another margarita?"

"Just a beer," she shouted back, barely taking her eyes off the foosball action. Jackson turned and went to the bar, stepping into an opening created when a very large motorcyclist turned to leave. He almost bumped Jackson, but Jackson moved to his left just in time to avoid contact. When he finally returned with the beer – having been passed over three times by the bartender – Maggie had joined one of the games. She expertly maneuvered the sticks and drew her men back and forth across the field, commenting on the action as she did.

"Oh, man!" she yelled as her opponent, who looked like a local resident, slammed a shot past her goalie and into the goal.

"Yes!" the local guy exclaimed, and then pointed at Maggie. "Never been beaten by a woman, and never will be."

"Hey, it's just one goal, Bub," Maggie replied, a little too familiar Jackson thought. Bub didn't seem to take offense, and they continued the game for about ten more minutes. Bub managed to keep his record in tact by winning 7-5. "You lucked out this time." Maggie called, as he was walking away, looking quite satisfied. She looked then at Jackson for what he thought was the first time since they had entered the bar.

"C'mon. Your turn to defend the male species," she said, but Jackson hesitated.

"I've never played this game. How did you get so good?" He asked.

"One of our neighbors had one in their basement, and I would play for hours down there with their son."

"Oh, that's good to know," Jackson said, as he stepped up and started spinning players. He practiced spinning and drawing the sticks, but lost his grip several times. "It's like rubbing your head and patting your stomach, or rubbing your stomach and patting your head. Whatever, I can't do either."

"What?" Maggie protested. "After all those stories you've told me about what a great athlete you were?"

"I don't see the correlation between this game and baseball, basketball or tennis," he objected. Just then, another guy approached the table, not a local, Jackson assumed, looking at his starched shirt, khaki shorts and loafers.

"You two going to play?" He asked, then looked at Maggie directly.

"You go ahead. I can't handle her," Jackson replied, and stepped back from the table. Maggie looked at him, surprised at first, but quickly turned her focus to the game. The new guy was a good player, too, and he and Maggie were quickly absorbed in the competition. Jackson decided it was not in his interest to watch, and went off to a corner to play a video game. He had some experience at that, but not much. He put in his quarters and immediately realized that he was not the man to save the galaxy from attacking spaceships. He kept misfiring and getting blown up by incoming missiles. This was not surprising, as he kept looking over his shoulder to see Maggie laughing, totally engrossed in her struggle with the college guy. After about his fifth look, he glanced back at his screen just in time to see his space ship explode and be given an ignoble epitaph, "GAME OVER." He reached into his pocket for more change when he heard a voice close in his left ear.

"Can I play with you?"

He was startled, and jumped slightly to his right before turning to see the speaker. Gaining his balance, he looked into the soft brown eyes of a very attractive brunette, but didn't answer her.

"Wanna play together?" she spoke again, gesturing with her head toward the screen. Again, Jackson didn't answer, but looked past her toward Maggie. Miraculously, he thought, she was leaving the foosball table and coming toward them. He started toward her, trying to move past the brunette, but there was little room to pass as the video box was stationed in a corner. Not wanting to brush against the brunette who was standing her ground, Jackson swayed to his left and bumped a table. It was a small café table that moved easily. The empty beer bottle sitting on it wobbled, and didn't stop wobbling until it had fallen over on the table and rolled off onto the concrete floor, bounced three times and done a drum roll vibration before finally coming to a stop. Jackson had watched it fall, as in a slow-motion movie stunt. Even with the noise of the music and the sounds from the rest of the bar, the rattling noise was loud enough to draw the look of many people in the game area. He was aware of their stares as he finally looked again directly into the eyes of the brunette, who was still staring at him. As Maggie stopped next to her, he spoke the only words that came to him.

"I'm married," he stammered. Before the brunette could respond, if she was going to respond, Maggie broke into hysterical laughter. He started to laugh himself, then added, "and here she is." He reached out to take her hand, trying mightily to regain even a hint of dignity. The brunette turned to let him pass without responding. Maggie was still laughing as they descended the steps outside.

"Smooth operator," she sang out loudly, but while taking his arm. "I'm lucky you didn't put those moves on me. We might not be married today." She giggled and hugged his neck as he kept walking, feigning resistance. She continued holding his arm as she added, "but I bet you remember my favorite line from the movie on our first date. 'Take me to bed or lose me forever!'" she said, and then laughed even louder.

XII

Much later that evening Jackson was reading again. When darkness had made it too difficult to see any longer on the balcony, Jackson had tried to bring a lamp outside, but had been engulfed in a swarm of bugs. Now he was propped up in bed, leaning toward the dim lamp and away from Maggie sleeping beside him. The sliding glass door remained open, but the screen and blinds were closed, keeping out the bugs and allowing in the puttering sounds from the port, along with a faint rush of wind and surf from the Gulf. It seemed to Jackson as if he were back in his old high-rise apartment in Dallas, where he often read in bed to similar sounds from the city streets below and the air conditioning units on the tops of the buildings that surrounded his twenty-first floor balcony.

With the comfort of familiarity and relaxation of knowing he could sleep as late as wanted, he was able to read quickly through much of his latest book. As he read, however, he became increasingly less comfortable, finding himself at first aggravated and then disturbed by the horrific story. The murder of a twelve year old black girl by a white man as payment for a black man's debt seemed preposterous, and made Jackson doubt the writer's credibility. However, he felt compelled to read on, grudgingly acknowledging to himself that this was often the reader's true gauge of the writer's skill.

By 2:30 a.m., he still felt no drowsiness. Rather, as he continued to read, he felt only greater tension. Was the writer being honest in creating such a despicable main character? Was he believable? Should Jackson admit the book was successful because of the reaction it provoked in him? Perhaps the grotesque story was the similarity the experts had seen between the author and Faulkner. To be truthful, Faulkner had created grotesque scenes of his own - Popeye and Temple Drake; Joe Christmas and Miss Burden; Wash Jones and Thomas Sutpen, as well as Jones' grand-daughter and great grand-daughter. Jackson couldn't recall being as offended – or disturbed - by those scenes as he felt now. Was he being harsher on this author due to his lack of stature? Did the greater degree of discomfort this book had caused him mean that this writer was better than Faulkner?

He had resolved none of these questions in his mind by 4:00 a.m., when he closed the book, appalled at the concluding scene, which Jackson thought must have been inspired by a massacre that had occurred five years earlier at a fast food restaurant in California. Though he had grown tired (weary was more like it), sleep was far from his mind. He got up from the bed softly, and began to pace. Concerned that he might wake Maggie, he clicked off the lamp, and in the darkness was immediately seized with fear and the expectation of being assaulted by the murderous Southerner. In a mild panic, he darted through the hall into the bathroom and quickly flipped on that light, which provided momentary security. He sat down on the toilet to steady himself, and recognized he was being ridiculous. It was only a story, and not, he thought, a very realistic one. Yet, his reaction told him it could be real - and reality was all he ever feared.

Even as a child, Jackson had never been frightened by

make-believe monsters, or even supernatural beings like ghosts. His terrors were of real life. His earliest nightmare, in fact, was of watching Jack Ruby gun down Lee Oswald live on television. He had no recollection of the Friday assassination of the president, but he remembered vividly the Sunday shooting, and the pained looked on Oswald's face broadcast into his own den. He could still recall the fear, however irrational, that Ruby would come to shoot him, too, even though he then lived nearly a thousand miles from Dallas. Several years later, he had the same fear when the Israeli athletes were taken hostage in Munich. This crisis, many thousands of miles away, was brought nearer in his imagination because he and his father had just moved into an apartment following his parents' divorce. His father was simply trying to survive the break-up, and would often leave Jackson after dinner and not return before Jackson was supposed to be asleep, perhaps not even until the next morning. Being left alone for most of the night – or even just his perception of being alone - greatly enhanced the specter of Arab terrorists for a young boy unable to turn away from the television that he watched ostensibly for protection. Even now, the two-toned, high-low whine of European sirens recall for him the possibility of international terrorism in Tennessee.

The terror he felt in this apartment on the Gulf of Mexico at thirty years old was less acute, but nevertheless disconcerting. The cause of his fear was the same. Could the world really produce such people and events? And, if so, (how could he deny it), when were they going to confront and befall him?

Jackson got up from the toilet and switched off the hallway light. Despite his determination not to, he immediately felt the panic of the dark. He stepped quickly into the bedroom and gently switched back on the lamp by the bed. Maggie still lay sleeping, covered fully again with the sheet, blanket and pillow. He picked up his pillow, which had collapsed from its upright position against the wall, and the image of the Southerner jumped out at him from the cover of the book. He snatched up the book and turned it over, and then could not stop himself from reading the text on the back cover: "A psychological spellbinder that will take your breath away, and probably interfere with your sleep." Well, he thought, maybe he wasn't being such a child after all. Even this justification, however, gave him no peace.

He turned the book again in his hands and walked to the corner of the room, which was serving as their closet. Four suitcases lay open on the floor, covered with clothes, both worn and unworn, folded and unfolded. Kneeling, he moved a pile of t-shirts and opened a small black bag that contained all of their reading material for the week. He placed the book deep into the bag, burying it beneath two hard-backs, another paperback, and several magazines. He then grabbed a few items from the pile of dirty laundry and piled them on top of the bag. He straightened, went to the slider, and then slowly and as silently as he could pulled the glass door toward him until it was closed. He pushed hard against it until the latch clicked loudly into the locked position. He returned to the bed and lay down under the sheet. He folded the part of the blanket on his side of the bed over Maggie, pulled the remaining sheet up to his neck and laid back against the pillow, which he had resituated against the wall to keep him in an upright, alert position. After a moment's mental debate, he snapped the bedside lamp off and lightly closed his eyes, but did not sleep.

Friday, August 4, 1989

XIII

Only once before in his life had Jackson seen such stars – when he had camped in the Grand Teton mountains in Wyoming. There, at high altitude, the stars felt close and comforting, like a blanket. Here, at sea level, the sky was so vast and the stars so distant that it felt like he was lost in space. He lay on his back on the deck of George Water's boat careening through the water, several miles out into the Gulf of Mexico. He felt like the world consisted only of stars, and even that he might be one of them. There were bright stars, dim stars, shooting stars – so many shooting stars that he thought of the video game where he had been virtually pounded the night before, only now he was inside the game. The beauty and majesty of the stars almost took Jackson's mind off of the actual pounding his body was now experiencing, as the boat slammed forward through waves that seemed to increase in height and force with each successive jolt.

Jackson lay on one side of the boat on a thick vinyl cushion covering a storage compartment. Maggie sat upright on a similar cushion on the other side of the boat, with the door to the cabin between them. In the darkness he could just make out her features – an expressionless face alternately glancing at him, the sky, and the water off the stern of the boat rushing back toward the shore, which was no longer visible, not even any lights. Jackson wanted to speak to her, but any communication would be difficult over the noise of the boat's motors and the pounding waves. Besides, there was nothing to say other than 'are you alright?' which would only have been a suggestion that he wasn't.

They had left the marina at 5:00 a.m. Neither he nor Maggie had any trouble being ready at that hour – Maggie because she had gone to bed early, and Jackson because he had barely slept at all. George had called the manager the night before and left word for them that the weather should be right for a great trip, especially for a couple of first-timers. When she had given them this comment, Jackson could clearly envision the grin on George's face when he said it. But since the experience remained the stated purpose for their visit, and also the consideration they had given for accepting George's offer of a free week's stay in his condominium, they knew they had to go through with it. Neither the knowledge they had gained through the week about George's reputation as a fisherman, nor the inconsistent reports of the strength and lasting effects of Hurricane Chantal, could excuse them from completing this task.

Whether through drowsiness or fear, Jackson and Maggie did not talk much as they dressed and drank coffee at an hour that they had not seen together since perhaps their first two dates. The mood those earlier mornings had been considerably lighter, although the conversation had been heavier. This morning there was virtually no conversation save a brief discussion about the merits of motion-sickness pills. Jackson had never taken them, preferring to test the uncertainty of his tolerance before submitting to (in his mind) the more certain danger of pills. Fortunately for him, he had proven to have a strong stomach, if not a courageous mind, when it came to air travel. Maggie, on the other hand, had often taken pills when flying. The idea of motion sickness while trapped in a metal tube 35,000 feet above the earth had always been abhorrent to her, and she gladly took the pills well in advance of any sign of weakness.

This adventure seemed different, and both found themselves on infirm ground. Jackson was so convinced that he could not compensate for the motion of the sea under any conditions – let alone the aftermath of a hurricane – that he quickly and forcibly chewed two tablets together with a bagel and a glass of milk. He then drank two cups of coffee as a final preventative, or encouragement. In contrast, Maggie simply could not bring herself to take the pills. So, she had sipped her coffee and nibbled a slice of toast, and waited for what would come.

Jackson could see her still waiting for something in the fading darkness over an hour later, bracing herself against the outside of the cabin trying to maintain her balance as the boat fought its way southeast into the Gulf of Mexico. He could now make out the strong line of her jaw, which was set but still showed no real emotion. The effects of the stars and noise gave way to another sense that demanded his attention. The smell of fuel coming from the outboard motors was the same sickly sweet aroma he got occasionally at gas pumps, only now it was not a momentary sensation. It was constant, and becoming pervasive. He cupped his hand over his face in an attempt to filter the fumes, but this did nothing to quiet the grumbling in his stomach. He was sure the turmoil there was from the smell, not the waves, so he turned over and raised up on the cushion enough to put his head over the side. The first impression of the wind and salt water spray was refreshing. The next was one of burning eyes and filmy skin. He leaned back and wiped his face with his t-shirt, but felt better. Like Maggie, he sat up and leaned his back against the cabin. The crashing of the boat through the waves jolted them both even more severely, and he couldn't stop himself from looking across to Maggie again.

He was surprised this time to see her looking back at him. This was the first time their eyes had met with recognition since passing through the jetties and assuming their positions below at George's direction. He could see that she was smiling, and the effect on him was therapeutic. He smiled back, as if to agree with her unspoken question - 'can you believe this?' Rather than answer, he simply shrugged his shoulders and raised his arms, palms up. Maggie's smile widened to a grin. Feeling empowered, Jackson leaned forward and looked up over his shoulder to the fly bridge. George stood rigidly upright, leaning forward against the wheel to brace himself for the recurring slamming of the waves. He had put on a yellow rain slicker and pants, and his clothing and stance reminded Jackson of a ski-jumper in mid-flight.

He wanted to speak to George, but with the motors, wind and waves, Jackson was certain that he could not make himself heard from below, even though the distance was not that far on George's twenty-eight foot Bertram. The fly bridge was customized, just as were the motors. Everything about George seemed special-ordered, and his boat was no exception. Only her name seemed borrowed, but *Satisfaction* made a totally appropriate connection between George and Mick Jagger.

Jackson did not feel confident enough to climb the ladder to the fly bridge. So, he turned his back against the cabin again, and re-joined Maggie in staring off the heaving stern in the direction of the shore and stability. They continued for perhaps another twenty minutes, which seemed like longer as the sounds and shakes from the waves increased. It was past dawn now, and Jackson could tell it was going to be a gray day. The sky, the air and the waves, all appeared gray. He could now make out the rolls of the waves as they moved past the boat and toward the shore. The white spume of the intersection of the wave and boat was the only other color visible. The effect of seeing the waves in addition to feeling them shook him emotionally as much as physically. He had no experience, of course, but the height and depth appeared menacing, and dangerous. He had no idea how far into the Gulf they were; he could see the agitated sea and nothing else. How close, he wondered, is the agitated sea to becoming truly angry? He wondered why George hadn't suggested they wear life jackets. Did George even carry life jackets? The irrational question came into his head without effort. Fishermen were safety conscious, right? The respect for the sea, and all that. But did George respect anything? What makes men – intelligent and even erudite men - shun caution and risk danger on the water. The poet Percy Bysshe Shelley came to mind. Why had he, an inexperienced sailor, stupidly rejected several warnings about an approaching storm before venturing out and getting himself and a companion drowned in the Mediterranean Sea when their sailboat capsized? Surely, Jackson hoped, George had more sense about the sea than a poet, even a great one.

He looked again at Maggie, and she still smiled back. It was not the knowing smile she had shown earlier, but there was no concern in it. She saw everything differently, he thought. He leaned forward and looked up at George again. This time George was looking back over his shoulder at the motors. As he was turning back to the horizon he glanced down and caught Jackson looking up at him. Jackson was not surprised when George flashed his bandito smile. His impossibly full mustache and thick hair were blown far back on his head by the wind and spray. He waved, but said nothing, and Jackson said nothing in return. He was bracing himself once again when the biggest jolt yet hit them. Jackson lost his balance and slipped off the cushion onto the deck of the boat. He quickly got to one knee, and felt Maggie's hand under his arm. He was about to stand when the next jolt came. Maggie fell against him and they both toppled onto the deck. As they tried to untangle, they both looked up at George, who was still locked in his jumper's position, looking straight ahead. From their backs at the bottom of the boat, George appeared to be several stories above them - either an authority figure watching over them, or the jumper having veered off course and about to land in the spectators, symbolizing the agony of defeat.

The boat bucked harder as Jackson and Maggie each crawled back to their opposite benches. Spray from the pounding waves had come over the sides and soaked the seats and they both immediately tried to stand again as soon as they had sat down. They almost joined hands as they each locked their knees and tried to balance like surfers riding serious waves. The sound of the motors changed noticeably from droning to a chugging as the propellers rose and fell with the waves, seeking solid water through which they could propel the boat. It was full light now and, as he gained a measure of balance and recognition, Jackson saw the entire horizon vibrating. As far as he could see, the water was coiling and crashing. The up and down movement of the boat felt like a teeter-totter ride, only one where his partner jumped off the other end each time he reached the apex of the lift, causing Jackson to slam repeatedly to the ground. After a particularly jolting drop that brought more spray from the sides, and even over the stern and the motors, Maggie finally spoke what he had been thinking.

"Are we there yet?" She yelled over the sound of the wind and the waves and the motors. Jackson was relieved to see her smile, having grown increasingly fearful that she would be angry with him for this ride. He would be even angrier with himself if they all got killed, but if Maggie was still in good humor, he would try to be, too.

"I don't know, because I don't know where we're going," he shouted back. "Wherever it is, I'll bet it looks just like this," he added. They both smiled, and together they looked up at George on the fly bridge. He was still leaning into the wheel, but their voices had apparently carried up to him, because he was now looking over his shoulder and down at them, bandito smile in full, windblown bloom.

"Having fun?" He yelled and tried to laugh, but was interrupted by another wave that pushed the boat sideways. More spray came over the sides, and Jackson felt that he had been hit by an actual wave as water dripped from his t-shirt. Maggie's hair, he noticed for the first time, was glistening and so damp in its pony tail that it looked as if she had just come up from a dip in the pool. Righting the boat once more, and keeping it steady through several smaller waves, George turned back to them.

"She's a little rougher than I expected," he yelled. Jackson and Maggie nodded up to him, and glanced at each other, thankful for confirmation that this ride was not what George had intended for them. They looked back up to see if it was going to end.

"I'm not sure it's going to get any smoother, so we could try to drop a few lines here, if you want." He had slowed the engines to help them hear his voice, but the decrease in power left the boat even more vulnerable to the waves. Before Jackson and Maggie could ask what they were both thinking –'how could we catch a fish in this?' – a wave rolled into the boat from the side and actually crested into the top of the motors – which promptly died. The shock of mechanical silence and roar of the natural wonder propelled Jackson past his immediate thought that they might be stranded. He had an instant vision of men struggling with the sea over the centuries, using whatever means they had to combat the elements. He wanted to feel proud. Before he could fully realize this, George had the motors restarted, and was pushing the throttles up. The roar of acceleration reminded Jackson that George was his means of triumph – that he and Maggie were totally dependent on George and his boat. He reached over and put his hand on her shoulder, and pointed up the ladder.

"Let's go up," he yelled. At least, he thought, he could get a better view of his rescue, or demise. Maggie betrayed no sense of urgency, but turned and carefully climbed the chrome ladder which was slippery from all of the spray, and still bucking with the waves. Jackson followed right after her, ready to catch her on his shoulders if she fell or tried to change her mind. The fly bridge was small, maybe three feet deep and six feet wide, but there was room for three people. Maggie stepped off the ladder, grabbed hold of the rail behind George and moved behind him to the far side. Jackson grabbed the same rail but stayed on George's right. George had lowered the plastic cover that served as a windshield, but still the spray was strong in their faces. George didn't seem fazed by it; nor did he object to their joining him.

"Sorry about the weather," he said, almost casually. "Bad for fishing." Maggie looked over at Jackson, as if she didn't comprehend the comment. Jackson decided to ask her question.

"Aren't you a little concerned about the effect of the weather on us, rather than the fish?" He tried to sound light and confident. George chuckled, but was prevented from answering by another large wave that pushed them off to the left (starboard? Jackson wondered).

"Nah!" George drawled. "This little squall is no danger to anything but my stomach. I was hoping we'd have fresh Mahi for dinner." Just then another wave hit them from the other side (port?), and the motors died again. Before Jackson could think of a quip ('You were saying?' seemed too obvious), George had them running again; but, now, he seemed to have come to a decision.

"Danger or no, there ain't gonna be any fishing today, I'm afraid. You all ready to go back?" He looked at Jackson, but it was Maggie who spoke.

"Before we turn back, I want to know if I've been out here long enough to know whether I am going to get sea sick." George and Jackson both looked surprised at the question, but only George could answer, smiling his smile again as he did.

"Maggie, honey, with these waves, if you were going to be sick it would have hit you before we even got through the jetties. That's the only reason I've kept going, because you both obviously have good sea legs." Maggie smiled broadly at Jackson, with an air of accomplishment.

"I'd rather feel great and catch no fish," Maggie said "than catch a whale and puke like a dog. Let's go home!" Jackson laughed back at her and then nodded to George, who began the rough task of turning the boat through the waves. Another glance at Maggie, and the confidant, satisfied smile on her face, reminded Jackson why he had loved her from the first moment he had seen those eyes.

XIV

The sun's rays spiked through the clouds just above the horizon as George steered the boat around, struggling to keep it steady as it bobbed through its own wake. The slash of orange and red light seemed three dimensional – it contrasted so with the gray clouds and dull water. It was also fleeting. As soon as George had gotten the boat turned northwest toward the port, the shadow cast by the glancing rays disappeared, leaving only a faint red haze in the eastern sky. George thought there would be rain.

"Better get back below," he said to both Jackson and Maggie. "The waves are going to push us along now, and we need to outrun this storm."

"Hasn't the storm passed?" Jackson asked, as he let Maggie go ahead of him down the ladder.

"Not this one, the next one," George answered vaguely, as he pointed back at the eastern sky which was now quite red. "You know, 'red sky at morning'...." He didn't finish the proverb as Jackson was already nodding his head and backing onto the first step of the ladder. He paused and responded.

"I know that one. It's in the Bible," Jackson said. "I just hope it doesn't mean we should expect one of biblical proportions." He shrugged when George didn't react, and continued his descent.

George wondered about an old sailor's axiom being in the Bible. Must be true, but Jackson surely knew it from Sunday school rather than from fishing experience, George assumed. The connection interested him. He shrugged, too, and looked down to see that his passengers had returned to their positions in the well. He pushed the throttles forward steadily, and the bow of the boat came up again. The higher attitude and the waves pushing forward made the boat even harder to steer, but George held its course straight, and even increased the speed. He looked back again to see Maggie and Jackson gesturing toward the impressive wake. Even in the aftermath of a hurricane and the approach of a squall, he could enjoy the beauty of a boat upon the sea. They seemed to him as naturally connected as the fish and the water.

He drove the motors hard for twenty minutes and felt very happy – practically in a trance with the blanket of wind and sea of noise – when he realized another sound was present. He heard a voice and looked down below, to where Maggie and Jackson sat motionless now, lolling on the cushions in trances of their own. He heard the voice again, this time in front of him, and realized it was coming from his radio. It was a distress call. He smoothly lessened the throttles and picked up his microphone hanging from a hook on the panel before him. The coiled cord stretched and the static jangled in the wind as George identified himself in response to the call. As the voice on the radio came back clearly, George recognized it immediately. It was Bill Fish, another man born into the oil business, but meant for life on the sea, in name and spirit.

"We've got engine trouble, and an injured man aboard. Can you help?"

"Where are you?" George responded quickly, an affirmative answer without using the affirmative. Bill responded with a longitude and latitude, and then added a descriptive coda, "about five miles out." George ascertained with a quick glance at his new Global Positioning Satellite system, the latest directional technology, that they were not that far away.

"About thirty minutes," he spoke again quickly into the radio, and then turned back to look at Maggie and Jackson, who had heard parts of the discussion. "Boat and passenger in distress. We need to give them a hand." George paused, as if recalling the warning he had spoken less than an hour earlier. "We'll be fine – probably they will, too." Immediately, the motors crescendoed again, and the boat turned south and east, almost 180 degrees from their prior course, and sliced smartly through the waves at an angle. The possibility of another storm still partially occupied George's mind, but now he was focused on the rescue and curious about the injury aboard. He was more surprised, though, at an experienced seaman like Bill Fish having boat problems. If it could happen to him.... George looked back and down at Jackson, but didn't complete the thought.

After twenty minutes, he picked up the microphone and asked for their position again. He expected to have them in sight soon. Hearing new coordinates, he veered further south and soon was certain that he could see the tower and rigging of Bill's boat – *Born To Fish.* George pushed the throttles harder and permitted nothing to distract him from that point on the horizon. In ten more minutes they were coming along side Bill's boat, a larger and newer Bertram than George's. George, Jackson and Maggie all looked with curiosity at the crew of four men to see which of them might be injured. Then a fifth man appeared in the cabin door, and hopped down the step and over to the starboard rail. As George held *Satisfaction* steady and inched her sideways to nuzzle Bill's boat, he was the first to see the trouble. The man sitting on the rail had crossed his left leg over his right, for balance perhaps, and his left foot hung limp. Light flashed off the silver chrome of a 12/0 circle hook slipped neatly through the top of his arch, as if placed there with care. A small trickle of dried blood extended down toward his toes. Maggie and Jackson caught sight of it together, and once again found themselves looking at each other in disbelief, but neither had an answer for the question this time.

"Good grief, Dusty, you know better than to stand barefoot around a hooked sailfish!" George called from his fly bridge. He had comprehended the incident immediately. Dusty was between Jackson and George's age, perhaps 35, and looked pale and unsteady. He started to swing his hooked foot over the side of Fish's boat and onto George's in one movement, but stopped short. He turned back and then attempted to swing both legs over, as one of the men on his boat stepped up to steady his back.

"Give him a hand, Jackie!" George snapped, sounding a little irritated. "I've got to try to keep the boat steady." Jackson awoke from his mild shock and stepped forward to meet the man's legs, but stopped short for fear of striking his foot as the boats bobbed in the waves. It was then that he realized that the sea had calmed somewhat – it must have or there would have been no way a man hooked in the foot with a sailfish tackle could crawl between boats in the open water. Jackson looked up at George again, as Dusty grasped his hand and propelled himself awkwardly into *Satisfaction*. He leaned forward almost into Jackson's arms, and then swiveled around and collapsed onto the cushioned bench where Jackson had been sitting most of the morning. Immediately George released the throttle, and the boats calmly drifted apart about ten feet.

"You guys going to be all right?" George shouted to the

man on the fly bridge across from him, louder than necessary in the calming waters.

"Fine," Bill Fish answered back, almost in a normal voice. "Just lost one engine. It'll take us a few hours to get back, and we didn't think Dusty should wait that long."

"We'll have him fixed up by the time you get in," George said, and everyone on both boats knew that it was true. "By the way, Dusty," he called down below him. "Was the fish worth it?" For the first time since they had arrived, Dusty smiled slightly, and nodded.

"About a hundred pound white marlin," Bill Fish called over. "Not bad for hurricane fishin!" George waved, and once again turned the boat westward. He looked down to see Maggie offering Dusty a drink of water, and putting a cushion behind his back. Jackson had scooted a small ice chest up to him, and carefully set it under his impaled foot. Seeing all settled, George pushed the throttles up again, and was surprised at the smooth acceleration. He remembered the approaching storm and looked back. He was surprised again to see that it had apparently passed north of them, for there was no redness anywhere now, only a darker gray mass off to his right. He focused again on his wake and was admiring its perfect origami shape when a flash of light caught his attention. He looked down to see Maggie standing up and pulling her camera back towards her. She must have knelt in the well to snap a close-up of Dusty's impaled foot. George smiled his smile at her spunk, then noticed that Jackson looked relaxed for the first time all morning.

XV

At 11:30 a.m., Bette took up her usual place on the marina deck, book in hand. The sun was very high and hot, so she decided to douse herself in the pool first. Dripping, she returned to her lounge chair, and was surprised to notice George's boat moored in its slip. She looked up to the balcony of George's unit, but neither Jackson nor Maggie was there, and the sliding doors were closed. Either they had caught a big one quickly, she thought, or George had actually admitted defeat. She was certain that she would have heard by now if there had been a big catch.

'I hope the kids didn't get too sick from the ride,' she thought further. Resisting the temptation to buzz George's unit in the elevator lobby, she resumed her reading position and tried to regain interest in the fight for Texas independence. Sam Houston had been all for that, just as he had been in support of admission to the Union as the 28th state. She was surprised to learn, however, that he was adamantly against secession. Indeed, Texas's vote to secede from the Union was perhaps the greatest political defeat for the only man ever to serve as governor of two different states, not to mention as a United States senator and president of an independent nation. Even such interesting and weighty historical matters, however, could not keep Bette's interest. She was more concerned for Jackson and Maggie – or just the present.

Making a decision, finally, she got up and went through the breezeway to the parking area and the entrance to the elevator lobby for George's unit. She was about to push the button when George emerged from the storage closet at the end of a row of doors facing the parking spaces. She waved to him, and went through the glass door on the opposite side of the lobby.

"Well, you're back early. Catch anything?" She decided not to tease him immediately about being beaten by the weather.

"Oh, about a 200 pounder," George smiled broadly, as he replied.

"What?" Bette answered, truly surprised. "You're kidding me!" She paused, but George kept smiling, so she added. "What was it, a sail?"

"Nah," George answered, "we caught us a *homo sapien*!" Now he couldn't keep from laughing.

"George, what *are* you talking about?" Bette demanded.

"I guess you didn't hear. We got beat to death for two hours, and we were coming back in when I got a distress call from Bill Fish's boat. We found him pretty quick, and he was down to one engine, but the real distress was Dusty Mather – he had a 12/0 circle hook through his foot."

"Oh!" Bette inhaled, and put her hand over her mouth. "Dusty knows better than that! What did he do, forget his shoes?"

"No, just his experience," George replied. "Anyway, it was a clean, solid catch. He wouldn't have gotten away if he had been on a line, that's for sure." He laughed again. "We helped him onto *Satisfaction,* and brought him in with us. Jackson and Maggie drove him over to the clinic. They ought to be back soon."

"How are they?" Bette asked. "Did they survive the pounding?"

"Oh, yea, no problem," George answered. "They've both got some sea legs, particularly Maggie. She seemed totally unfazed by it, and I'm telling you, it was pretty rough. I kept waiting for them to complain, but they never did. So we kept going for about two hours. I think the waves may have cracked the hull of my boat."

"They should have cracked your skull," Bette was smiling as she said this, and George smiled, too. Just then Jackson and Maggie's car appeared around the corner of the building and eased into the parking space for George's unit, in front of the storage closet where George and Bette stood.

"So, how's the catch of the day?" George asked, as they were still getting out of the car.

"Still kicking," Jackson answered.

"And he's got some new jewelry," Maggie added. "They cut the hook with fence cutters, and Dusty says he's going to wear the loop around his neck."

"They ought to stick the business end in his head," Bette said. "Let that be a lesson to you kids. Even experienced fishermen can be stupid." She turned and looked at George before continuing. "Getting hooks through their feet, or going fishing in the aftermath of a hurricane."

"Oh, Bette," George said, sheepishly, for him.

"I'm shocked. How about you?" Maggie said, and then looked at Jackson.

"No comment," Jackson said.

"If that's the best defense I can get from my lawyer, I'm outta here," George said.

"Don't go away mad," Bette interrupted him. "I was thinking we could all have lunch."

"Nah, I've got boats to build," George answered.

"And I need some sleep. I was up late last night and early this morning," Jackson added.

"You all go dancing?" Bette inquired.

"I tried," Maggie laughed, "but Jackson decided he would rather stay up with a book than dance all night with me."

"Guilty," Jackson admitted, "but if you'll let me sleep now, I promise I will try again tonight." He then blinked, and started to withdraw the offer, but Maggie accepted before he could.

"Deal," she said, and she gave him a quick kiss. Turning to Bette, she said, "I'll have lunch with you, if that's okay."

"Ooh, the best – girl talk!" Bette said.

George and Jackson said goodbye, and the women started to get in Maggie's car, before deciding to walk to the port. Bette suggested Tortuga's and, after first objecting that she had just been there the night before, Maggie relented.

"You can get a salad, or some fish." Bette suggested. "Stay away from the burgers." In fifteen minutes they were seated on the patio, the lower deck this time. The sun was directly overhead, but the umbrellas and gulf breeze made the temperature bearable. The view made it more than worth the discomfort.

"I just love the Coast," Bette observed, looking wistfully at the boats moored in the marina right in front of them, and those speeding down the ship channel beyond. "I can't describe the feeling, but I've always had it – since the first time my Daddy brought me here to fish." Now, she looked intently at the water, but this time without seeing.

"When was that?" Maggie asked, innocently.

"Oh, child, don't ask me that! You'll ruin the memory." Maggie was surprised by the rebuke, but then Bette laughed. "I'm teasing, honey. It was a long time ago, and I need to admit it. I get down here in the summer now, though, and I feel nothing's changed. I expect to hear Daddy's voice calling me – 'Bet! Let's go fishing!'" She paused again, then continued. "I have to be reminded that he died over ten years ago. And I see you, and realize you could be my daughter. What are you, 25?" she asked.

"Twenty-six," Maggie answered.

"I thought so. I've got a son older than you, and a daughter a year younger." Bette pronounced, and noticed Maggie's surprise. "Ah, I didn't strike you as the motherly type, did I?"

"No, you didn't," Maggie answered, directly, and then waited for a reaction from Bette that did not come. They sat silently for a few minutes, and then gave their orders to a girl much younger than Maggie, but very pretty.

"You see," Bette whispered as the waitress walked away, "I can't escape the evidence of my age. That girl's *mother* is ten years younger than me!"

"Hey, you look great, and I don't think I've met anyone in a long while who acts as young as you do," Maggie said.

"Foolish, you mean? That's what Bob says."

"No! I don't think you're foolish. That's silly."

"Girls just want to have fun, right?" Bette winked at her, and lit a cigarette with the same smart movements Jackson had observed the day before. Maggie paused another instant, before responding.

"I love that song, and I used to believe it, but I think I'm losing some of the desire. I don't know if it's because of Jackson, or just me."

"That doesn't sound good. You guys seem really happy to me," Bette said.

"Oh, we are," Maggie said, "that's not what I meant. I was referring to your continuing desire to have fun – act young. I think I'm gaining a desire to act grown-up."

"Old, you mean," Bette exhaled smoke, emphatically.

"You may think of it like that, but I don't. Take reading, for example. I never used to read at all. It was so *boring*, but now I love sitting for hours with a good book – particularly in a setting like this." She looked out at the port as Bette had earlier.

"Yes, we've established that you are a reader. I'm surprised that's a new thing, though." She put the cigarette to her lips, and inhaled, also emphatically.

"Very new, and definitely Jackson's influence," Maggie admitted, "but, I'm okay with it. I don't read much of the stuff he likes – is obsessed with – but, I'm working my way past the romance-novel stage. The point is that, once, you couldn't pay me to read a book, and now it is one of my favorite past times. I might even pass up dancing to stay home and read. You tell me if that is growing old, or up."

"Now child, you're too young to hang up your dancing shoes. You've got lots of years to sit at home reading," Bette counseled.

"You're right, but, truthfully, Jackson's not much of a dancer."

"You said you all went dancing last night?" Bette countered.

"I said we 'sort of' went dancing. We stopped at Barracuda's after eating dinner here. I played foosball with a couple of guys, and Jackson played a video game. We never made it to the dance floor."

"Why not?" Bette wondered.

"Well, I'm not totally sure, but I think Jackson was in shock from a striking brunette that wanted to play the video game with him." Bette looked puzzled at Maggie's broad smile, and she explained. "All he could think to say to her was, 'I'm married,' and then almost knocked over a table trying to get away from her!" Maggie broke into complete laughter.

"How cute!" Bette joined her. "That could make up for missing a dance or two."

"Yes, he's always doing that. Just when I am about to get mad at him, or decide that he's a total loser, he'll do something incredibly sweet, and make me love him even more."

"That's really good. I don't see that kind of understanding in many kids your age. They usually aren't even paying that much attention to their spouses." The young waitress brought their lunches. They ate quietly for a few minutes. Bette thought of her own marriage, and the differences she saw in Maggie and her own daughter. She decided to continue the discussion.

"I think you've got something special going, from what I've observed."

"In twenty-four hours?" Maggie asked.

"Well, it's actually been four days. I watched you for three days, and now I've known you for one. That's not long, but I've seen a lot of relationships, and I think I know when one is different. Take your willingness, even eagerness, to take up reading over other interests you've had. That's quite a change, and more importantly you are happy about it. You aren't changing just for Jackson, you are changing for yourself – even if Jackson may have started it. That's rare these days. Most kids get married and hardly even think about what their spouses like. If they do, they either just leave them to it, or join in just for the sake of the relationship. That lasts for a few months or maybe a year or so, and then trouble starts." She paused, thinking of the many examples she knew of this process. "How long have you two been married?" she asked.

"We just passed two years," Maggie answered.

"Well, it's still early, I guess," Bette seemed to agree with Maggie's analysis, "but I think the signs are very good."

"Thanks for the encouragement. Believe it or not, I really don't know Jackson that well. I'm still learning about him, and about marriage, of course."

"So you didn't date for long before you got married?" Bette asked.

"Ten months," Maggie responded, "and we were engaged for seven of those months."

"You are kidding me!" Bette insisted, dropping her fork on her plate.

"No, I'm not. Jackson sort of proposed on our second date. I wasn't sure he was serious, but I wasn't bothered by the thought. Then I went back to Houston for my teaching job, and the distance kind of proved to both of us that we really felt what we thought we did. We met in late July and got officially engaged on Labor Day. We spent the next nine months flying back and forth between Houston and Dallas on the weekends." She stopped so that Bette could absorb this information.

"Now I'm really impressed. You've been married for over two years, but you've known each other for less than three! That is very unusual. I can see why you would say that you are still getting to know him."

"I've got an even better excuse, though. Remember, we were living in different cities the entire time. So, when we got married and went on a two-week honeymoon to Europe, it was the most consecutive days we had ever been together."

"Didn't that scare you?" Bette asked.

"Not at first. I've had moments of uncertainty, sure, but like I said, each time I start to form a negative opinion something will happen to change it to a positive. Do you know what he did for my birthday less than a month after we met? He took me to a designer trunk show at Neiman's and bought me an outfit. I even got to meet the designer." Bette didn't speak, but dropped her jaw. "I know," Maggie said, "it was really wonderful, in a weird sort of way." She paused again, before adding, "but not as weird as the first time we had a fight."

"Oh, I'm sure a guy like Jackson must have come up with a good peace offering," Bette guessed, "but why was it weird?"

"Because I can't figure out how he did it." Maggie nodded. "It was late one Sunday, when I was about to fly back to Houston for the week. I can't even remember what we argued about, probably just the tension created by having to leave each other for another week. Anyway, I caught the last plane out of Love Field around 9 p.m., Sunday, before we really had time to make-up. But," she paused for emphasis, "when I got to my classroom at 8 a.m., the next morning, there were fresh flowers sitting on my desk, and an apology note." She paused as Bette's face showed the appropriate mixture of surprise and respect, before adding, "I still to this day don't know how he pulled that off." Bette again shook her head, showing appropriate disbelief and preparing to comment. "And," Maggie interrupted her, "the more amazing part of the story is that those fresh flowers kept coming each Monday morning for the rest of our engagement, and they still arrive every week at our house, only now they come home with Jackson every Friday night."

"Oh, honey, that is too much!" Bette couldn't keep from verbalizing her surprise this time.

"Yes, I know," Maggie nodded. "I'm actually kind of tired of having to arrange them every week. Jackson's no good at that."

"That's not what I meant," Bette protested, "and you can't be serious that you are tired of receiving flowers every week. You don't deserve them, then." Maggie shrugged, and Bette leaned forward. "Now, I've really got to defend Jackson. I was going to say that the designer thing and the flowers after fighting was just typical Dallas-guy stuff, but to keep it up for what, three years now?" Maggie nodded reluctantly. "Honey, you've got a keeper." Bette lightly slapped Maggie's wrist.

They both thought for a moment or two, as the waitress took away their lunch plates and offered them desserts. Bette declined, Maggie accepted.

"You don't seem to have to worry about your weight or your husband," Bette said. Maggie dismissed her with a wave, but didn't speak. "I'm the opposite on both counts," Bette continued. "The years change your body, and your relationships. I'm not complaining about either. I've been blessed, but I find myself quite envious of you. You're young and pretty, and seem to be enjoying your marriage to a handsome lawyer from Dallas. Not bad."

Oh, stop it," Maggie insisted, but with a smile. "You're making me sound like a TV character. Besides, I'm not that pretty, and Jackson's not what most would consider handsome – although I certainly think so," she added quickly.

"Well, I'll leave the final determination to you two," Bette concluded, "but I wish we had a TV show today centered around a young couple that is as happy as you guys are – it would be good for society. Of course, no one would watch it or believe it - except me, of course." She smiled broadly, as she deftly lit yet another cigarette.

XVI

Jackson woke in the full afternoon light that filled the condo, and was immediately confused. He looked at his watch, and saw that he had been asleep for only a little more than an hour. The effect was to shift the stiffness from his brain to his body. He turned over on his back, rubbed his eyes, and still felt the motion of the pounding waves. He lay in bed for ten minutes, thinking that this would be a good time to have room service, since he needed some refreshment badly. He felt like he had a hangover, but with Maggie absent he knew the usual service wasn't available. He had to get out of bed.

He stretched, rolled over, and forced himself to stand. He put on his swim trunks and dug a clean t-shirt out of his bag. He decided to go down to the pool to wait for Maggie to return from lunch. He was surprised to realize that he still was not hungry. Must be the sea sickness medicine, he thought. Passing through the kitchen, he picked up a bag of chips off the counter, just in case, and took a soda and a beer from the refrigerator.

After only one and a half laps in the pool, he got out and lay on his stomach on a lounge chair. The sun was still almost directly overhead, and he knew that he should not lay there for long without applying sunscreen, but he was still very tired, and he hated to apply the greasy lotion. His next thoughts were dreams of waves and the boat rocking – only this time the boat was not breaking through the waves. It felt like it was breaking up. He was holding tightly to the tower support as he felt the queasy, roller-coaster type emptiness in his stomach. He knew the boat was going over, and wondered where Maggie was. He felt his body tense and jerk as his hands gripped the railing tighter.

"Jackson!" Someone was calling his name. He caught himself just as the boat was coming over his head, and he opened his eyes to see Maggie and Bette standing over him in the glare of the sun. "You are going to fry sleeping out in this sun," Maggie said, "and I bet you didn't put any lotion on."

He felt the heat on his face even as she was speaking, and he released the tight hold he had on the arms of the lounge chair. He reached under the chair to find his watch in his shoe. He was relieved to see that he had only been there for about twenty minutes. He stretched again, and sat up to put his shirt on.

"No problem," he finally managed to respond. "I've only been out here a few minutes. How was lunch?"

"Great, if you like Tortuga's," Maggie said.

"Great, if you like talking about husbands," Bette added.

"That's two reasons I'm glad I didn't join you," Jackson responded, first to Bette, and then looked at Maggie. "You want to lay out, or take a nap?"

"I could use a swim. It ought to help me wake up. I don't want to nap this late." She paused, and then spoke to Bette. "Want to join us for a game of cards, or something?"

"Sounds good," Bette answered. "Give me ten minutes to see Bob, and get changed." She turned quickly and went around the corner to her elevator lobby.

"Should I come up with you?" Jackson looked at Maggie, and smiled.

"Forget it," she laughed, "she said ten minutes. Be patient."

"You know me better than to expect that, but I'll try," he answered, trying, in fact, at that moment.

"Actually, Bette and I were just discussing how little I knew about you when we got married, and I admitted I've still got a lot to learn." Maggie looked down at him with more of a frown than curiosity.

"I think I'm fairly predictable on this point," Jackson said.

"That's true," she said, and turned back to him. "You win," she added, and took his hand to pull him up out of the chair.

"Really?" Jackson asked.

"Don't sound so shocked. It'll ruin the effect." Maggie put her arm around his waist as they walked toward the stairs.

About thirty minutes later they descended the same stairs and found Bette lying on a chair beside the one Jackson had been using. Maggie took Jackson's chair, and Jackson aligned another one with these, turning it west away from the port and toward the afternoon sun.

"Sorry we took so long," Jackson said, "I decided I was hungry." He looked at Bette, and she smiled back at him, betraying no judgment.

"What are you reading now?" He asked, looking at the book in her lap, and deciding to change the subject quickly.

"Oh, another big novel by that Western writer," Bette replied, "I picked it up at the library this morning while you all were fishing with George. I gave up on Sam Houston's struggle to control his fellow Texans."

"We weren't doing much fishing this morning, but we did manage to control George before we all got drowned," Jackson said. "We could have spent the time better at the library with you. I don't know that book. May I see it?" He reached across Maggie's body and took the hard bound book from Bette. It was over two inches thick. He read the title aloud, *Nobody's Patsy.* "I haven't read it," he said. "Another epic tale, I assume, at least from the size of it."

"Ok, if you guys are going to talk books all afternoon, we ought to change places," Maggie complained. "Besides, I thought this morning was fun!"

"Yes, George told me you were quite the sea dog. He said it was really rough, but that it didn't even phase you two," Bette said, sounding impressed.

"I was under the influence of drugs," Jackson explained. "Maggie decided to do her pioneer woman routine. Just another example of how much tougher she is than me."

"Didn't I just tell you to stop being pathetic?" Maggie said. "Besides, all Texas women are strong, and particularly Texas A&M women!"

"Hey," Bette challenged her. "It's okay for the woman to be the stronger one in the relationship – at least in some areas. Besides, from what I heard at lunch, it sounds like Jackson showed some strength of will at the beginning of your relationship."

"Thanks, Bette," Jackson accepted her defense, while looking at Maggie, "but I don't know if Maggie will agree with you on that. I'm not sure what she told you, but it took me all night sitting in my car at White Rock Lake on our first date just to get up the nerve to kiss her." Maggie giggled as he finished his admission.

"What?" Bette asked sharply as she sat up in her chair. "What did you do?" She repeated the question as she reached across Maggie's chest and took the book back from Jackson. Jackson gave it to her, and looked at Maggie.

"You didn't tell her about that?" He asked, surprised.

"No." Maggie answered. "I spared her the details. We went straight to analyzing you." She spoke the last word sharply, as if pointing a finger at him, or sticking him with a pin.

"Oh, great," Jackson said.

"Now, stop it you two," Bette interrupted. "Tell me what you did at the lake," she added, insistently, as she began flipping through the pages of the novel. Jackson hesitated, and Maggie spoke.

"You brought it up. You tell her," she said, as she adjusted her swim suit top and closed her eyes against the sun.

"Ok, I'll try to make myself sound aggressive." He sat upright and turned toward Bette with his feet on the deck. It was a better position from which to tell the story, and he got to look across Maggie's body. "We met on a Saturday night, at a firm - my law firm - recruiting party. Maggie's brother and I were associates in the same firm at that time. I was really interested in her from the moment we were introduced. We talked a lot that night, but I didn't ask her out. I wanted to be cool, you know. So the next day I organized another firm social event – dinner and a movie – and called Maggie's brother to see if he and his wife wanted to join us."

"He had never invited them to any other event," Maggie interjected, without opening her eyes.

"That's true, and I wasn't really inviting them then, either," Jackson admitted. "I wanted to see Maggie, but I was playing it cool, right?"

"Oh, right," Bette agreed, still looking through the big book.

"So, her brother declined the invitation, but immediately suggested that Maggie might like to go, instead." He stopped, as Bette looked up at him, and then punched Maggie's shoulder.

"Sounds like Jackson wasn't the only one trying to play it cool," she said. Maggie grinned, but kept her eyes closed, and didn't speak.

"I've never gotten the full story on that response – whether it was pre-planned - but I remember thinking that my own plan was working out well. I couldn't imagine it would lead to here," Jackson said, as he reached over and put his hand on Maggie's arm. She didn't move, or open her eyes, but her grin had not faded. "Anyway, I picked her up in my red Italian convertible, and we met up with our group of about a dozen people at a restaurant. I only remember a few of the people that were there. Mostly, I remember just wanting to be with Maggie. There was something about her that I found very attractive." He looked down at her, but Maggie still kept her eyes closed, and Bette, still looking through her book, didn't notice. "Anyway," Jackson continued, "we talked at dinner and, I knew something was different about her. It wasn't just a physical attraction, although that was there, too."

"They're better be more to this story than that," Maggie interjected this time, still without opening her eyes. Bette laughed.

"You can skip that part," Bette said. "I've watched you two, and I was young once you know.'

"You're still young!" Maggie objected.

"Thank you, honey. Now," Bette looked again at Jackson, "you were saying how interested you were in this beautiful mind."

"Right," Jackson started again. "I didn't mean to give you the *War and Peace* version. I'll switch to the Cliffs Notes. We just started talking, and everybody – everything – else faded out of the picture. It lasted through the dinner, through the movie, through drinks with the others after the movie, and then at another bar after that, when we finally ditched the rest of the group, and finally till about 6 a.m., at the lake, where we sat in my convertible and kept talking."

"And, on the retaining wall in front of someone's house," Maggie added, eyes still closed.

"Right," Jackson agreed. "I remember the wall. I think you got out to sit on it just to give yourself a chance to think about the deep questions I was asking you - about your family and whether you were really as close as you claimed to be." Maggie responded by opening her eyes, finally, and turned to Bette.

"It wasn't a typical first date, I'll admit, either in setting or conversation." She paused. "Sure, I'd been parking before, but not to have my family relationships groped."

"Amazing," Bette said, with a serious but distracted tone, as she continued to look through the novel, only now she held it open and appeared to be scanning each line of the two facing pages.

"It was an amazing moment for me," Jackson admitted. "I think it was the only time I had ever been totally myself with a girl, and I was amazed that she didn't laugh or run. She even seemed to like me. It was a miracle." He paused, too, and Bette finally looked up from the book with an odd expression, just as he continued. "I know it sounds odd, but that's what happened, and I want to remember it always. I've joked to Maggie that I'm never selling that car. It's my tangible reminder of falling in love with her."

"Hmm," Bette said again, this time looking specifically at Jackson. "Are you sure you have never read this book?" She held up the thick novel, still open to the pages she had been studying.

"Yes," Jackson answered. "I mean, I'm sure I haven't. Why?"

"Listen to this," Bette said, and started to read from the book: '*They could easily afford another car, but Jim was sentimental about the Ford and stubbornly refused to sell it. They had discovered each other in the car, and he had got it bound up with their love in some way. They spent their first full night together parked in the car on a hill near White Rock Lake, in Dallas, kissing and talking.*'"

Maggie sat straight up in her chair, and looked gape-mouthed at Bette. She then turned to Jackson.

"And all this time I thought you came up with that idea on your own. I should have known that you got it from a book." She sounded more than slightly perturbed.

"I didn't!" Jackson insisted in response. "I told you, I have never read that book." He stopped, and then adopted a less urgent tone. "I know we weren't the first couple to go parking or even to fall in love at White Rock Lake on a moonlit night, but that doesn't lessen the magic – at least not for me. And, the fact that the same scene appears in a story by a major novelist just proves that we had a 'story-book' romance. Right?" He stopped, and looked anxiously at Maggie for agreement, but she looked at Bette.

"What do you think? *Is* he a true romantic, or just a plagiarist?" She asked this mostly in a mock tone, but Bette responded seriously.

"Oh, definitely a romantic," she said, winking at Jackson. "Listen, child. I've been around long enough to understand that any man who cares enough to remember how he fell in love with you – not to mention one willing to tell others the story – is worthy of some kind of complimentary title: romantic, prince, saint, dinosaur." She laughed at herself, but in a way meant to underscore her point, rather than undermine it. Maggie thought for a few seconds before turning back to Jackson.

"Ok. I guess one of us has to be the historian of our relationship. It's not like anyone is ever going to write a book about us. And it doesn't matter that someone else imagined – or even lived – our story before us. It was special to me, too, regardless." She turned back to Bette once more. "I agree with you about his romanticism, but it doesn't really matter. I'm going to keep him, even if I discover he is a fraud. I told him that already. I knew what I was doing when I promised before God 'for better or for worse.'" She finished with a broad smile, aimed directly at Jackson.

"Hey, at least my car wasn't a Ford," Jackson protested. "Surely Pininfarina styling counts for something."

XVII

"Okay, that's enough agonizing reappraisal for one day, not to mention ultra violet rays," Maggie said. She struggled out of her chair and gathered her things. She looked down at Jackson. "You know, I never said things like that before we met." Jackson started to speak, but Maggie held up her hand, palm forward. "Stop," she said, "no commentary, just take it as a compliment that you are influencing me, and leave it to me to decide if I meant it that way. I'm going to take a nap. Why don't you stay out here and keep Bette company? You owe her that much."

"Ok, I'll be glad to, if she doesn't mind, of course," Jackson answered, after a brief pause. They both looked at Bette.

"Absolutely," she responded to Jackson. "I've been waiting to get you alone, and really pick your brain about literature." She looked up at Maggie. "You just go get your beauty rest, honey. I'll take good care of him."

"Thanks," Maggie said, and started to walk away toward the elevator lobby.

"Two-four," Jackson called. Maggie turned and smiled back at him, and answered quickly.

"Two-four," She said, and then disappeared around the corner.

"Toofer?" Bette repeated with a question mark. Jackson looked down with a shy smile.

"No," he said, somewhat embarrassed. "it's two, four." He signed the numbers with his fingers. I guess we aren't going to have any secrets from you by the time we leave here." Bette's look indicated that she did not follow his explanation, so he continued. "It's how we say 'I love you.' We've always said that, whenever we are leaving each other or getting off the phone. Usually, I would say 'I love you' first, and she would respond with 'I love you, too.' After a while I decided to get the last word in, so I started responding to her with 'I love you, too, forever.' Sometime after that, I don't know how long, or even which of us started it, the whole exchange was simply shortened to 'Too, for.' I'm also not sure which one of us realized the whole expression could be signed with one hand, 'two-four'." He made the hand motion again.

"I'm sure it was you," Bette cracked, and Jackson understood.

"You would think so, wouldn't you? But, I really don't remember. I guess I'm not much of a historian after all. We should ask Maggie how she remembers it." After another pause, he added. "I'm just glad she still uses it. You may have noticed that she's not the most romantic person."

"Oh, I wouldn't say that with such conviction," Bette observed. "I think it may just be that her sense of romance seems thin when compared to yours. I think that she is closer to you on that score than she wants you to think."

"I'm glad you think so," Jackson said. "She can skewer me pretty good when the opportunity arises, which unfortunately is all too often."

"We girls have to keep our mystery about us any way we can," Bette concluded. "Now, tell me, what are you reading today?" Jackson reached under his chair, and pulled from under his towel a leather bound Bible. "Well!" Bette exhaled, "you surprise me again. I can't say that I've ever seen anyone reading that book on this dock." Jackson nodded his head in agreement, but did not speak. He opened the Bible and flipped through the pages, instead. "So," Bette inquired, "is there a particular purpose for your study, or just the general search for Truth?"

"Well," Jackson hesitated, "I've got a lot of general knowledge, but I'm trying to understand the particulars better."

"That sounds more like a lawyer's answer than a Believer's," Bette snapped.

"Good point," Jackson said, "and, essentially, a correct one." He leaned over again and pulled another book from underneath his chair, a thick one, and showed it to Bette. The large print on the front of what looked to her like a text book, read "Systematic Theology."

"You're kidding me!" She exclaimed sharply, and then giggled. "No offense intended." Jackson waved off her apology, and she asked, "Why are you studying these deep topics? Are you thinking of going into the ministry?"

"Not really," Jackson answered. "I'm thinking that we are all in the ministry. I don't mean that to be preaching, but it's true. I've come to realize lately that if you call yourself a Christian – or even if you don't – you've still got some serious responsibilities." He stopped short, although Bette could tell he was prepared to say more.

"Okay," she observed with her own hesitancy, "this is not the literary discussion I was expecting, but it could be interesting. I'll bite. You know I went to Catholic schools, so I shouldn't shy away from a religious discussion."

"No offense, but my perception of most Catholics is that they don't just shy away from a religious discussion, they run from it." Jackson spoke quickly, perhaps before he had considered the potential impact of such an assertion, Bette thought. She decided not to react directly.

"Oh, I suspect all denominations have their members who are unwilling – more likely, unable – to discuss their beliefs," she said, as she reached under her own chair, but pulled out her cigarette case rather than a book. She performed her lighting mime that Jackson had come to expect, and enjoyed watching.

"That's what I meant," Jackson said, after waiting for her to exhale the first drag. "You're right that it cuts across religions."

"Are you suggesting that Catholics and Protestants practice different religions?" Bette asked. Jackson looked up at her with concern.

"I'm not about to start that discussion," he said. "I don't know enough yet to respond intelligently and, even if I did, I don't know you well enough yet to discuss it. Maggie would kill me if I destroyed a new friendship." Bette listened to him with a blank look, not sure if she was disappointed, or glad that Jackson had declined the debate, but she liked what he said about Maggie.

"Ok," she replied after an instant. "I doubt that you aren't qualified to discuss it, but I'll accept your demurrer."

"Don't tell me you went to law school, too? I haven't heard that term used since I studied for the bar exam," Jackson said.

"Oh, didn't I tell you? Bob's a lawyer. I feel like I should be licensed, too, considering all that I have learned putting him through school, and then working at his office all these years." She looked up almost wistfully at the sky.

"You certainly picked up the terminology, and although I never practiced that old state court procedural stuff, I think you used you it correctly – not that I'm surprised about that, of course."

"Oh, of course you're surprised," Bette corrected him in a light tone. "You pegged me for a faded blonde Dallas socialite who does nothing but read a few books between tennis lessons and lunches at the club with the girls." She stopped, and could see that Jackson was flustered. "See, you can't think how to respond, because I'm right, right?"

"No, no," was all Jackson could manage to say in response, at least immediately. Bette giggled as he tried to recover. "I, we've, only just met you, so I don't know enough to form that kind of opinion," Jackson said. "Not that I would, even if I knew more," he added, realizing that he could still be misinterpreted. Bette laughed again, and Jackson kept up his struggle. "Actually, Maggie and I have been fascinated by your interest in us. You're not like anyone we know. You've got a style and personality that seems to be from another era – and I mean that positively." He stopped, trying to avoid another potential insult, Bette thought.

"Okay, okay; you can stop groveling. I'm not mad. You kids amuse me. I guess it's only fair that I amuse you some, too. I must say, though, that I'm surprised that I could fluster you so easily. I figured your courtroom experience would have trained you better. No offense, just an observation." This time, she was afraid she had gone too far.

"No offense taken," Jackson said. "I'm still young and learning, although I have been told that I'm very quick on my feet in court. But I don't think I've been in front of any judges like you. You're interesting and surprising and, of course, you're a woman." Jackson left his meaning unclear, and Bette challenged him.

"What has that got to do with anything?" She asked. Jackson was ready to respond.

"I know the answer should be 'nothing,' but I can't say that I feel the same way when I am in front of a woman judge as I do before a man. *But,"* he emphasized, "before you conclude that I'm a chauvinist, you should know that I simply consider it another character trait, just like all the other personality traits I take into consideration in preparing my arguments. All of the judges are different, and gender is just one of the potential differences." He stopped, and Bette could tell that he hoped he had convinced her.

"Okay, I'll accept that. I guess you are pretty quick on your feet, or on your back." She nodded at his lounging position, but immediately put her hand to her mouth in embarrassment. "Oops! That didn't sound right. Sorry." Jackson grinned, but again waved off her remark.

"I said you were interesting, but perhaps mischievous is a better word."

"Oh, I like that," she admitted. "Now, how did we get into this discussion?"

"I ducked your religion question," Jackson reminded her, "and a pretty good job I did."

"I'll say," Bette agreed, and then paused before continuing, "but even if you don't want to discuss it, I can still give you my views. I definitely had my problems with the Sisters, but that was a discipline thing. It wasn't until I was older, in my late 20's, that I began to question the doctrine. There's a lot about the Bible that doesn't make sense to me, but the Church's effort to put it into practice often makes even less sense. I started asking questions about some of the rules, and the answers I got from the clergy weren't very convincing. Some of them had at least a basis in Scripture, but most of it just seemed to be made up to suit their needs." She stopped to see if Jackson had changed his mind about joining the discussion. He had.

"I can agree with you on that point, and there isn't a lot of difference between the Catholics and Protestants there. Luther broke with the Church because he believed that the Pope was only interested in fleecing his flock for money to support the building of the Vatican. And, of course, the Catholics accused Luther of breaking away just so he could get married. It's hard to know what the true personal motivations were, or are, in religious matters. So, lately, I've been trying to get to the heart of the beliefs, ignoring as best as I can the human element. That's what I've been doing with this book." He pointed to the theology treatise.

"Have you reached your own conclusions?" Bette asked.

"Oh, not yet. Even I'm not arrogant enough to think I can resolve these ancient disputes by age thirty. I'm just trying to get convinced in my own mind, right now." He shook his head, somewhat in disillusionment, Bette thought. "In fact, I'm trying to get convinced about a lot of things right now. I keep having this feeling that I'm supposed to be doing something, but I can't quite decide what it is."

"Sounds like professional restlessness to me," Bette observed.

"You could think so," Jackson admitted, "but, actually, I'm pretty happy with my profession. And besides, I've had this feeling for a long time, since long before I became a lawyer. I just can't get a clear picture of what it is that I'm supposed to be doing differently. Do you ever have that feeling?"

"No," Bette answered immediately, although she continued to consider the question. "I guess I've always been pretty happy with where I was, and what I was doing. I'm certainly happy now, I can say that, because I'm here. I love being here in the summer. This is a magical place to me." She looked around at the green port and the blue sky. In the mid-afternoon, it was very quiet, with only a few sea gulls making their presence known. "When I'm here, I think about many things - but not to change what I'm doing, just to review it, and reflect on it. I think about my Daddy, my children, and Bob." She paused long enough for Jackson to interject.

"I didn't know you had children," he said.

"Oh, yes. Two, almost as old as you and Maggie. They give me lots to reflect on, I can tell you that." She paused again.

"Maggie and I haven't decided about children yet. We agreed to wait five years before seriously considering the issue." Bette snapped out of her reminiscence.

"Now, there you go again, thinking like a lawyer. Children aren't issues. Their people. They *create* issues, sure, but they are not issues in the abstract." Bette was surprised by the conviction she heard in her voice. Jackson acted as if he was, too.

"Well, to be technical, they are considered "issue" in the context of estate planning and probate law," Jackson said. "I guess Bob does not do that kind of law, but anyway, I get that you are speaking as a mother now, not as a legal assistant, but you should know that it's not just me that feels this way. Maggie agrees totally. You can ask her."

"I will, and I'll tell her the same thing. You kids are great together, but I assure you that you will regret it if you don't have children. Maybe that's the purpose you've been looking for. I certainly can say that my children, as flawed as they are, have filled spaces in my life that I didn't even know were there." She knew she was preaching now, but didn't care. "Now I can sit here and enjoy myself, knowing that I gave everything I've learned to them. You'll probably laugh, but I believe my purpose in life was to raise my kids, to teach them right from wrong, and have them be positive additions to society – and I'm not talking about the country club. We each need to instill in our children a sense of responsibility. If parents don't do it, who will?" She stopped, again aware of her preachy tone and unsure if Jackson was actually listening. He was.

"I got that kind of teaching from my father," Jackson said. "It wasn't overt, but I'm sure I do things today because of what I saw him do – little things, but they are the *right* things. You know, opening doors for others, doing my share of stuff around the house, driving the speed limit - just little things, but what most people would characterize as being 'responsible.' Where my Dad got it from is an interesting question, because he pretty much grew up on his own, to hear him tell the story. Anyway, he instilled in me a sense of right and wrong through his example – from watching him around the house, to going with him to church three times a week for most of my childhood. It's funny, though. I picked up these little habits from him that most people would consider doing "good," but I have come to realize that we have very different views on that theologically. John Calvin would say that Paul teaches us that any desire to do good only comes from above. I agree with him, but I'm not sure my Dad does. Even if I'm right – or Calvin is - I still have to acknowledge that Dad's teaching was effective, because I'm certain that he is the source of my personality traits that reflect the golden rule – and I'm not talking about 'he who has the gold makes the rules.' Like many people, I catch myself doing things that are *exactly* like I have seen my father do them, and these are usually good things, little acts of kindness. So, that must mean that either I'm wrong on my doctrinal beliefs, or that perhaps we both are, and maybe even Calvin and Paul were." He finally paused what he realized had become a speech, and then asked her, "Does that make any sense?"

"No," Bette said without hesitation, but then she broke into a laugh, and continued, "I thought we were talking about my purpose in life, and that we weren't going to have a discussion about religion. Isn't that what you wanted?"

"I thought so," Jackson answered. "I guess I'm not sure what I want – or what I think."

"Well, you just keep trying hard to figure it out," Bette encouraged him. "That's a good thing." Jackson nodded, and

Bette added, "I'm not going to stop you from analyzing the issues to death, if you want. We certainly need more people who are willing to think deeply about these ideas, but my view is that it's still going to come down – at the end of the day – to faith. What do you believe in enough to have faith in? Or do you believe in anything? I've told my kids that I can't make up their minds for them, but I'll be really mad at them if they don't make up their minds for themselves."

"Make up whose mind, about what?" A voice asked from behind them. Both Bette and Jackson turned in their chairs to see George standing on the pier extending out beside his boat.

"George Waters! Didn't anyone ever tell you it is not polite to listen in on other peoples' conversation?" Bette asked.

"Hey, I wasn't listening in. I was just standing here, and you were talking. I think that excuses me from being impolite." He came back onto the main deck and walked over to their chairs. "I didn't understand what you were saying anyway. Just what are you trying to make up your mind about?" He asked Bette, and then grinned at Jackson.

"Where we are going to eat dinner," Bette answered, also grinning at Jackson. "Do you have an expert opinion about that?"

"Sure. Right here," George answered, and pointed down to the dock below his feet. "I came back to get some fish out of the freezer. We can grill it and eat out here on the dock."

"I think maybe we should consult him on more issues," Jackson said. "He seems to be a man capable of quick decisions."

"Let's hold off until after dinner," Bette said. "I want a little more time to think about our discussion." She raised her hand to let George help her out of her chair.

"I can hardly wait to hear what I'm missing," George said.

"Nothing, and everything, I think," Bette told him. "I'm

going up to take a shower before you cook me dinner. Nice talking with you, Jackson." She picked up her books and cigarettes, and quickly disappeared around the corner to her elevator lobby.

"You going in, too?" George asked Jackson.

"No, I don't want to wake Maggie up. Want to join me in a little sun worshipping?"

"Nah. I'm handsome enough as I am. I'll see you at dinner." George turned and soon disappeared around a corner in the other direction. The sun was partly blocked by the building now, and Jackson turned his chair to face the port again. He sat quietly, looking out at the few boats cruising the channel and the occasional one passing by in the port. He started to day-dream again, but this time not about a future life upon the sea, but rather his current one in a federal courtroom. He recalled his last argument with a black-robed bankruptcy judge, sitting high above him in a dark paneled chamber. The judge was a woman, and she was not pleased with Jackson, or at least his arguments. He had struggled to defend his position, and he cringed at the condescending comments he had received from the bench. Then a male voice interrupted his remembrance in a booming, amplified command.

"This is the United States Coast Guard. Disperse immediately. You are impeding a federal waterway. Disperse immediately!" Jackson looked across the water toward the jetties, and could see a large white ship with a slash of orange running vertically from deck to hull, about a third of the way back from the bow. Several uniformed sailors stood on deck. Jackson was surprised to see that they wore dark blue uniforms, instead of white.

"Disperse immediately!" The voice boomed again, like a fog horn. "This is your final warning." It was only then that Jackson's attention turned to the object of the warning. In the channel across the entrance to the port were at least a dozen shrimp boats jostling side by side in a sort of line dance. Beyond them were many more boats – both pleasure and commercial – backed up in the channel as if at the scene of a traffic accident. Farther beyond them, Jackson noticed many more shrimp boats coming up the intra-coastal channel from Aransas Pass toward the Tarpon port. Dozens of people had gathered on the jetties and the point by the ferry landing to watch.

"They're really doing it," Bette said in an excited voice, as she reappeared suddenly next to Jackson on the dock, binoculars to her eyes.

"Doing what?" Jackson asked.

"Blockading the port," she answered, her voice rising with even greater excitement. "They're protesting the new T.E.D. regulations."

"Really?" Maggie said, joining them just as suddenly, and sounding even more excited than Bette. Just then the air horn blasted again and the voice returned.

"You have been warned. You are violating federal regulations and have refused to desist. Prepare to be boarded."

"They're going to board their boats?" Jackson asked Bette, as if he did not believe what he had heard.

"That's what the man said," Bette answered, amused. "This could get ugly," she added in a more serious tone. She raised the binoculars to her eyes as the Coast Guard ship moved forward toward the shrimp boats. She could see several smaller official craft rushing forward beside the larger ship, each with five or six guardsmen aboard. The line of shrimp boats had now grown to at least two dozen. "This is going to be really interesting," she said, and handed the binoculars to Maggie. "Here, take a look." Maggie put the glasses to her eyes as the voice returned.

"You are under arrest by the United States Coast Guard.

Do not resist." Maggie could not locate the speaker on the deck of the Coast Guard ship, but noticed several of the sailors moving around holding what looked like very large ropes. "All shrimp vessel crew, please assemble on deck with your hands in front of you. Do *not* resist arrest," the voice repeated its warning with even greater emphasis. Maggie panned over the channel to the armada of shrimp vessels and focused on the deck of the one closest to the Coast Guard ship. Several shrimpers had, in fact, assembled on its deck.

"They appear to be complying. They're lining up on deck. Uh oh!" She exclaimed, suddenly. "I don't think that's what the Coast Guard had in mind." She laughed out loud as she handed the binoculars to Jackson. He took them from her and quickly found a row of about 15 men in his field of vision. They had turned their backs away from the Coast Guard ship, and were bending over, exposing their bare bottoms to the sailors.

"They're mooning them!" Jackson almost shouted.

"Let me see that!" Bette exclaimed, and took the glasses from him quickly. By the time she had focused on the shrimp boat, the sailors had responded with the large hoses Maggie had seen them unrolling. Water fired swiftly across the distance of twenty yards or so between the decks of the ship and shrimp boats. Several men fell, and two were pushed sideways over the port side and into the channel. "Oh my!" Bette sucked in her breath. They're hitting them with the water cannon and two just went overboard!" Shouts could be heard from the other boats, and from the spectators on the jetties. Bette saw three smaller craft move quickly toward the hull of one shrimp boat with the guardsmen holding out hooks and life preservers. A couple of them in wet suits went over the side. "Looks like a rescue job is in progress," she said.

"I bet it's hard to swim with your pants around your

ankles," Jackson offered his own observation, and looked at Maggie. 'And I bet it is cold, too,' he thought.

"I think we have a get-a-way action in addition to the rescue operation," Maggie joined in. "Look." Several of the shrimp boats had separated from the formation and were moving away from the entrance to the channel. A couple of the smaller Coast Guard craft moved through the opening and took up a position in the center of the channel. This did not stop the shrimp boats from continuing to move. Suddenly, several of them started swiftly up the channel toward the Gulf.

"Stop immediately!" The voice returned again. "This is the United States Coast Guard. You are ordered to stop immediately!"

"Can you believe that?" Bette asked. "They're actually making a run for it!"

"I assume the Coast Guard will get all their registration numbers," Jackson said. "They sure can't stop the boats with the water cannon, and I assume they won't use anything more explosive." Several more boats were moving now, some down the channel, others across toward the intracoastal waterway. Horns began to sound from the other boats that had gathered in the port and channel. Cheers came up from the crowd on the jetties and the point, perhaps one hundred strong now. Several small craft zipped around in circles seemingly in an effort to corral the much larger shrimp boats, but the efforts went unheeded. The Coast Guard ship moved on through the now open jetties, turned clockwise toward the Gulf, and surged forward at full power.

"It appears that they have decided to go after one of them, at least," Maggie said. "Maybe they know who the ringleader is."

"Maybe the guys they pulled out of the channel told them," Jackson said. As quickly as the show had begun, it was over. The boats still in the channel and the port moved orderly in the usual fashion, and the people on the jetties and the point fanned out in the park area, as they would on any summer day.

"Well, that *was* interesting. I may have to buy a paper tomorrow just to see those pictures," George spoke for the first time. He had come from his storage unit around the corner and was carrying a platter of fish filets.

"You may have to go to the supermarket counter to get the best shots," Maggie said.

"So, counselor," Bette said, "what do you think of that as a strategy against federal regulation?"

"I would have advised against it," Jackson replied in a professional tone. "Not likely to obtain the remedy they are seeking," he added.

"It probably was fun, though," Maggie offered, "at least until they got blown into the water."

"Better than getting blown out of the water," George said. "All this excitement work up an appetite for anyone?"

"I have an appetite for fish you cook anytime, George," Bette replied, turning her back to the port and taking a seat on the dock. Did you know that was about to happen?"

"Of course not!" George said, with his usual grin. "If I had, don't you think I would have been out there in my boat?"

"I guess that's right," Bette nodded. "I just figured you might have planned it for them, and then got smart and decided to watch it from the sidelines."

"I guess I should be flattered by that, but I can't take the credit or the blame. I'm not that dedicated to anything." George turned away from them and went down the dock toward the grill, but then stopped and called back. "Jackson, can you grab that bag of mesquite wood out of the unit? It's in the pantry in the kitchen." Jackson got up quickly, without answering, and went up the stairs toward the unit.

"Well!" Bette sighed to Maggie. "It has been an exciting afternoon. First, I get to debate theology with Jackson, and then I get to see a shrimper's bare backside get washed overboard into the channel. I'd call that the sublime and ridiculous, but I'm just not sure which is which."

"Jackson made you talk about theology?" Maggie asked, as she took a seat next to Maggie. "I knew I shouldn't have left him alone with you. He just doesn't know when to stop."

"Now, honey," Bette waved her hand at Maggie, "don't go blaming your sweet husband. He tried to avoid it, but I egged him on."

"Is that true?" Maggie asked, surprised.

"Not exactly, but close enough." Bette waved again. "He's got some interesting ideas, and so I let him know a few of mine."

I'm sure I'll regret this question, but I guess I have to ask what you all talked about, specifically," Maggie said.

"Oh nothing truly heretical," Bette answered. "I just told him my belief that everyone's got a purpose in life, and that if you look for it long enough you'll figure yours out. God'll let you know."

"That doesn't sound too radical to me," Maggie said. "Surely Jackson didn't call that heresy?"

"No, he agreed with me. I just think he's upset that God hasn't let him know what his purpose is yet."

"Don't I know that," Maggie agreed.

"I think I made him feel even worse when I told him that I didn't learn my purpose until after it was finished."

"Really? What was it?"

"Raising my kids," Bette replied. "I don't know when I realized it, or how, but I'm as sure of it now as I am that the sky is blue and our port is green." She looked up first, and then out to the now calm water.

"That's nice." Maggie could think of nothing more to

observe, after an awkward pause. Before she could try to say more, Jackson reappeared from the unit carrying the bag of wood. He started toward the end of the dock as George emerged from behind the palm tree hiding the barbeque pit on a little spit of beach beside the port. He handed the bag off to George.

"Why do you girls look so serious?" Jackson asked, as he came toward them.

"Because we're talking about you," Bette said directly.

"That'll teach you to ask a woman a question you don't know the answer to," George said, as he set the bag down on the dock next to a small cooler. He opened the cooler and took out a long-necked bottle of beer. "I thought they taught you that in law school?"

"They don't teach such practical things in law school - maybe about witnesses in a case, but not about women in real life." Jackson shrugged, and accepted the beer bottle as George held it out to him.

"Well, then, law school or no law school, you should just know not to lead with your chin."

"When did you become so wise in dealing with women?" Bette asked George.

"I don't know," George fingered his mustache, "maybe during all the hours I've spent fishing. You've got a lot of time to think, waiting for that big strike. You ask yourself over and over what the fish might be doing or thinking out there in the big blue ocean, hoping you can come up with an idea that'll make your paths cross. And if your paths do cross, you hope you're using a bait that she'll be interested in. Of course, you don't really know, because you can't exactly ask her ahead of time, but maybe you've had other experiences that will help you." He paused while a grin formed at the corners of his mustache, then glanced first at Bette, then at Maggie, and finally fixed his eyes on Jackson. "Sound familiar?"

"I've never been deep-sea fishing – until this morning, of course, and I guess I still haven't actually. Anyway, I think I get your meaning," Jackson said, with his own smile forming. "You're saying fish, like women, never tell you what they want, you just have to observe their behavior and make as good a guess as you can, based on the other women you've caught? I mean fish," Jackson quickly corrected himself, while shaking the grin off his face.

"You are a quick study!" George slapped Jackson on his shoulder. "I need to be sure and tell your bosses that."

"I think we're being insulted, more than Jackson's being complimented," Bette said to Maggie.

"I think you're right," Maggie agreed, and turned to George, "but if Jackson is so quick to pick up on your point, why hasn't he learned it before now? He has been leading with his chin for many years with us enigmatic women."

"I might could answer that if I knew what 'enigmatic' meant," George said. "Help me out, here, counselor." Jackson took a long drink from his beer, long enough to try to formulate in his mind the meaning of the word. A large yacht glided by them in the port, and George waved. A thin man on the fly bridge swung his hand over his head in an exaggerated salute.

"Let's see," Jackson began, "'enigmatic' – mysterious, ambiguous, unknowable?" He gave each word an increasingly questioning inflection.

"You're too technical," George responded. "I was thinking something more descriptive and earthy.'"

"Hey!" Bette and Maggie protested jointly. "That's not very nice." Bette added. "You can think that about me – maybe – but not about my new friend, Maggie." George tipped his beer to her in his most sincere apology, picked up the bag of wood, and started back down the dock to the grill.

"No, that's not a term I've ever associated with Maggie," Jackson observed. "And I don't think I would use it to describe you, either," he pointed at Bette with his beer bottle.

"That's awfully nice of you," Bette sniffed.

"I'd just call you 'frank'," George called back over his shoulder.

"As if you never say what you mean!" Bette called after him. "We're a lot alike, you know!"

"God help you then," was George's reply, although he had disappeared again behind the palm tree.

"He has, as a matter of fact," Bette answered, in a normal voice and only for Jackson's benefit. She then turned to Maggie. "Like I was telling Jackson this afternoon, I'm learning more and more about God as I grow older." She paused as George reappeared and approached them again. "You know, you ought to give God a little more attention," she added. George rolled his eyes.

"Oh, I have as a matter of fact. I was just thinking this morning – 'God, how am I going to take Jackie and Maggie fishing if this hurricane doesn't go away?' – and what happens? Just look at the water." He pointed out to the port that had become as calm as a lake. "It's a sign, obviously. *He* wants us to go fishin' tomorrow." George pointed his finger in the air. "I love it when He does that."

Jackson and Maggie caught each other's look of surprise and uncertainty. Jackson knew it was his duty to speak.

"So, you think it's okay to try again tomorrow?" He tried to sound like he was encouraged.

"Oh, sure. Look at it." George turned again to the port and the other three followed him with their eyes. "They'll be really frisky tomorrow."

"Is that learned from your fishing, or your dating experience?" Maggie asked. Bette laughed out loud.

"Don't answer that, George," she put her hand out. "I'll vouch for you in the fishing department, and the other should be left alone." She turned to Maggie. "Honey, if George says it's good fishing weather, you can take it as the Gospel."

"Why did you have to bring faith into it?" Jackson asked.

XVIII

"Did you intend to talk about religion so much?" Maggie asked Jackson as they walked south along the beach. They had driven over after dinner and parked along the jetty, and were now walking in the damp packed sand, zig-zagging right toward the dunes and left back toward the surf as the waves rolled up with varying force. This was all that remained of the storm that had disrupted their fishing trip, and its final assault was not threatening. The waves were breaking about fifty yards out, and occasionally they would rise to two or three feet – decent waves for this part of the Gulf, but nothing to alarm any villagers or even the campers whose tents lined the public section of the beach near the jetties. In the last light of the summer evening, Jackson and Maggie were not alone on the beach. In addition to campers, several families were still playing in the water. A few eternally hopeful surfers made optimistic efforts to ride the day's final waves.

As they walked, Jackson looked south and west at the last streak of sunset mingling with the sand stirring in the air. The hazy picture with the muffled sound of the waves and wind seemed to fit their mood. Maggie had spoken not with anger, but with uncertainty.

"Haven't you noticed that I seem to be talking about

religion all the time these days?" Jackson finally answered her. "Others just don't seem to share my interest."

"I don't know. Bette seemed to be interested," Maggie replied, thinking that she was, too, but she wasn't sure how to say so. "She filled me in on your afternoon conversation while we ate dinner. She said she needed more time to think about what you said. I guess that's why I was surprised that you all talked so much about it tonight."

"You *do* know me well enough, don't you, to recognize when I'm still working through my ideas?" Jackson asked. Maggie didn't respond, so Jackson continued. "I'm still vague on many points, and I need all the input I can get. I especially like getting it from people who don't expect to be asked. I think you get a truer opinion that way."

"But isn't it just as likely to be half-baked?" Maggie asked.

"Maybe," Jackson admitted, "but I've come to learn in my practice that my first off-the-cuff answer is usually right, or at least as right as the one I come up with after studying the issue for days. The more I think about theology, the harder it is for me to explain to others what I've thought. Several hours in the sun and several margaritas don't help."

"Not to mention Jimmy Buffett's music playing in the background all day and all night," Maggie observed. "I didn't know George was as big a fan as you – either that or he was using it to keep himself out of your conversation with Bette."

"Probably a little of both, but he did seem rather focused on the music tonight, didn't he?" Jackson agreed. "Of course, anyone that has George's view of life would have to love Jimmy Buffett – and probably *not* love Jesus. Although, I have to admit, I've never discussed either point with him."

"That's the first time I've heard you admit that the two are inconsistent." Maggie said. "I've been thinking it for a long time, and I assume you know it, but I wasn't sure you would admit it." She stopped, but Jackson didn't answer immediately, and she continued. "I know you're changing. You've been changing since the day we met – maybe even since before we met – but you're definitely different from when we met. Back then, I don't know if it would have dawned on you that these two interests of yours don't really go together." Jackson stepped quickly to his right to avoid a wave, and almost tripped them both. He grabbed Maggie's arm to balance them, and then stood still, looking back up the beach from where they had come. It was past dusk now, and they could just see the outline of an oil tanker as it entered the jetties from the Gulf.

"We'd better turn back," he said. After a few steps, when Maggie was about to conclude that he was not going to respond to her charges, Jackson did. "I think the main difference you see in me now is that I am thinking about religion a lot more than I was. I don't know if I'm thinking about Jimmy Buffett less – maybe so – but I'm certainly not ready to admit that the two are not compatible. I will admit that most people think they aren't, including Jimmy Buffett, probably. Of course, I don't know that it would be any more difficult to convince the literary critics of America that Buffett's a great writer, than it would be to convince him or you that he's a theologian.'

"Neither is harder than the other, they're both impossible," Maggie said.

"But with God all things are possible, right?" Jackson countered. "Look at us. Who would have ever thought that we would be a good match? It was obviously Divine intervention just for you to be interested in me."

"Oh, don't start that again," Maggie complained. "Remember, I was amused by your borderline pathetic side when we met, but now that I'm part of your life, it is no longer amusing or justifiable."

"Okay, okay," Jackson protested. "Don't jump to

conclusions. I was just observing the unlikely nature of our attraction. You can agree with me on that without having to decide that I'm still pathetic. I still don't understand why it is important to you that I was, in the first place. How was that attractive to you?" He seemed genuinely interested in the answer, but Maggie decided to dodge the question.

"And I don't understand why it was so important to you for me to be impressed by your car," she insisted. "I would think that you would be pleased that I was caught up in you, not red steel and black leather." Jackson started to respond, but she didn't let him. "No, don't explain. It just shows that we still have a few more things to learn about each other. I don't think it would be healthy to have everything figured out in the first three years."

"Well, you were the one who started our first conversation about God," Jackson said.

"I was just trying to keep the conversation interesting," Maggie responded, "and I'm still doing that, only now we talk about you, God and Jimmy Buffett – the Holy Trinity of my life."

"If that's true, then you're the one who needs to be thinking about your religion – and you left out baseball," Jackson added.

"You know what I mean," she persisted. "What are you planning on doing with this intensive study?"

"Why do I have to *do* anything with it?" he asked, sounding a bit perplexed Maggie thought, although his emphasis may have come from the effort to elude another wave. This one caught them both, as the Gulf was in complete darkness now. The water was warm and they stopped to feel the pull of the tide against their calves as the wave receded. "Why can't I go on worshipping them both?" he continued. "Do *you* think it is a sin to love Jimmy Buffett's music?"

"You're the theologian in the family," Maggie answered immediately. "You figure it out."

"Okay, then. I'll let you know when I find the answer," Jackson said. "Right now, I couldn't say anything other than that I would find it harder to stop listening to Buffett's music than to stop studying the Scriptures."

'That's no surprise,' Maggie thought to herself, 'since you do more listening than you do studying.' She was about to express the thought as they reached their car, but she decided to remain quiet when Jackson put the key in the lock and opened the door for her, as he always did.

"I forgot to tell you," Jackson said, "George changed his mind again about fishing. He still thinks it's too rough to go out in the Gulf, but he insisted that I go bay-fishing with him tomorrow. He said he owes it to me after this morning." He closed her door and walked around to the driver's side and got in. "He also said he owed it to you *not* to invite you."

"I accept his non-invitation," Maggie said with glee. "What time do you leave?"

"He said he'd pick me up on the dock around 6," Jackson said, with a grimace.

"That early?" Maggie responded, with another look of glee. "Then you need to go straight to bed and get some sleep. You need to save your strength for the fish."

"I still hate fishing," Jackson said.

XIX

As Jackson and Maggie pulled into their assigned parking place at the condo complex, the headlights of their Chevy Blazer exposed George's backside. As he leaned into the freezer, he was framed by the open door in his storage unit. George saw and felt the lights, but did not hurry to raise up or turn around to greet them. Let 'em stare, he thought. After both Maggie and Jackson's doors crunched closed, he heard a low whistle from the passenger side.

"I thought you'd never notice," George said, finally straightening and turning to meet Maggie's smile with his own. "It's really cold in that freezer and very hard on my back. That's a lot of work for an old man to get a little attention from a pretty young girl."

"You're not an old man, and I'm not a young girl," Maggie responded, as George turned from her to shake Jackson's hand.

"I'd say you're a pretty woman, and he's a dirty man, old or not," Jackson said, pointing to George's t-shirt that bore the signs of grilling a large amount of fish earlier in the evening.

"Dirty cook, dirty old man, just trying to play all my parts," George said. "Speaking of which, Bette and I decided we want to see that dancing you promised Maggie earlier. Ready to go back to Barracuda's?" Jackson flinched, George was sure, but then tried to hide his reaction by glancing at his watch.

"Well, it's almost 10," Jackson hesitated. "You're making me go fishing again early tomorrow, so I was going to try to get some sleep." He looked at Maggie, clearly hoping for support. "We've already had quite a day – and you said you were tired." His voice trailed off, and he looked at Maggie for support. George decided not to let her help him.

"Hey, I'm the old man here, and I'm still going." He turned to Maggie. "You're not going to let him out of this are you? Didn't he promise he'd take you dancing tonight?" George could tell she was trying to decide quickly whether to agree with him as she wanted to for her own sake, or disagree with him to protect her husband. She started to answer, but again George interrupted.

"Okay, I'm pulling host rank. My place is off limits till midnight. That gives us a couple of hours to see what this uptight lawyer's got," he punched Jackson on the arm and did a little jig, "and that will still give him plenty of time for beauty sleep before we head out to fish with Bubba in the morning." Jackson shrugged and Maggie grinned. George laughed, knowing that he had given her what she wanted without putting her in Jackson's dog house. He, on the other hand, was going to have to make it up to Jackson, but he already had a plan for that, too.

"Who's Bubba?" Jackson asked.

"Oh, just an old fishing buddy of mine who's passing through. He's a poor substitute for Maggie, but I guess we've got no choice in the matter." He looked at Maggie, and she shook her head decisively. "Okay!" he ordered. "Let me get Bette, and we'll be dancing in no time. We can stay even later now that Maggie can sleep late!" He turned and marched around the corner, reaching behind his back to scratch his behind through his swim trunks as he went. Twenty minutes later the four of them were climbing the steps to the neon-framed front door of the club, which was held open by the backside of the same woman who had waved Maggie and Jackson in the night before. This time she spoke to George first.

"Hello, George. Glad you dressed up for us this evening," she said, as she pointed to the dirty t-shirt that he had not changed.

"Just trying to fit the image of your club," George replied.

"Fair enough," the woman nodded in agreement. "You responsible for these children tonight?" She asked, looking at Bette rather than Jackson and Maggie.

"Patsy, George responded, "you know I'm not responsible for anything or anybody, including myself," and he walked on past her into the flashing lights and blaring music inside the club. Bette and Maggie followed him without hesitation, but Jackson reached for his wallet.

"Forget it," Patsy growled dismissively, putting her hand on his shoulder and guiding him into the club. For an instant Jackson thought she would pat him on the behind. She didn't. Inside, Jackson automatically looked to his left, hoping to see Maggie engaged in another foosball battle, but the table was occupied by a couple of local guys. He turned and looked down the length of the crowded bar and saw Bette talking to a man about her age and size, handsome with tanned skin and fine salt and pepper hair, neatly trimmed. They were smiling, and Bette was pointing toward the dance floor. Jackson's eyes followed her direction. On the dance floor he saw George grinning at him in his best bandito leer as he danced with Maggie – or at least in the same general area with her. George actually seemed to be in his own world, spinning and bending his body in a remote connection to the music. Maggie was making an effort to coordinate with him, but George was his own show. Jackson keep his eye on them, even as he moved over to where Bette was standing by the bar.

"Do you know Will?' Bette strained to ask him over the din. She put her arm on the man's shoulder, which was level with her own. Jackson shook his head 'no,' but held out his hand to shake Will's and shouted to him over the music.

"I'm Jackson. That's my wife out there with George." Will shook Jackson's hand firmly, but didn't speak. Instead he gestured at the beer bottle in his hand and pointed at Jackson who this time shook his head 'yes.' In an instant Will turned and caught the attention of the bar tender. A moment later he handed Jackson a long-necked bottle of beer. He tipped his bottle to Jackson in a salute and took a long drink. Jackson did the same, but before he could finish he felt a light punch in his stomach that made him hunch over, and nearly caused him to spit out his beer. George laughed, and pushed on past him to the bar. Maggie moved to Jackson's side, snatched the bottle from his hand and took a long drink.

"Want one of your own?" Jackson shouted, but before she could respond Will held out another bottle, and Maggie took it with a smile of thanks. "This is Will," Jackson shouted again. Again, Will replied only with a nod of his head and slight but warm smile, followed by a salute with his beer bottle. Maggie responded in kind, and then looked quickly to Jackson. At that moment the music stopped abruptly and an unnatural hush rushed into the room. Suddenly able to be heard, most of the people instinctively lowered their voices from a shout to a whisper, and looked around self-consciously, but not George.

"Well! After fishin', dancin's one of my favorite things – all kinds of dancin'!" he called out, loudly.

"It looked like you were doing all kinds of dancing at one time just now," Jackson said, quietly.

"It was a sight better than what you were doing," George

fired back. "I couldn't leave this beautiful lady unescorted on the dance floor in this joint." He put his arm around Maggie for an instant.

"You're dancing style appears to escort all of the ladies at the same time," Bette offered, but before George could respond, an amplified voice blasted into all corners of the room.

"Ladies and gentlemen! Welcome to Barracuda's, a world class bar because we have all classes of patrons. We hope you are enjoying yourself tonight, and are ready for the main event – Barracuda's Bikini Bingo!" A mild response, relative to the volume of the microphone, greeted this rhetorical question. George saw Jackson and Maggie look at each other uncertainly. He glanced at Will, who seemed to notice as well, but Will again said nothing. George stepped away from the bar to the edge of the now empty dance floor, and howled.

"There's our guest host for the evening! Let's hear it for George Waters!" George howled again, as the crowd joined in. George turned back toward them in time to catch Maggie and Jackson looking at each other again. The voice continued. "Before we bring out our five contestants, let's review the rules for any of you that may be here for the first time. Each of the contestants will draw a letter from our special pitcher of beer – B-I-N-G or O. They will then appear in that order and act out a word chosen for them by you, the audience, that starts with the same letter and describes an aspect of life here on our beautiful island. And, remember, as always, parts of the body are not eligible, even though they are, undoubtedly an essential element of life on our beautiful island." A few boos came from the crowd, but the speaker ignored them and continued. "After all contestants have finished, your applause will determine the winner who will receive a $50 bill! Are we high rollers, or what!" The crowd applauded again, as Maggie and Jackson rolled their eyes at each other. George saw Jackson shrug as if to say 'it was your idea to come.' He interrupted their thoughts with another howl, and Bette put her hands over her eyes. Will looked on, without judgment.

"Ok!" The voice continued, "without further ado, let's bring out tonight's contestants. Give them a big welcome, the girls of Tarpon! At least for tonight." A door in the back corner of the dance floor opened, and five young women marched out as the music shot back into the room and pumped energy into their walk. They did a quick circuit of the dance floor, and the crowd pressed forward in a bunch with George still in front, howling again. They were all wearing bikini swim suits and appeared reasonably attractive, but with apparently varying degrees of commitment to the show. Jackson leaned in to comment to Maggie, but was prevented by the return of the voice, now even louder in order to be heard over the music.

"Okay, ladies! Thank you for that fine entrance, and for your participation tonight. Let's first let the folks get to know you a little better. Please step forward as I call your name, take a letter from the pitcher, and then hand it to our guest host. George, come on out and join the ladies!" George stepped out onto the dance floor, to several hoots from the crowd, and began hugging each of the contestants. As he reached the end of the row, a waitress came out from behind the bar carrying a glass pitcher three-quarters full of beer. She held out the pitcher toward George as she handed him five bottle caps. He proceeded to drop them into the pitcher one at a time, as the crowd called out with increasing enthusiasm, "B!" "I!" "N!" "G!" "OOOOO!!" The waitress then handed the pitcher to George, who immediately put it to his lips and took a long drink.

"Okay, George, leave some for the contestants to draw from!" The voice pleaded. George lowered the pitcher and wiped his mouth on the sleeve of his dirty t-shirt. "Contestant Number One," the voice continued, "Mandy, please step forward!" A brunette in an electric orange colored bikini bottom and an equally electric green top, stepped forward, cautiously. "Mandy is from Tyler, Texas – the Rose Capital of the country – I think you'll agree she's quite a flower, right? She's a junior at Sam Houston State University, and enjoys horseback riding and beach volleyball!" A few hoots came from the crowd, along with some applause. "Choose your letter, Mandy!" Still cautiously, she dipped her hand into the pitcher of beer as George held it out to her, grinning broadly. Mandy kept her distance from George, but stumbled slightly as she tried to grasp a bottle cap from arm's length. Finally, she pulled her hand from the pitcher and handed a dripping cap to George. She giggled softly, her first sound, or show of emotion.

"N!" George yelled. "What does that stand for in our community?"

"Naked!" a man at the bar yelled, and the crowd roared its approval. "Nature," a woman called, with less conviction but intensity. "Au, Naturel," an older man called out, and the voice answered.

"There is the kind of sophistication we welcome on our island. 'Au, naturel,' it is!" Mandy responded with a broader smile, and then licked her fingers that still held traces of the beer. The voice returned when the crowd finally quieted. "Next contestant, please!" Mandy returned to her place in line with a more confident gait.

"Please welcome Suzy, from Corpus Christi!" A taller, lankier girl of about the same age came forward, not as cautious as Mandy had been at first. "Suzy is a graduate of King High School, and currently works in a law office. She likes dancing and Oprah!" The crowd reacted modestly to this information, but perked up as Suzy strutted in a circle around

George and then stopped, facing him, and leaned forward, as the crowd hooted. Responding to the encouragement, Suzy jammed her hand into the pitcher and pulled out a top, along with a good amount of beer, and smacked George with both in the chest. He recovered awkwardly, but laughed loudly as he read the letter.

"B! Which we all know stands for ..."

"Bikini!" A group of young men yelled in unison. Suzy seemed to agree, as she laughed and took a model's turn before the crowd. George noticed Maggie and Jackson exchanging more questioning glances, as Suzy returned to her place in line, and the voice continued.

"Our third contestant is Danielle! She's twenty-one years old, and from Naw-lynns! Let's give this Cajun queen a big Texas welcome! Danielle strode casually toward George and gave him a meaningful kiss on the check, pausing at the point of contact long enough for the crowd to respond. She then smoothly plucked a bottle cap from the pitcher and handed it to George with another almost graceful movement. George seemed stunned by her action, but slowly smiled again, although in an almost blushing manner, as if even he wasn't confident of where he was about to go.

"O" stands for..." his voice trailed off.

A slight murmur followed from the crowd, and the voice joined in quickly.

"Okay, okay, this is not a family show, but do try for a little decency, folks."

"We are a little decent!" A guy at the bar called out, "about as decent as this show." Maggie, Jackson and Bette all nodded in agreement.

"Opportunity!" One of the bar tenders yelled, as if trying to force decency on the show, and the island. Danielle looked puzzled for an instant, and then quickly took her finger and mimed writing her phone number on her palm to modest applause.

"The next contestant," the voice continued hurriedly, "is Jesse. She's twenty-two and from Fort Worth. Let's hear it for Jesse!" He tried to regain his momentum. The crowd gave a modest reply as the slightly overweight girl stumbled toward George in a poorly fitting bikini and heels, obviously not accustomed to walking in heels even when fully dressed, and not before an audience. George caught her arm and steadied her, but spilled some beer from the pitcher. Jesse quickly reached into the pitcher and pulled out a bottle cap.

"G!" George called, and then placed the bottle cap on his head like a beanie. A woman in the crowd called out.

"George!"

"Onnnkk!" the voice interrupted, "the judges rule that is not a valid answer."

"Great Heron," said another voice from the bar area, but not loud enough for George or Jesse to hear, or at least to have to acknowledge.

"How about G-?" a local woman in front started to say as another buzzer sound drowned out her voice.

"I think I've about seen enough," Maggie said to Jackson and Bette. "I don't think I want to know how this ends."

"Well, after this next girl gets her word from George," Bette explained anyway, "they all will march around the dance floor acting out their word to music."

"Then, I know I've seen enough. You are coming with me," Maggie informed Jackson, as she started for the door.

"Absolutely," he said, without hesitation, and stood up behind her as the voice continued.

"...last contestant is Donna, from right here in Tarpon. Let's hear it for the local girl who gets the letter 'I'. We all know what that stands for, right?"

Jackson and Maggie waved goodbye to Bette and Will

as Donna was waving to her hometown crowd. George saw them move and quicken their steps before the audience could answer the voice's question. Still, the crowd's response carried to them outside.

"Oh, please!" Maggie complained to Jackson. "Can you believe those people? And your friend George is the Master of Ceremonies!"

"Pretty sad, I'll admit, but I don't think you should condemn George. He's just having a little fun." Just then the door to the club opened, and Bette and Will appeared.

"Wait up," Bette called. "We've seen enough, too, and I think George will be along shortly. One of the girls used him to demonstrate her word, and that seemed a little much even for him."

"I don't want to know which one," Maggie interrupted, and held up her hand as if to stop her from explaining, but then managed a laugh. "I guess that's what I get for wanting to go dancing with him."

"No, I would say that's what I get," Jackson interrupted her, "for not taking you dancing myself."

"Oh, I wouldn't blame either of you, or even George," Bette insisted. "That setting is just a little young and raw for us old folks. George will agree, if he ever gets out of there. You agree, Will?" Before Will could answer her, the door to the club opened again, and George ambled out casually, although looking frazzled. Seeing his friends gathered and waiting for him, he put his hands over his eyes, then his ears, and finally his mouth, as he descended the steps and approached them.

"That was fun, wasn't it?" he said, and smiled, a little sheepishly, Maggie thought.

XX

George continued walking, and before anyone could answer, he was past them heading toward the condo. Bette was the first to call out.

"George! Wait up!" George turned, but did not stop walking.

"I've got to get some sleep. Jackson and I have a big date tomorrow morning."

"You mean *this* morning," Jackson said, looking at his watch, as the group caught up with George. They walked the short distance to the complex in silence. Stepping over the chain blocking the entrance, George spoke again.

"You ready for some action, Jackson?" George grinned.

"Never," Jackson replied flatly, looking at Maggie.

"Well, some is coming, I can feeeell it!" George practically screamed the last syllables, as the group reached his truck in the parking lot of the complex. "I will see you at the end of the dock at 6 *this* morning – assuming I can find Bubba." He pulled his keys from deep in his baggy shorts pocket, found the correct one and unlocked the door.

"You're not driving back to Corpus now?" Maggie asked, concerned. "You can stay with us in your place." George turned and smiled, as if he liked the notion, but then shook his head.

"Nah. I'm sleeping on the boat. It's docked down at the Moorings at the house Bubba's renting. Thanks for the offer, though." He grinned this time, and then got in his truck and rumbled away.

"I hope he's safe just going down the state highway," Maggie expressed her concern with a shake of her head.

"Oh, he'll be fine," Bette said. "It's Jackson I'd be concerned about." She turned to him. "You better get some rest. George always runs hardest the day after he's been partying. Don't know how he does it, but he always does."

"Thanks for the warning. I'm hoping to get a few hours of sleep. You ready?" He took Maggie's arm.

"Oh, I don't know." She moved away from his grasp and walked to the edge of the marina. "It's such a beautiful night – or it was until about thirty minutes ago. Anyway, *I* don't have to get up early to go fishing. Why don't you go on. I think I'll sit here on the dock for a while and recover, if Bette will join me." She looked around at Bette.

"Absolutely! Bob's probably been asleep for two hours already. He won't know if I come in at midnight, or daybreak." At that moment both Bette and Maggie realized that they had not considered everyone. Will stood quietly beside Bette, not making a move to stay or go. Looking awkwardly at Maggie, Bette spoke first. "What's your plan, Will?"

"No plan," Will replied firmly. Bette looked cautiously at Maggie again. After another instant Maggie nodded her head, then turned and walked to a table near the pool. The only sound was the tinking of the boat riggings against metal and the gurgling of the sauna next to the pool. She then glanced out to the port again, when the low sound of a barge's horn came dimly across the water. When she turned back to sit, Will was there to pull out her chair for her.

"Who are you, exactly?" She asked.

"No one you know," Will answered quietly.

"Maggie," Jackson called, as he reached the corner of the building. "don't stay out too long."

"I'll be fine. Just go on to sleep," she called back, realizing that her words to both Will and Jackson carried an edge that was unintended. She felt agitated and wasn't sure why, until she thought of the night club.

"Bette told me that you two were never apart," Will gestured toward the corner of the building, as Jackson disappeared from view.

"Not much since she's known us, that's for sure," Maggie observed, looking at Bette and sounding less strident.

"They just sit around reading all day, and then dance all night," Bette said. "Well, not always in public," she added.

"No, I didn't get any public dancing in with Jackson today, but that was about the only thing that I didn't experience tonight." She shook her head. "Does that go on every night?"

"What?" Will asked, sounding sincerely unsure of her question.

"That!" she pointed in the direction of the club, as if they could still hear the voice and see George holding the pitcher out for each of the contestants.

"The contest? Only once a week during the summer," Will said, after taking another drink from his beer. "Not your cup of tea, I guess."

"You could say that," she spat back, her edge returning. "I'm not sure who I was more disgusted by, the contestants or the audience."

"Don't forget their host – and yours," Bette added.

"Oh, yeah. What am I supposed to make of that? I thought George was only 'eccentric' on the water," Maggie responded, again sounding on edge.

"He was just trying to have a little fun," Will said, and then added before either Maggie or Bette could speak. "Maybe he went a little overboard, but he was getting some strong pushes from behind."

"And from the front," Bette observed.

"So you were having fun, then?" Maggie questioned Will.

"Oh, I don't know if I'd call it fun, but I wasn't offended by it." He paused, but again neither Maggie nor Bette spoke. The riggings tinked and the sauna gurgled. Out in the channel another barge chugged by softly, and its horn sounded a melancholy bass note as Will continued. "Not all the girls in the world have what you have, Maggie, inside or out. Few are smart enough to even want it. So, I wouldn't let their choices in life – even if you think they're poor choices – cause you to lose much sleep." Will took another drink of beer, and Maggie again looked at Bette demanding to know without asking, 'Who is this guy?' Bette answered when Maggie hadn't really intended her to.

"Will's a retired goat rancher from the edge of the Texas Hill Country."

"Really?" Maggie responded back to Will, again not expecting an answer.

"Partly true," Will shrugged, and took another sip of his beer.

"Which part isn't true?" Bette challenged him.

"Oh, those parts are both true, but they aren't complete. I ranched up in the Hill Country, and I consider myself retired from that, but I'm actually from Dallas. I'll always think of that as home, for good or evil."

"Really?" Bette replied this time, equally intrigued as Maggie had been a moment earlier. "How is it that I never knew that? What part of Dallas?"

"I don't recall you ever asking," Will said, again through a sip of beer. "The good part," he added after swallowing, "not far from where you went to school, I think."

"Well, I don't recall ever thinking about that. You've

always been a rancher in my eyes, but now that you say 'Dallas' I can see that, too. You always seemed a little too refined for the goats, but I couldn't put my finger on it until now. Of course, you never say much about anything, so I didn't have a lot to go on."

"Again, I don't recall you asking," Will said.

"Right, and it wouldn't be like you to volunteer the information." She paused. "Okay, though, I get it now." Bette waved her hand from her forehead toward him in a salute. "You're just always so quiet, I learned to picture you out in the rocky pastures of West Texas silently tending your goats. It's hard to picture you in the neon lights of Dallas."

"They were sheep, actually, and there weren't many neon lights in Dallas when I lived there, external ones anyway. I think what you are admitting is that I might be a little different person, and from a different background, than what you thought. I'd say the same is true for those girls over at Barracuda's." He looked at Maggie.

"So, we're back to that, are we?" Maggie responded, while leaning up in her chair as if to go. "You're not going to leave it alone until I admit to being arrogant and condescending, right?"

"I don't think I called you either of those things," Will smiled. "I was just asking you to consider a different perspective." Will looked at her with his slight smile, but she did not respond. "Perhaps," he shifted in his chair to put his empty beer bottle on the table, "I shouldn't have made my comments personal to you. I don't know what advantages or disadvantages you've had in life – even though I can make some assumptions. Let's put it in a little more global context. Who knows how many people died in Tiananmen Square in China just asking for a little freedom – maybe the freedom to dance in public. On the other hand, you've got people in the Middle East claiming that the U.S. is the root of all evil."

"I don't think the display we saw tonight would do much to convince them otherwise," Maggie interrupted him.

"Can you really be that judgmental?" Will answered, but in as light a tone as he could manage. Maggie rose from her chair immediately, and Bette stiffened in hers.

"Let me get back to you on that," Maggie said, but without anger. She managed a slight smile as Will rose, too, but did not extend his hand. "Maybe tomorrow," Maggie added, and then looked at Bette who had relaxed back in her chair. "Good night, Bette. It's been an interesting evening." She started toward the breezeway leading to the elevator. When she had turned the corner out of view, Bette spoke.

"You were a little hard on her, weren't you?" She asked.

"Not intentionally," Will answered. "I was just exploring her feelings about the bikini contest. Perhaps she was taking it a little too seriously, or more seriously than even the girls who were actually participating, but I didn't intend to make it a matter of world politics."

"I never knew you were such a sociologist, or world affairs expert." Bette said.

"You can learn a lot watching sheep for twenty-five years, which is a good thing considering there were over two million sheep and fewer than two thousand people in my county.

"And you preferred that over Dallas?"

"I don't know if I did at the time I left, although I was interested in trying it when the opportunity arose. Dallas in the 60's was a disconcerting place. How else could you describe a place that's two best-known landmarks were the Texas School Book Depository and the original Neiman-Marcus? I'd say that represents about the two worse elements of society, wouldn't you?"

"What about the Cowboys and J.R. Ewing? Bette offered.

"Are you offering that to support my point?" Will asked, with a smile.

"Good point," was all that Bette could think of as a response.

"Cowboys were still poor working stiffs back then," Will said. "The 'Cowboys' were barely known outside of Fair Park, and the Cotton Bowl was just known as a college football stadium. Now, of course, it is again since the Cowboys moved out to Irving. That was typical, to me, for Dallas. It is supposed to be this 'can-do' city, but they let a nowhere suburb like Irving steal 'America's Team.' The same thing happened when the baseball team moved from D.C. to Arlington, another nowhere suburb. Maybe you can't judge a city by its sports teams, but Dallas is identified with two that it doesn't even really possess. The same goes for the cowboy image. There were never any herds in Dallas. They just stole Fort Worth's heritage. That has to say something."

"Well, I'm not a big sports fan, or a civic historian," Bette observed, "and I can't say I developed a real love for Dallas while I was there, but I don't hate it like you seem to. Hate may be too strong. Disgust may be more accurate."

"Like Maggie felt for the bikini contest?" Will grinned. "Yes, that's probably true. A sense that people's values are not like yours, and that yours are the ones out of whack. I guess I do sort of owe Maggie an apology."

"Oh, I doubt that you offended her," Bette waved her hand at Will, "but tell me more about you. You bailed out of Dallas and became a rancher. Wasn't that a shock to your system, even if you were ready for a change?"

"It wasn't a shock after college in Austin in the '60's. That was more of a contrast to my upbringing than ranching was. There were no hippies in Dallas, and very few liberals. I think seeing both sides actually prepared me for ranching. I concluded that neither of them knew what they were talking about. I knew I didn't want the pressure of money and social standing you face in Dallas, and I sure didn't like the drugs and poverty of the bohemian lifestyle in Austin. Ranching avoids all of those ills. You don't make much money, but you don't starve. There is no society to speak of, but you've got plenty of room and solitude so you don't need drugs. Ranching is an honored Texas institution, and people in the Hill Country don't look down on it, however you do it."

"You did well enough," Bette offered.

"That's a good description. Well enough to come down here and buy a place by the Gulf, and maybe see a few people for a change.

"Or some college girls in bikinis," Bette added.

"That, too," Will nodded, and took the final swig from his second beer. "I might even get me a small ranch in the Coastal Bend for when I've had enough of this decadent city life." Bette looked away from him toward the dark port. There were no boats moving or even any breeze now, and virtually no sound, until she sighed.

"It's funny to hear you describe Dallas as putting social pressure on you," she said, drawing a deep drag on yet another cigarette. "I heard Jackson say that his experience was just the opposite. He described Nashville like that, but he said when he got to Dallas, it was all about whether you could do the job you're given, rather than who's your daddy."

"Well, it's probably changed some since I left twenty-five years ago, but I also think he'll see more of it the longer he lives there, and the higher his income level goes. New money can be just as judgmental as old money, maybe worse."

"Perhaps," Bette exhaled a cloud of smoke, "but I liked Jackson's way of describing how he's been judged in Texas. He called it the 'Alamo test' - what can you do when the Mexicans come over the wall."

"Die?" Will suggested.

"Hopefully not," Bette laughed, "but he did mention that there are more Tennessee flags in the Alamo memorial room than any other state. He's from Tennessee, you know, just like Davy Crockett. Davy took care of the Mexicans, even if he died doing it. And rangers like Gus McCrae took care of the Indians."

"Uh, Bette," Will interrupted, "you're mixing fact and fiction there."

"Oh, right. I forget Gus wasn't the real person," she said, sheepishly.

"You are thinking of Charles Goodnight, among many others," Will said, politely.

"Right again. He came here from somewhere else, too, Missouri or Illinois, I think," Bette speculated, "seeking his fortune. Maggie says Jackson's still looking for his purpose in coming here."

"Why not her? She seems like a good one to come for," Will speculated this time.

"He seems to be taking pretty good care of her, I admit. They don't seem to be going too fast or too slow, just about right. I don't think they'll have to bail out of Dallas to survive."

"More power to them, but I think they will find it harder and harder. Neutral is not a gear that Dallasites tolerate."

"You're probably right," Bette stubbed out her cigarette, slipped back on her sandals and rose to leave. "Thankfully, it is the only gear on this island."

"It's the right gear anywhere for me," Will concluded, standing and bowing, as Bette laughed and walked away.

XXI

Jackson was sitting upright in bed when Maggie returned to the condo. In the lamplight she could see that his eyes were closed and a book was resting open, face-down on his chest. She was used to seeing him this way, but typically it was from her side of the bed, through the haze of her own sleepy eyes. She would often wake up to find his light still on, but him fast asleep in the upright position. She could not understand why he wouldn't just turn out the light and go to sleep like normal people, instead of always having to read as if he was sleeping, and then sleep as if he was reading. She was pondering this question anew when Jackson opened his eyes.

"Hey," he said, softly.

"Hey," she said. "Why didn't you just go to bed?"

"I was just resting my eyes, waiting for you. What were you guys talking about?"

"Oh, just about Will leaving Dallas to become a rancher." She paused, trying to decide whether she should tell Jackson about Will's affront, but instead added as she began to undress, "he's an interesting guy, and I think he's got Dallas pegged pretty well, even though I've only lived there a few years. It took him over twenty to get out."

"So you want me to leave Dallas and become a rancher?"

Jackson was fully awake now, and sat up straighter in bed. Maggie was walking toward the bathroom, but stopped to answer him.

"The leaving Dallas part sounds interesting, but not the ranching part. We have to eat, and maybe save some money for children someday." She continued on into the bathroom and turned on the water to wash her face. When she looked up from the sink, Jackson's face was in the mirror.

"What? You don't think I could make a living as a rancher?" He asked, and then reached for his toothbrush.

"No," Maggie answered. Seeing the contortion of Jackson's face, she turned to face him. "What? You disagree with that?" When Jackson responded only by snapping the toothpaste tube from the counter, the tension she had felt since watching the show at Barracuda's was released in a bark at him. "What do you know about ranching? Have you ever even been on a ranch?" Jackson looked back up at her, blankly, but responded.

"Nothing, and no," he answered both questions truthfully. "but I could learn."

"From who? Or is it 'from whom?' Mr. English Major." Maggie followed her sarcastic questions with a comment offered in a more incredulous tone. "You don't even know anyone who owns a ranch." Jackson didn't answer any of these, immediately, although she could see his mind working. After a moment's pause, she pushed past him out of the bathroom. He caught her arm and practically yelled into her ear.

"Mac!" He named an attorney he had met in Tennessee whose family owned one of the largest remaining cattle ranches in Texas. "I'm sure he could get me a job, and find someone to teach me," Jackson added, following her into the bedroom.

"I can't believe we are having this conversation at all, let alone at 1 in the morning," Maggie responded as she crawled into the bed and looked at the clock on George's nightstand. "I'm going to sleep, and you should, too, if you want any rest before George crashes into the dock to get you." Jackson didn't respond and didn't move, but stood on his side of the bed looking down at her. "What?" She asked finally. "You want me to consider this a serious conversation?" Jackson didn't roll his eyes exactly, but he raised his head and turned it to the side slightly as he would if he had rolled his eyes. Maggie knew she could go three directions from here: ignore him and wait to see if he forced her to finish the "discussion;" explain that she really didn't want to be a rancher's wife, irrespective of his abilities; or, admit that she didn't believe for a minute that he could make a living as rancher. She made up her mind quickly, choosing option two, but then actually hit closer to option three. "Look, she said with the most seriousness she could muster at that hour and on this topic, "if I had wanted to be a rancher's wife, I would have married Davis." Jackson reacted immediately, even faster than she had realized what a mistake she had made.

"So, you finally admit that my being a lawyer was part of your attraction to me. And, on top of that, you admit that you don't think I'm man enough to do anything else, particularly anything manly like being a rancher. I don't know which makes me madder – that you really don't believe in me, or that you've lied about it for three years."

"Oh, come on!" Maggie snapped back. She knew she was mostly to blame for setting Jackson off, but his response was so absurd she couldn't bring herself to apologize, and her words kept coming out with a sharper edge than she intended. "Are you drunk? You'd have to be to actually believe what you just said. I have not lied to you ever. You're the one that started out our relationship with a lie, remember? And besides, I've always pointed out what you can't do – the subject of ranching just hasn't come up before, at least not directly. Sure, we've joked about Davis, but I assure you, that not wanting to be a rancher's wife was *not* the only reason I didn't marry him. He was totally worthless then, and I'm sure he is today."

"Like I said," Jackson finally cut in, "my lawyer's salary was important to you."

"Stop!" Maggie almost screamed. "I didn't say that, and you know it. Can't you see the difference between wanting a husband who will do something with his life, and just wanting the fruits of his labor? And besides, it's not like we're rich, or anything."

"Oh," Jackson reacted to this comment so physically that he had to turn around in a circle to release the energy. "So now I'm not even a good enough lawyer for you! We're really getting to the truth here. I don't know why you wouldn't want me to try ranching if you think I'm just a mediocre lawyer." Maggie wanted to snap back at him again, but something helped her refrain. Jackson, too, took a deep breath, and did not continue. After a very long second or two, Maggie spoke. Still her words found a wound.

"Well, you may be right if that is as good an analysis as you can make of the situation."

Again Jackson responded physically before audibly. His body jerked around again, but not completely this time. He stopped his turn, and after a pause, reached for the handle of the sliding glass door and pulled it open sharply. Without a word he stepped out onto the balcony and out of sight. Maggie again debated with herself about which way to go from here. She still believed it to be a ridiculous argument, but she knew that it was now partly her fault. She could turn off the light and go to sleep, hoping that when Jackson returned from fishing later in the day it would be forgotten. Or, she could follow him onto the balcony and – perhaps – lower the tension. Of course, she could also end up causing a public scene in the early morning hours. Yelling from their balcony would carry all around the complex, and perhaps across the still water to most of the port. Which would Jackson want her to do? In the past, she had always tried to withdraw from arguments and cool down. Jackson was the one who always forced it to some conclusion, even if it wasn't an immediate resolution. He was the one that needed closure, even if it meant escalating the conflict first. She would much prefer to sleep on it and take her chances with the passage of time, but she knew that this could take a few days. She hated that part at any time, but certainly did not want to endure it on their vacation. That decided it. She threw off the covers and started to pull on her shorts. Her extra-large sleep t-shirt hung down to her thighs, and she dropped her shorts back to the floor. Might as well use whatever I've got, she thought. She tried to adopt the professional patience she used in preparing for conferences with parents of her kindergarten students, and walked through the open door onto the balcony. Jackson was sitting in the director's chair, looking out to the channel. Maggie noticed the flash of a barge search light as it came toward them from the intra-coastal channel, beyond the port. She wondered what it was like to guide that massive weight in the dark against unpredictable hidden currents. Involuntarily, she thought of the Exxon *Valdez*. Jackson looked up at her, as if he had been wondering the same thing. She looked to him as unmanageable as a barge.

"Can we back up a minute?" She asked, in the best conciliatory tone she could muster.

"Don't you mean about thirty minutes?" He answered, also in a soft tone, but a wary one.

"Or even three years and thirty minutes," she replied, and Jackson forced himself to smile. "Have I ever given you the impression that I married you for money or position?"

She asked, then immediately added "no, wait, no questions, just answers." She put her arms around his shoulders from behind his chair. He took her wrist with his hand over his heart. "I've always told you," Maggie continued, "even this week right here on this balcony, that I married you – fell in love with you – because of *you*." She poked his head with her index finger. "What's in here, not here." She tried to touch his back pocket through the seat of the chair. "Well, this was a definite asset." She tried to pinch him through his shorts. Jackson squirmed and reached back behind his chair to try to pinch her back. He discovered that he could, and she didn't resist, even when the barge light flashed across them, beginning its turn from the intracoastal into the Corpus Christi channel. She hugged him tighter, and he finally answered her.

"I thought you said you loved me because I was so pathetic," he said.

"You were, and still are in the same way – pathetically wonderful. I don't know why that makes me love you more."

"But don't you see that's what this argument is all about?" His tone was serious again, but not angry.

"No, I don't see," Maggie answered truthfully. "Can you explain it to me without getting mad at me?"

"I'm trying, but it's obviously difficult." He paused, before continuing. "It's hard to appreciate being loved because I'm pathetic. A guy wants to be loved – admired actually – because of what he's capable of, not because of his failures." Maggie started to answer, but realized that Jackson wasn't ready for a reply. "It may seem endearing to you in some weird way," he continued, "but it's frustrating to me, and embarrassing, sometimes even humiliating when you point out to others my ineptitude." Maggie let go of her embrace and sighed. She came around to his side and leaned over the railing. She wondered if Jackson would put his hand under her shirt, but he didn't. Instead, he spoke again. "I know what you're going to say – that you're just teasing me, and that I'm way too sensitive. You're probably right, but I'm not able to look at it that way, at least not yet." He paused again, and then added, "I don't think I'm asking too much. You don't have to pump me up all the time; in fact, you know I hate that about as much as the teasing." She turned to face him and he did put his hand on her hip, outside of her shirt. "Just try not to expose my shortcomings so purposefully, will you?"

"You make me sound like some sadistic witch," she said.

"I'm not saying you enjoy it," Jackson answered, "but now that you know how much it bugs me, if you keep doing it, then your description might be accurate."

"Oh, come on," she said, again without edge. "You're not as sensitive as that, even if I didn't cut you any slack at all. But thanks for explaining it to me like this. It helps me to understand just how pathetic you really are." She hugged him again, and pulled his hand under her shirt to make sure he knew she was teasing him in a new way.

"Okay, so I am," he admitted, rubbing her leg lightly, "but I think every guy is – whether he admits it or not – even if he isn't a 'sensitive' guy. I don't mind being vulnerable, I just don't want to be stupid or incompetent." Maggie leaned back from his chest, and looked directly into Jackson's eyes.

"You're serious, aren't you. It *really* bugs you that you can't do everything."

"Yes," Jackson admitted, "but especially when you make fun of whatever it is I can't do." Maggie backed away from him, and turned again to look into the port. "Why does that surprise you?" Jackson asked, and then continued before she could answer. "I'm a guy; I'm human – practically." He managed a short laugh, but Maggie didn't respond. "Look," he said with an air of conclusion, "Jackson Browne has a song where he says *don't confront me with my failures; I have not forgotten them.* That's true for me, too, and probably every guy. I know what I can't do, and I'm more than a little bothered by you pointing it out to me and others – particularly in a mocking tone, even if you mean it as teasing." Maggie turned to him again quickly, and Jackson flinched. "Surely you're not shocked by that?"

"No," she said. "I guess I just hadn't realized that you do have some 'Texan' in you. I am surprised that you actually want to *be* Gus McCrae. I'm also surprised to hear you live by the quotes of someone other than Jimmy Buffett."

"Oh, Jimmy's got a song about this, too." Jackson started to sing, as best he could: *They say he learned to be a cowboy; they say he learned to rope and ride, but I wonder if he ever thinks about the tears his woman cried. Livingston's gone to Texas, and he'll be gone awhile.*"

"The only problem is that you're the woman in that song." Maggie said, before she could stop herself. Jackson looked at her seriously, but wasn't angry.

"You may be right, but can't you just keep it to yourself?" He asked. "I really can't deal with critics, even one I'm married to – maybe *especially* one that I'm married to, and I'm going to be that way until I can understand why you married me. You insist that it was not for my car – or what that said about me – and that it was not for my profession and the money it might bring. I know it couldn't be for my looks, and I wouldn't want it to be." His voice trailed off, although he had intended to stop her from arguing with him on that point.

"Look," she said, "I've told you that I think you're handsome, and obviously I find you attractive, but I'm learning that nothing I say will answer this question for you. You've got to come to believe that I love you, and you've got to have faith in that belief. Your struggle with that fact has worried me, because I thought it meant that I'm not giving you enough to have faith in. But now I see that it's not about me. Your faith in us has to come from you, not me. I'm here for you, and I have been ever since you recanted the soap story, and that is how I knew that I loved you, that I was willing to forgive you. So as it relates to our marriage, I don't care if you are a lawyer or a rancher or a preacher or a bum. I promised 'for better or for worse', remember? And I meant it. I don't know how else to convince you that nothing you say or do will change that."

Jackson sat without moving, almost without breathing. He wanted to say something, but he knew that Maggie did not want him to, at least not until he could tell her that he understood.

Saturday, August 5, 1989

XXII

Jackson stepped out onto the balcony, into the dim light rising from lamps on the pier. It was only 5:30 a.m., but already several boats were at that moment puttering past him toward the jetties. Although not fully conscious, he was pleased with himself for merely being awake. He did not want George to have to wake him up. He was not accustomed to being up at this hour, and certainly not for two days in a row. At least today's bay fishing should be less eventful, he thought.

Jackson had agreed to go only after confirming that he was not the sole reason for George's effort. Indeed, George assured him that he was already planning to fish with Bubba, whoever he might be. Jackson thought it odd that anyone would be just passing through this island, but apparently Bubba and George had done a lot of fishing together in the Gulf in years past, and then lost touch for several years. George seemed particularly excited about having Jackson along for the trip, so he agreed to go - convincing himself that George needed him to come along to help avoid any awkward moments with his old friend. Even so, Jackson was apprehensive as he stood on the balcony and took a big gulp of black coffee. It wasn't fear he felt this time, but embarrassment. With a couple of experienced fishermen,

Jackson knew he would be the odd-man-out for reasons even beyond George and Bubba's old friendship. He remembered the previous night's argument with Maggie - actually, that morning's - and slumped into the director's chair, feeling the weight of all that she had challenged him to accept.

The sky was slightly brighter, but the port was even busier thirty minutes later when Jackson recognized George's boat sliding around the point of the jetties. The boat approached the dock quietly, until the water churned as George reversed the engines and deftly backed the 28-foot boat into its slip. The sound and movement returned Jackson quickly to the rocking Gulf waters, and he braced his knees against the railing involuntarily. George looked up and waved for him to come down. Jackson walked quickly through the condo and down the stairs to the marina, where George was already tying one of the ropes to the cleat on the stern of the boat. He pointed to the other rope out of his reach on the dock, and Jackson quickly handed it over. George repeated the same knot, and then fairly leapt up the ladder to the bridge and cut the idling engines.

"Morning. Ready to go fishin'!" Even before sunrise George spoke in his usual emphatic tone, that was not questioning.

"If we must," Jackson shrugged. "Speaking of 'we,' where's your friend?"

"Oh, he's asleep in the cabin. He woke *me* up about 5. I don't think he'd been to bed yet, or at least not to sleep. Let me grab some light tackle, and we'll be off." He stepped onto the dock and disappeared around the corner of the building. Jackson looked at the dark tinted windows of the cabin, and saw only his own reflection in the spotlight from the lamps on the pier.

By 6:20 a.m., a red glow was now visible on the Gulf's horizon, as Jackson stood on the fly bridge. George turned the boat out of the jetties and pushed the throttle forward firmly. The bow of the Bertram rose quickly and assumed its haughty, nose-in-the-air posture as the twin outboard engines dug deep into the steel-gray water and propelled them across the channel. The morning air was heavy with moisture and smells of the Gulf. Neither of them spoke for about 10 minutes as the sun's rays finally shot over the horizon and into the sky like laser beams.

"God never did anything more right that make the sunrise!" George proclaimed. Startled, Jackson nevertheless responded quickly.

"'Let there be light,' He said, and He saw that it was good."

"He could have stopped there," George concluded.

"Well, actually, Genesis says that He separated the light and dark before he made the sun and moon...." Jackson broke off as he saw the look George was aiming directly at him. Ten minutes later, with the sun higher and its rays brighter, George slowed the engines and turned the boat down a side channel, where a pontoon dock bobbed as their wake preceded them. Tied to the far side was an 18-foot flat top skiff that Jackson recognized as one of George's designs. He had seen one just like it in the warehouse only four days before - if not this same one.

"Go down and tell Bubba it's time to go fishin!" George chirped excitedly, and Jackson obeyed immediately. He climbed down from the bridge, as George sidled the larger boat parallel with the pier in the very narrow cut. He was coming down the ladder himself as Jackson slid open the raised cabin door and stood face to chest with the words "My head hurts, my feet stink, and I don't love Jesus." Startled, if not offended, he stepped back as the chest came forward and stepped down from the cabin. Then Jackson found himself looking directly into the semi-conscious eyes of Jimmy Buffett.

George had watched this dance out of the corner of his eye as he tied the boat to the dock. "Uh, Jackson, I don't think you've met my old friend, Bubba, Bubba Buffett; most people call him Jimmy." Jackson stood staring at George, and then turned blankly back to Jimmy just as he moved on past him to the gulf side of the boat. Jackson was about to speak just as he realized what Jimmy was doing there, and instead turned back to George with a look that screamed silently, "How could you NOT tell me?" George smiled his bandito smile and moved past Jackson to the cabin door. As he opened it fully, he said in his loud voice, "Yep, Bubba and I go way back. We met first in Colorado in what, '78 or '79?" When Bubba did not respond, Jackson felt obligated to.

"Fishing?" Jackson asked weakly. George reappeared from the cabin, as Jimmy turned from his business, and they both passed Jackson again.

"Skiing," Jimmy said, as he stepped back into the cabin. Jackson's head was spinning already, and the constant movement of waves and men made him weak in the knees. For an instant he felt that he might be seasick for the first time. George helped stabilize him, whether intentionally, Jackson did not know, by handing him a pair of rods and reels.

"Here, take these and put them in the skiff. You know where to stow them?" George didn't wait for an answer, and Jackson didn't give one, but rather focused all his energy and concentration on stepping up out of the boat onto the pontoon and then carefully down again onto the skiff. His mind was still swirling as he tried to set each rod into the holders George had shown him earlier in the week, when he had demonstrated his design at the warehouse. George suddenly appeared behind him and completed the task for him, without further comment, which said enough.

"Ready, Bubba?" he turned, and called back into the

cabin of the larger boat. Jimmy reappeared with a cup in one hand and a duffle bag in the other. He now wore a baseball cap and expensive sunglasses with reflective lenses. Looking at Jimmy directly for the first time, Jackson saw only his own reflection. George looked at the bag and said in a tone that caught Jackson's attention, "Zero tolerance, you know." Jimmy smiled for the first time, and replied.

"Man, George, it *has* been a long time. I've grown up." He stepped onto the skiff and laid open the bag on the console: lip balm, suntan lotion, sunflower seeds, two cassettes, a book of poetry, a sketch pad, several pens and a hand-held recorder. "Satisfied?" He asked.

"No. *Satisfaction!*" George fairly yelled, as he tossed off the lines of the skiff onto the pier right below the name emblazoned on the hull of the Bertram. "Let's go fishin!" He put the skiff in gear and turned her away from the sun toward the back bays. Even as they headed for shallow water with three people on the 18- foot skiff, George raced the ninety horse power Mercury engine full throttle, with Jimmy braced beside him. Jackson was forced to sit in front, on the molded console, and was pushed back by the force of the salty air. Thoughts flew through his head as fast as the wind blew past his face. Racing west with the sun's rays, the boat appeared to be chasing its shadow. Even as he stared blankly ahead, Jackson could not escape the outline of the figures looming behind him.

XXIII

Blinking against the insistent morning rays, even through the tinted glass and her tented sleeping habits, the light forced Maggie awake. Consciousness came slowly, grasping first the high-pitched sound of seagulls and then the low rumble of diesel engines grinding past her in the port. Next came solitude, recognizing that Jackson was gone, fishing. Fishing? Oh, yes, with George and an old friend. Poor, Jackson.

Uncovering, she stretched and felt pleased, surprised to find herself in a self-appraising mood. Where's my coffee, she thought. Jackson usually brings it. He forced her to join him at first, and then hooked her like a junkie to the ritual need. Another of Jackson's needs beginning to be her own - but much slower than the caffeine. How do I tell him, show him, we are different? She wondered. No fault, not his or mine - just different. She must keep trying.

Thoughts continued to come as she dressed and shuffled into the kitchen. Funny, it's the only time he really talks to me. What would cause that? Nervousness? Dependence? Freedom? Tediousness? She should find a way to talk back. Weird contrast - one must seek total focus, the other total distraction. Why analyze this? Oh, yeah, last night's argument.

Hot coffee cup in hand – she was surprised to find that the pot was still on and the coffee not burned - she walked out onto the balcony and felt the thick heat. Facing due east, George's unit absorbed the morning sun's rays that felt good for about ten seconds. The boats kept streaming by - big, small, beautiful, embarrassing. Who are these people? What is the allure? As big a mystery as the other. Guys. Jackson, of course, is only really interested in one. He does the other out of a sense of manhood. Could the opposite be true for the real fishermen? Why am I stuck on this subject? Maybe Jackson is getting through after all.

Returning to the bedroom to retrieve a book, she tried to read on the balcony, but the heat was too intense. Returning to the bedroom, she tilted the blinds and laid back on the unmade bed. Even in the half-light, it was too hot. She sighed and rose again, this time returning to the kitchen, a galley that reminded her of her apartment after graduating from college - an independent woman. I needed that accomplishment, she thought - first a degree, then a job in a great district, and supporting myself. Well, mostly - Dad had to help with the car and, sometimes, by month's end, gas. Groceries I could do without. Still, I was getting by, mostly on my own doing. Imagine that.

Jackson said he would never have been interested in her, at least not long-term, without that independence. He meant her personality, but it showed in her actual achievement of independence. Had she been motivated, unconsciously, by that when she finally felt the need, compulsion, desire to get her degree? How many guys had she known to that point who even cared about their own education, let alone hers? If she had been motivated by that kind of recognition – and reward – did that make her degree an Mrs.? No. She was happy teaching - being alone. She wasn't looking for him when it happened. So, why did she agree immediately? Had to, she guessed. As Jackson says, that Lyle says: "You can't resist it when it happens to you." But what's *it*?

Abandoning her questioning, she put on her two-piece bathing suit. With a book and towel in hand, she descended to the pool deck. Stretched out facing east into the sun, she looked over the top of her book to the port, half-expecting to see Jackson coming in early. Not yet. She glanced up at Bette's windows, but saw no one there. If fact, there wasn't a soul anywhere in the complex, that she could see. Twenty-four units in a measure of paradise, and no one home. People have their homes backwards, as to which should be first and which should be second, she thought. Or, perhaps most of the units are now owned by the banks, and the banks are owned by the government, as Jackson explained. He's always pointing out the office buildings in Dallas that have been foreclosed on now that the economy has crashed. He sees his work everywhere, whether he's driving up the toll way or laying on the beach. Of course, it's always bad news for someone when he shows up – legal pathology he calls it.

This is the first full vacation since the honeymoon, and of course he keeps getting on the phone here. In a way, even the fishing trips are work - certainly today's is for him. He can be obsessed with the office - like insisting on going there straight from the airport after their honeymoon. That's reality, she thought - from sleeping together in one of the best hotels in Paris, to sleeping by myself on a bench outside his office building in Dallas.

Still, we had been in Europe for two weeks. Could we have done the one without him doing the other? Not likely, but I just can't comprehend the pressure that makes Tuesday night so much more important than Wednesday morning. What could he have done that night anyway - at the office, at least?

She realized that she had been turning pages in her book as she turned these questions in her mind - comprehending neither the meaning of the words nor the answers to the questions. She closed the book and her eyes. Her mind remained open. Something Jackson had been singing earlier in the week arrived there suddenly: *He always seemed kind of sad to me, and I asked him why that was, and he told me it's because, in my contract there's this clause that says it's my job to be worried half to death and that's the thing people expect in me. It's my job, and without it I'd be less than what I expect from me.* Should she be surprised she could sing all the words herself? Was that Jackson, or just the truthfulness of the song?

The sun continued to glare at her as she closed her eyes tighter, and was soon asleep.

XXIV

George was proud of himself. Jackson had never suspected that he knew Jimmy Buffett. He's playing it pretty cool, though, George thought, as he looked at Jackson sitting up in the front of the boat, as if to ignore them. Of course, Jimmy had barely shown himself to be alive - let alone being interested in getting up close and personal with a fan. He hasn't changed much, George thought. He had half-expected him to have grown up a little by now. 'But,' George admitted to himself, 'I haven't, so I don't know why I expected it from him. Of course, he's probably richer than I am, and obviously more famous.' He wondered whether either fact should make Jimmy more responsible, or permit him to be less so?

Now, moving northwest through the intracoastal channel, George abruptly cut the motor and turned the skiff due west into a narrow cut that seemed to appear on his command. There was no marker, natural or man-made, but George knew where it was - where he was - precisely. The boat righted itself from the arc and settled into a soft rocking motion as it floated deeper into the cut and out of the channel. George kept the throttle at the lowest level as they moved slowly deeper into the cut.

"Weeelll, gentlemen," he said after a few minutes, "ready to catch some fiiiisssh?" As usual, he did not wait for an answer, as he cut the engine completely and came around the console. "Jackson, grab a rod. You know what to do with it." Unanswered, his assertion drifted into a question. "Well, we'll leave Bubba to his own self, and I'll coach you." He reached down and pulled a rod from the holder along the bow. "Here, take this one. It's guaranteed to nail a tarpon," he said, with a grin.

"Cut it out, George," Jimmy croaked. "If he catches a tarpon today, I'll swim back to Florida."

"Now, don't go putting yourself out like that on our account. And, don't go doubting a friend of mine. You can insult your other fans anytime you want, but not someone who is a fan of yours, and a friend of mine."

"Who said I was a fan of his?" Jackson said, trying to join in.

"Good point," George said, and then returned to Jimmy, as he picked up his own rod and reel. "So, Bubba, you don't talk to your fans anymore?" He asked, in a teasing tone. "You just too big for that? Does that mean you don't consider me to be a fan?"

"Hey, I talk to fans *all* the time. I hope you're a fan, and him, too," Jimmy said, shrugging at Jackson. "I just thought you and I were going fishing." He shook his head and moved past Jackson to step off the front of the skiff.

"Hey, don't blame him," George said, refusing to yield the field. "He hasn't said a word to you, and he didn't even want to come fishing. He also didn't know who my long-lost friend was, did you, Jackie? You may still not know - or care." When Jackson didn't answer, George continued. "Come on. Let's go catch a tarpon! It'd serve Bubba right." He stepped off the side of the boat into knee deep water. Smiling broadly at Jackson, he said, "Let's show him that being rich and famous don't mean nothing to a fish."

On second thought, George realized that the day might

not work out quite the way he had hoped. It depended now on Jackson. At least, I got a few good hooks into Bubba, George mused, having assumed that he could still take it. Feeling what for him constituted concern, George decided to focus on catching a fish, any fish. That would break the ice, one way or another.

"Let's wade on out here and cast back into that grass over there," he said. "See the way the water kind of piles up against it even though there really isn't any wake? That shows there's something moving under the surface, but then you probably knew that. Here we go."

With a gentle roll of his wrist and grip of his thumb, George deposited the end of his line exactly where he intended. He purposefully but deliberately reeled it in until the bait and hook reappeared. "Your turn. He's waiting for you. No, no, not that way! Like this." He turned the rod in Jackson's hand. "There you go, that's it. Now, just let it hang there. You just got to let them come to you."

George climbed back up in the boat to look out on the water, and perhaps increase the chance of catching any fish. He wondered what Jimmy was doing, and turned to see that he had waded over to the other side of the cut. He caught himself just before he called out another insult. Better to let him sulk in silence, George decided.

Jackson was also thinking. How am I supposed to know how these things work? Where does such knowledge come from? Should I have read a book, or hired an expert, like in the practice of law? You would think that if I can figure out matters that involve millions of dollars, I could learn how to hold a fishing pole, rod, correctly. But I don't want to have to learn it. I want to just know. A real man doesn't have to read a book to fish, does he? It's in his blood - passed directly from his father and grandfather. But I can't blame them for my ignorance. I could have read a book. He finally surrendered.

"Wait, George. Help me out here. This rod seems different than the one I used in the Gulf."

"That's because it is - lighter and shorter. Meant for accurate casts and smaller fish. Back here you aren't just throwing it in the ocean. Here, let me show you." He stepped back into the water and took the rod from Jackson's hand. Turning in one motion he swiftly deposited the line along the bank. Pausing, George let the line go slack and then swiftly jerked the rod toward his shoulder, creating a forward arc like a rainbow. "You see? Nothing to it." He reeled in the small redfish, slipped it off the hook and returned it to the water without another word. Jackson did not speak, either, but his face clearly asked 'how?'

"Oh, I saw him over there when I was in the boat. The water rippled, and a shadow moved. He was just lolling, not very interested, but I got his attention. Now, you do it."

"But I don't see any lolling fish," Jackson said, looking at the water as he might study a wall full of law books. "I might even miss them if they jumped."

"Look over there," George pointed. "What do you see?"

"Water."

"Okay, that's right. Now, is it all the same shade of green?"

"George, I'm green/brown color-blind. Will lighter or darker do?

"That's what I meant. Do you see any shadows in the water?

"There are shadows everywhere. How do I know one's a fish?

"You just know." George coached. Jackson sent him a frustrated look. "No, really, you can see other signs. Look for ripples, look for light reflecting off their fins. Look for dirt rising in the water - any sign of motion."

"I'm looking, but all I see is water, grass and sky. I'm just a big-picture guy." Casting and recasting. Trying and retrying.

Not learning, just repeating. 'Insanity is doing the same thing over and over again and expecting a different result.' Einstein was smart enough to know. Suddenly, Jackson felt the tension and jerked the rod as he had seen George do, creating the rainbow. "Hey! I've got something!"

"Alright, alright!" George perked up. "Not so hard. You'll rip it right out of his mouth. Smooth pull and steady crank. Keep pressure on the line, but not too much. Just dance with him right up to the boat. Not so jerky. Man, you need to get some rhythm. Keep it up, alright. Got 'em!"

George pulled the net up out of the mushrooming dirt and under a fish. It jerked, as the net came out of the water and light shot off the glistening scales. Jackson thought of his favorite poet - like shining from shook foil.

"See," George said, "you know how."

"No. Either you did that, or I'm just lucky. I had no idea a fish was out there, and he obviously didn't know I was here."

"Oh, you're just warming up. Luck or skill, there's a fish in the boat." He held it up high, and then returned it to the water on its side cradled in his enormous hands, like a diamond necklace. Frozen for an instant as water filled its gills, the fish then kicked out of his grasp and was gone beneath the surface. "Go tell your friend the tarpon we're here and we're not leaving without him! Okay, Jackie, time to get serrioussss!"

"Is there anyone as serious as me?" Jackson asked. George laughed fully.

"That's funny," he said.

Jackson smiled, too, but actually wondered whether he was too serious, because he didn't take the time to study about fishing. Or was that just laziness? More questions crowded his mind. Would it be "seriousness" to spend good hours of my life learning to spot a fish lolling in the shallows? Does that give me a triumph over the fish? Does that make me a better man, or just a man? Is it less serious that I spend those hours listening to and thinking about Jimmy Buffett songs? What would Bubba say? What *has* he said about that?' Jackson stared across the water, surprised not to see written there a lyric that was appropriate. He saw, instead, the backside of Jimmy Buffett himself, as he was casting away from them, perhaps trying to escape from them. I'm going to have to talk to him eventually, Jackson realized. I always imagined meeting him, but I wish I had spent more time imagining what I would say if I did. I guess now I will really find out if I am good on my feet.

XXV

Jackson and George climbed back onto the skiff, and George poled over to meet Jimmy. He had stopped casting and was hunched over as if he were sick. As he turned toward them, Jackson could see that he was working on his gear.

"Lousy expensive equipment. It's always tangling," Jimmy said, sounding disgusted.

"Just like a woman," George chuckled. Jimmy looked up.

"I'd prefer not to go into that topic, you know," he said.

"Welll, then, what can we talk about?" George took up the opportunity. "Jackson, you've caught a fish, and Jimmy hasn't. So, what would you like to talk about? You've been reading all week - anything good? Bubba's a reader, if you can believe that. Right Bubba?" Jimmy looked at George again, but this time with less hostility.

"Yeah, next to fishing it's my favorite thing to do. Well, maybe third. Or even fourth. I guess I've got to count singing." He looked at Jackson, and smiled for the first time.

"I think you should. Your songs are important. At least they are to me." Jackson looked serious, suddenly.

"Oh yeah? Great," Jimmy responded casually.

"No, I mean very important." This time Jackson sounded serious.

"You mean like, life and death important?" George chuckled, as Jackson kept his gaze on Jimmy.

"Well, I have described him as one of America's best poets of the second half of the 20th century."

"Who were you talking to, your shrink?" Jimmy asked.

"Anyone who would listen - which is a lot of people. You know, you're a cult figure - although someone as famous as you are shouldn't really be considered a cult figure, but since you've achieved your notoriety with very little public notice outside of your followers, you probably qualify as a cult." Jimmy stopped messing with his rod, and looked up at George.

"I'm not sure that's a good thing," he said, more to George than Jackson.

"Regardless," Jackson plunged forward, "it's true, but it's also more complicated than that. Cult figures are usually understood by their followers as something they really are not, and usually they are less than expected, but you are the opposite. You - or at least your songs, I don't know you yet - are so much more meaningful than most of your fans – probably ninety percent - know. I think of you as a poet first, and a drunken troubadour second. Of course, there isn't always a difference between the two." Jackson stopped, as he realized Jimmy was looking at him sharply, showing surprise, but also some interest.

"So, you think I'm a serious writer because my songs are important to you?" Jimmy asked. "And you think about ten percent of my fans agree with you?" George turned now to look at them both, as he noted a sincere tone in Jimmy's voice. The conversation suddenly seemed two-sided.

"That doesn't begin to explain it," Jackson answered. "You see, I've always had this love of literature. It pokes me in places I need to be prodded. It's unsettling and comforting at the same time. Your music is the same way. It takes me to places I long to see, but that already feel familiar. I know most people who listen to your music just like to get drunk and dance, but I'm listening to your words. There is truth, often profound truth, in every one of your songs. Even the ones the drunks are yelling for. Name any one of the hundred-fifty or so, and I'll prove my point."

"No, I don't think I want to go down that path," Jimmy said, and turned back to focus on his reel.

"Yeah, I know it sounds silly, maybe even frightening to you. I told myself - and my wife - that I would never say these things to you," Jackson answered.

"You knew I was going to be here?" Jimmy looked back up quickly. "George, you said you didn't tell him!"

"No, he didn't tell me," Jackson answered, just as quickly. "I didn't know you would be here. Believe it or not, my wife and I have had conversations about me having a conversation with you."

"Okay, now I'm getting a little worried," Jimmy said, looking at George.

"But you don't need to," Jackson insisted. "This isn't about you - it's about what your music means to me. It's the same thing those drunken dancers experience, only mine is an internal struggle, rather than an external wiggle."

"Hey, that's not bad. Can I use that?" Jimmy actually laughed for the first time since they had met.

"You can do better," Jackson said, now feeling he could actually engage him in a conversation. "In fact, you *do* better. I've always taken your music seriously. I first heard it in '76 when I visited my brother in college. I liked *Changes in Latitudes* so much, he gave me the album. I then went out and bought all of your earlier ones, and pretty soon you were all that I was listening to. The next year, I went to college myself, and my first English paper was a comparison of that song with Faulkner's short story, "A Rose for Emily." My professor's only comments were: 'This is sick. This is great!' Right above a big, red 'A.' Jackson paused for an instant, but neither Jimmy nor George interrupted, so he pressed on. "This was before I knew anything about you personally - that you are from the South, and that you like Faulkner, too. Boy, I was excited when I heard "If I could just get it on paper." Hearing you mention Faulkner made me feel vindicated as a literary critic, but this is not just about shared interests. It's the fact that your songs evoke the same feelings in me as Faulkner's stories. He said that the only thing worth writing about is the 'human heart in conflict with itself.' You do that, you know." Finally, Jackson stopped.

"Well, I can't say that I've ever thought of it precisely," Jimmy answered slowly, almost reluctantly, "but, of course, I'd like to. I'm flattered, if not a bit skeptical, about being compared to Faulkner. I don't think many people agree with you - certainly not even 10% of my following."

"I think you would be surprised. I've talked about your music with many fans, and I don't get any strong arguments against my position. Okay, maybe glassy looks from some, like my wife, but I believe at least some others think and feel as I do. Maybe some of the writers in Mississippi. They should anyway. Your songs have described the Gulf Coast just as Faulkner's work described his little postage-stamp of earth in North Mississippi. Think of "Biloxi" and "Creola" and "Pascagoula Run" and others. Of course, I may have thought about it more than others – well, I'm sure I have - and perhaps I can articulate the idea better than others, but the proof is in the words - your words."

"Well, this may be one time I'm practically at a loss for words," Jimmy said, after a brief silence. "I appreciate what you are saying and, of course, I want to be taken seriously as a writer. That's why I wrote a book, but I am still surprised by the depth of analysis you've described." His tone showed only a polite sincerity, Jackson thought.

"That's great, but truthfully, I'm not talking about your fiction writing. It's okay, but not nearly as effective as your songwriting, in my opinion."

"Ok, I guess I should have kept my mouth shut," Jimmy said.

"No, I mean, you're more of a poet than a short-story writer – which is good. You know, those that can't write poems, write novels...." He stopped and let Jimmy shake his head with understanding. "Anyway, this is just about my reaction to your work - what it means in my life. I'm not a deconstructionist, but there is something to the idea that art is in the mind of the audience. I get mad when people doubt that you are trying to say anything meaningful, because that means they aren't listening to what you are saying. I tried to explain this to my wife just a few days ago. If she, and others, would truly listen to your words, they would know what I feel. It's what I'm reacting to - truth. You are telling me that there is a way to live my life that I've forfeited, either through some kind of personal defeat or just professional ambition, or even inattention. Whatever, you're saying that I can still have it. I'm not talking about the dancing and dining. I'm thinking of the poet who lived before his time, the cowboy with Brahma fear, the twelve-volt man, about going to Texas. Of course, that's about the only bit of your doctrine that I've followed. The ideas you represent are attractive to me, and others, but they're just part of what I'm looking for. There's one thing missing and I've filled it with words of other prophets."

"Oh yeah? Who?" Jimmy asked, truly interested now, both Jackson and George perceived.

"Have you ever heard the saying 'Look, you scoffers, wonder and perish, for I am going to do something in your days that you would never believe even if someone told you'?"

"No," Jimmy responded quickly, "but it sounds like something I would have said to some folks in Nashville about fifteen years ago." He scoffed, before asking, "Where's it from?"

"Well, it comes up in several works, from the mouths of a couple of very interesting guys. You really want to hear about them?"

"Sure. You've got my attention now," Jimmy said, as he sat down on the deck of the skiff with his feet in the water. Then he turned to George. "Where did you find this guy, George?"

"He's my lawyer; if can you believe that," George replied, with his own scoff.

XXVI

George! Jimmy thought. I just wanted to go fishing. He should have known better than to invite a fan, particularly this psychoanalyst, but I have to admit, he has said some interesting things about me, or at least my work. I guess George thought I would be flattered, if George thought at all, which was unlikely. Or he may have intended to show me how much attention I am getting out there, even that I don't often hear about.

Of course, I wasn't so famous back when we first knew each other. I wasn't famous at all. At least Jackson has a different perspective. It beats the drunks falling over themselves, and me; it is an interesting change. In fact, he may be right about one thing. I always have felt a little melancholy about my work - not just that no one plays my meaningful songs on the radio, or takes me seriously as a writer. Those things used to hurt, but profit is a good medicine for the ego. But now, I want to make more of the work. Is it as good as it could be? Am I saying all that I really want to say? Jackson has heard it, even from the beginning, and he's tried to respond to it, but even he can't define it precisely. Can I? Maybe I should listen to him a bit. I've never listened to critics. I've never listened to fans. I've never listened to anyone! That's how I got where I am - following my intuition. That's why I'm so smug. I did it my way. I need to cover that tune. But what did Jackson say? "Look, sucker, you won't believe what I'm going to do even if I tell you?" That's my life. I wonder where he got that. I guess I'll have to find out. Maybe I can write a new song about it.

XXVII

This is more like it, George thought, as he took a seat on the deck, and handed Jimmy a bottle of beer. Jackson's warming up. He's talking like this is life or death stuff - and Bubba actually seems interested. He ought to. It's his life's work Jackson is talking about.

"Have you ever read Habakkuk?" Jackson asked, not addressing either of them specifically. Jimmy didn't respond, apparently lost in his own thought, so Jackson turned to George? "Have you?"

"Can't say as I have," George admitted. "You know I'm not a reader, unless, of course, it has to do with fishing - which is what I thought we had come to do today." He climbed behind the console of the skiff, and started the motor. "You guys can philosophize all you want back at the dock, but I am ready to try another spot." He moved the throttle gently and the skiff drifted softly into the middle of the cut. "And, if we catch Mr. Tarpon, you'll have an epic tale on your hands!"

"Oh, cut it out, George," Jimmy barked, as he swung his feet up out of the water. "You know there are no tarpon left around here. They hardly ever catch one these days even in the Keys."

"You might be right, Bubba, but I've got a feeling some unusual things are going on around here." He shot a smile at Jackson. "What do you say we scoot around that cut over there, and try a few more casts?"

"Okay by me," Jackson volunteered quickly. "It'll give you guys some time to figure out who Habakkuk is."

"Don't count on it," George responded, smiling this time at Jimmy. "He never did have much of an attention span unless you're a fish, or maybe a woman. No, just a fish."

"George," Jimmy shrugged, "I'm telling you, I've changed."

"Right," George said. "I guess you were changing even while you were lying on the pier at 5 this morning."

"Well, I'm *trying* to change," Jimmy protested. "There's a time for everything, you know."

"I've heard that," George said.

"Yeah; it's in the Bible." Jackson said. "I'm sure that's where you've read it."

"About as likely as Bubba getting it from there," George laughed again.

"Well," Jackson said, "It's from Solomon, and I've been trying to tell Jimmy how smart he is."

"Oh, don't give me that," George said, a little more seriously than he had intended, but he did not apologize to Jackson. Instead, he looked at Jimmy. "Sorry, Jimmy, but I'm not buying what he's selling you." George accelerated the engine briefly and then backed off to troll toward the new cut. "Jackie, stop selling, and keep fishing. Go ahead and throw your line in. Usually the churning scares the fish away, but you never know. We might get lucky." Jackson tried to be casual as he stepped past Jimmy to the stern. He kept his attention on the rod as he sent the line off the back of the boat into to the small wake. "So, just what were you doing last night, Bubba?" George asked, with a sincere tone that was just soft enough to make Jackson think this was a conversation intended to be between just George and Jimmy. The sound of the trolling motor and the wash of the wake, as well as Jackson being behind and turned away from the direction they were speaking, made their words unintelligible, regardless of whether George intended it or not.

"Songwriting?" Jimmy tried. George chuckled.

"I think you've written that song already – and sung it over and over."

"It is getting kind of old, I'll admit. Or *I* am." He looked back at Jackson, stepped closer to George and lowered his voice, unsure if Jackson could hear. "I've tried to get her to come back, you know. She just won't. Either I've destroyed her ability to believe in me, or she never really loved me."

"It could be worse," George said.

"Yeah? How so?" Jimmy asked, surprised.

"It could be both," George started to laugh, but stopped when he saw that Jimmy didn't. He added, "I always thought you were an odd match - she being a debutante and all, but then I remembered my own wife, and figured it wasn't so - impossible."

"Your wife was a socialite?"

"Was and is. Memphis belle, pure bred."

"I bet it was a fine time when she brought you home for dinner. Did you have that mustache then?" Jimmy asked, and George nodded with his bandito grin.

"Her Daddy fought about as hard as a tarpon on a fly rod," George said.

"Help!" Jackson shouted.

"What?" George looked back at Jackson. He was bending over trying to catch his balance, to keep from falling in the water. George reached for Jackson's shoulder and asked "Did you hurt yourself or what?" It was only then that he noticed Jackson's rod bent over more than Jackson, and heard the line screaming from the reel. "Yee Haw!" George yelled. "There's only one fish in this water that makes that sound!" He righted Jackson, and shot a wicked smile back at Jimmy, who had taken over the controls. "I haven't heard it in a long time, but I still know it when I do!" Jimmy didn't respond, and didn't look as if he could. "Well, don't look so shocked." George grinned broadly, stretching his mustache to its full breadth. "I told you Jackson was going to do it, and you didn't believe me. You might as well call me Habakkuk!"

XXVIII

'I better go wake her,' Bette thought, as she walked onto her balcony and looked for the third time down to where Maggie was sleeping. She's going to fry sleeping out there in this morning sun. Of course, kids today don't care. Not like in my day when we were supposed to look like Snow White, and were forbidden to even show our arms or legs in the house, much less parade them out in public, golden-brown and offered like some fast food. We even had to sleep in full-length nightgowns. Now they sleep outside in essentially panties and a bra – and sometimes not even that! Shock? Nostalgia? Jealousy? Envy? She wasn't sure which. Perhaps all of that.

She walked back through her condo and picked up a towel, book and cigarettes. She quietly closed the door behind her, hoping not to wake Bob, who was now back asleep after his own morning fishing excursion. She descended the steps to the dock and thought unavoidably of her "coming out" party – how she had nervously walked down the grand staircase at her parents' country club, appearing in a beautiful gown before all of their friends, and a few that would become hers. Was this where she expected to be thirty years later? Probably not, but she knew she was better off now than wherever it was she might have hoped, or her parents expected her, to be.

The sun was almost directly overhead now, and as she moved out from the shadows of the building into the light, she put on her sunglasses. She noticed that Maggie had turned over on her stomach, and was pleased that she would not have to decide whether, or how to, wake her. She knew that waking in full sunlight is like being hit in the head with a bat, coupling blinding light with a dull thud.

"So, glad to see you're alive," she said, deciding to start in the middle of a conversation. Maggie raised her torso stiffly, blinking against the light and attempting to hold her unfastened bikini top.

"Was there a doubt?" She muttered.

"Well, I guess not, but you were laying pretty still on your back for a long time. I've been watching, of course." She smiled, as she laid out her towel on the chaise nearest Maggie. "I was surprised to see you alone. You two aren't still arguing, are you?" She asked, as Maggie gave her a surprised look. "Oh, don't worry," Bette waved her hand, "we all have disagreements. I learned to spot them a long time ago."

"Another skill of yours," Maggie said, as she squirmed and felt the tightness in her skin, suggesting the beginning of sunburn. "Jackson went fishing with George and Bubba, whoever he is," she explained.

"That's a good way to put it, when he's a friend of George's," Bette said.

"Right. I don't know who he is, or even if it is a 'he', come to think of it." Maggie was fully awake now, perhaps from the sun, or perhaps from the realization that "Bubba" could be a woman, at least in George's world.

"Don't tell me. Oh my!" Bette sat up and spat out, half-excited and half-sarcastic.

"What? What is it?" Maggie sat up too, and caught her

top just before it dropped. She was still squinting, but could see Bette smiling in an odd way.

"Jimmy Buffett!" She exclaimed, through her smile.

"I know, Jackson's obsessed with him." Maggie relaxed. "I'm sure you've heard us listening to his music all week. I am sorry if you're tired of hearing it."

"No, not that," Bette insisted. "George's friend, the guy Jackson is fishing with; I bet it's Jimmy Buffett!"

"Oh, Bette, now you've been in the sun too long. What would Jimmy Buffett be doing fishing in Tarpon, Texas? Jackson says he's fished all over the world. I'm sure he could find a better place than here - and a better guide than George Waters. The guy almost got me and Jackson drowned yesterday, and you predicted it!"

"Well, you're right about George being a little dangerous, but you're wrong about there being a better guide. George is an expert fisherman, and he told me once a long time ago that he used to fish with Buffett when he had money and Buffett didn't. He also told me that he had a surprise for Jackson that he could hardly keep secret. Call *me* eccentric, but something just clicked in my head, and I bet I'm right!"

"I think something's come loose in your head," Maggie put her finger to her own head, "but I don't know whether to hope you're right or wrong. Obviously, it would be cool if you're right, but if you are, I'm sure Jackson is a basket case right this minute. I'd pray for him if I knew what to ask for." Bette smirked.

"I know how that goes," she paused, and then added, "maybe I'm right; maybe I'm wrong. We'll just have to sit here and wait for them to return. I wouldn't mind meeting Jimmy Buffett myself. Maybe we could get drunk and."

"Bette!" Maggie interrupted.

"Just kidding." Bette laughed. "I'm sure he gets that all the time. Maybe you do, too, if Jackson's such a big fan of his."

"Oh, he is, but not like that." Bette looked at her, puzzled. "It's a long story," Maggie started to explain. "Jackson doesn't like him for that stuff. He likes his *real* music."

"What?" Bette asked. "You mean like the ones about the cheeseburgers and the margaritas?"

"Well, not really those, either. I don't know. You'll have to hear it from him. He thinks it's poetry. You heard him talk about Gus like he was a *real* hero."

"Oh, yeah; I was surprised by his ideas about that book. Don't tell me he thinks that deeply about Jimmy Buffett's songs!"

"Deeper."

"Well, I'll just have to hear about that! I pride myself on always being open to other peoples' perspectives, and the idea of Jimmy Buffett being a deep thinker is definitely a new view to me."

"It was new to me, too – still is, I guess," admitted Maggie, "but it's not to Jackson. He's felt like that ever since I've known him – ever since he discovered Buffett's music in high school – and he seems to be more moved by him with every new album. We've talked about it some, but I think he's still struggling to understand it, or at least to get to where it doesn't embarrass him. I know it would shock him to actually meet Buffett. Just maybe, that would clear everything up in his mind. I don't know."

"In about five minutes you will," Bette said. "There's George's boat, coming through the jetties now."

Maggie looked up to see the *Satisfaction* bobbing, seemingly on the rocks, as it floated through the jetties that formed the port. She turned back to Bette, her heart suddenly racing.

"You don't really think he's with them?" Hearing the half-excited, half-concerned tone in her own voice made Maggie turn back to look at the boat before Bette could respond.

"Knowing George, I wouldn't be surprised. In his own way, he's as unpredictable – and as unexplainable – as Jimmy Buffett. George comes from money, you know, but he looks and acts like a shrimper. Buffett grew up on the docks in Mobile, I think, but he's making good money marketing the mentality of the beach bum. But Jackson thinks he's a poet, eh? That's an encounter I'd like to see myself."

George's boat came toward them without evidence of anyone on board. It wasn't until the bow cleared the piling at the entrance to the marina that George's head appeared on the fly bridge. Just like George, thought Bette, probably doing shots with Jimmy in the cabin. But no one else was in sight. George stood up now, his arms shifting slightly as he reversed the engines and swung the bow away from them, preparing to back into the slip. It was only then that Jackson came into view, emerging from the cabin and giving them a polite wave as he reached for the ropes on the dock.

"Yee haw!" George yelled, as he cut the motors. Maggie and Bette, already leaning forward in their chaises in anticipation, jumped in unison and scrambled in opposite directions to their feet. As she gained her balance, Maggie clutched uncertainly at her chest, trying to remember if she had fastened her top. "Yee haw!" George yelled, again. "What a day, eh, Jackie?" Jackson looked up at him and smiled, then turned to meet Bette and Maggie.

"What is it? Did you see him?" Maggie asked, not directly to Jackson or George.

"See him?" George yelled back, as he jumped down the ladder from the fly bridge. "We brought him home!"

"I knew it!" Bette said, looking smartly at Maggie. Maggie looked somewhat bewildered at Jackson, who finally spoke.

"We brought you back a little surprise. Well, actually, it is a big surprise. Did you hear already?" He asked shyly.

Maggie looked at Bette again, her excitement escalating. "Bette said so, but I couldn't believe her. He's on the boat?"

"Yep," Jackson grinned, but looked inquiringly at Bette. "How did you hear?"

"I just guessed," Bette admitted. "Can we meet him?"

"Meet him? Well, he's dead," George interjected, "but I guess he might still be able to give you a smile!" He laughed as he disappeared into the cabin. Maggie and Bette looked at each other, startled, as George yelled from inside. "Come on, Jackie. Give me a hand. This is your catch." Jackson looked down and shook his head, as Bette and Maggie both looked at him.

"Alright, if you insist on being modest," George called as he struggled out of the cabin, straining to present a glistening silver fish, over three feet long with scales like armor plates and a lower jaw that resembled a heavy-duty front loader. "Here he is!" George said, proudly.

Maggie's face sank. "You got me this excited over a fish?

"Honey, that's no ordinary fish," Bette screamed. "That's a tarpon!"

XXIX

I never thought of myself as a prophet, but this is some evidence, George thought. Of course, he had just been teasing Jimmy with the talk about catching a tarpon. Then, Jackson actually caught one. Man, I've never even caught one! George exclaimed in his head. But, should I count this one as mine? Clearly Jackson wouldn't have caught it without me, but then, I was talking to Jimmy about his love life when Jackson hooked it – or it hooked itself. I guess it's his, though. I'll have to settle for having prophesied it.

"It sure is a tarpon – seventy or eighty pounds, I'd say," George drawled, as he heaved the shining silver trophy onto the dock.

"Incredible!" Bette exclaimed coming closer, and kneeling. "I've only seen one of these in my life. It's gorgeous." She looked up at George, by-passing Jackson. "George, you never cease to amaze me. I didn't think anyone around here would ever catch a tarpon again. I should have known it would be you; you're just the man for this to happen to."

"Now, I think that's a compliment," George said, scratching his head, as he stepped up onto the dock and stood beside her, "but either way, you're wrong. This is Jackie's fish."

"No way!" Maggie's interest suddenly returned. "You caught this?" She asked, accusingly, of Jackson, who now stood alone in the boat. Before he could decide how to respond, George answered emphatically.

"Yes, ma'am! All by himself, while Jimmy and I were shooting the breeze." He glanced with a smile at Jackson. "Pretty good fisherman you got yourself there, Maggie. I figure that's the first tarpon seen in Tarpon in about twenty years. What do you think, Bette?"

"I'd say closer to thirty. The last one we caught was before I got out of finishing school." Bette said. George grinned at the reference.

"They taught you how to fish at that school?" He asked, amused.

"Of course not," Bette said. "They would be mortified by how much I know about fishing."

"Wait!" Maggie interrupted again, this time looking at George. "You said you were talking to 'Jimmy.' Jimmy who?" Once again Jackson smiled, starting to speak, but as his smile turned into a laugh, George cut in again.

"You know. My long, lost friend Jimmy. I know him as 'Bubba,' actually, but he said he prefers 'Jimmy' when around new acquaintances, like Jackson." George shot another bandito grin toward Jackson. "He went fishing with us, and was as amazed as I was at what Jackie did. Also, somewhat by what Jackie said." He laughed again, and then turned completely around to see Jackson, who he thought seemed amused rather than frustrated at not being able to speak. "Although, *I* was the one who told him we were going to catch a tarpon, right Jackie?" He looked at the prophecy fulfilled on the dock. By now, several others had approached the dock and were gathering around the catch. Word spreads quickly on the island, George thought. I wonder which is the bigger story?

"But Jimmy *who*?" Maggie fairly pleaded for an answer, bringing George back to the moment.

"Oh, sorry. Jimmy Buffett. We knew each other a long time ago in Florida and Colorado. Funny, we never fished together in Texas before today. You know him?" George deadpanned.

"I told you!" Bette laughed, and punched Maggie. "That's George, for you," she said, shaking her head.

"I know *a* Jimmy Buffett, or at least of him," Maggie started, clearly still not believing what she heard, which clearly amused George. "Is there more than one?" Maggie asked.

"Probably. I don't know. This one likes to fish. What else was it he said he liked, Jackie? Women?" He looked at Jackson, who was also grinning.

"Reading," Jackson answered.

"That's right! You guys got into that stuff about that Habakkuk guy," George shrugged. Jackson laughed out loud now, and looked again at Maggie, who was still bewildered and starting to look angry. He decided he better get on with the story.

"Yes, he likes to read Faulkner, even likes to sing about him – even wrote a song about him."

"Right again," said George. "This Jimmy Buffett likes to read *and* write songs, even sings them, too." He paused, also checking Maggie's disposition, and sensing it was time for the punchline. He could tell that she simply did not know how to respond, and he decided to help. "Maggie, Jackie told me he wrote a paper in college comparing a Faulkner short story to one of Jimmy Buffett's songs. Is that true?" With this, Maggie finally believed, and resolved to settle the issue.

"Are you two pulling my leg – or all three of you?" She turned to include Bette. With no response, she continued, "Are you telling me that you have just been fishing with Jimmy Buffett, and that Jackson told him about his obsession with his music and then caught a tarpon?"

"Whale of a story, isn't it?" said George. "Even better because it's true." Maggie shrieked. Wow, I bet that's the first time she's done that since she was about 13, George thought. Maggie jumped down into the boat and grabbed Jackson around the shoulders, half-hugging, half-throttling him.

"You went fishing with Jimmy Buffett? You finally got what you've been dreaming about all these years!" Jackson shrugged, still not responding to her excitement. Maggie didn't seem to notice, but turned her enthusiasm to George. "How could you pull this off without telling us?" Then remembering, she turned to Bette who now stood before a small crowd that had gathered to see the fish, but were now staying to listen to the story. "How could you not tell us, Bette?"

"Honestly, I didn't know," she protested. "I just guessed, just now as we were sitting here on the dock." Bette tried to sound convincing. "Call it luck or female intuition, but it probably was from many years of having George surprise me with his antics. This is just like something he would do." She looked admiringly at George. "In fact, this is vintage George, the totally unexpected. Imagine – Jimmy Buffett and a tarpon return to Tarpon on the same day, and both of them in George's boat." She paused, then added, "If someone had told me this would happen I wouldn't have believed it, unless George said he was going to do it."

"Wow, Bette, you're making me out to be some kind of prophet," George said, and glanced at Jackson. "All I did was meet up with an old fishing buddy, and then watch a new fishing buddy catch a fish. Is it my doing that one of those is Jimmy Buffett, and the other was a tarpon?" George smirked, realizing that he had asked himself the same question only a few minutes earlier. "Who *is* responsible?" He wondered again, aloud this time.

"Well," Maggie piped in, as she climbed back onto the

dock, "to answer your earlier question, yes, it is true that Jackson wrote that paper about Faulkner and Buffett. I've never read it, but I've heard the story so many times, and I've talked to Jackson about the connection so many times, I know it must be true. That's probably better than actually reading it, but I would still like to sometime." She looked at her husband with affection and growing admiration.

"I would, too," a voice behind her interrupted. Maggie turned to see a smiling Jimmy Buffett, standing two feet from her.

XXX

"You must be Maggie," Jimmy said, almost shyly.

"Oh, my," Maggie managed. "You're *the* Jimmy Buffett."

"That's true, I do believe," he laughed. "And, I'll tell you something else that's true," he added, as he looked around at the crowd now gathered to see the prize fish and the public figure. "That's some husband you've got there." He gestured at Jackson. Maggie turned to smile at her husband, and then stopped, deciding to keep focused on Jimmy.

"I agree with you," she said, "but I've had to fight you for his affection since the day we met, and now it's only going to be worse."

"Oh," Jimmy winced, but continued smiling. "I've been accused of messing with a few marriages in my day, but never for being too close to the husband." The crowd, mostly men, laughed together. Jimmy looked around. "I guess I shouldn't have said that. These people might get the wrong idea – all the way around."

"Too late; they all know you by reputation," George joined back in, "but like I said out there," he pointed toward the back bays, "it could be worse." Jimmy gave him a knowing look.

"I hope not, for my sake," Jimmy paused, and then added, "I better get out of here and let Jackson take the spotlight for his historic catch. Have you weighed it yet?" He looked at Jackson.

"No," Jackson spoke for the first time since Jimmy had appeared.

"Well, you need to do that, Jackie. It is okay if I call you Jackie?" Jimmy asked sincerely.

"Sure, Bubba," Jackson deadpanned, and then looked at George who broke into his trademark howl.

"Okay, I'll see you guys later, uh – and girls," he nodded at Maggie and Bette. "Meet where and when we agreed, right George?"

"Whatever you say, Bubba," George replied, as the crowd parted and Jimmy disappeared through it, moving quickly while thinking that George had not changed a bit. He always was just like me, and always did surround himself with really interesting people. I should be flattered by that realization. He then ducked into the passenger side of a black Town Car, with darkly tinted windows. The door was held and then closed by a middle-aged man in a dark suit. One lucky fisherman, too, Jimmy acknowledged to himself.

XXXI

"If that isn't just like you. You actually have your dream come true, and you interrupt it by catching the first tarpon this town's seen in thirty years! Can't you do anything normal?"

Maggie's tone was gently mocking, but with an air of truthful accusation. She and Jackson were back in the condo after spending another hour at the dock with more gawkers – at the fish, not Buffett – and even a visit from a reporter for the island's weekly newspaper. The *Jetty Caller* came out on Thursdays, and thus wouldn't be published again for five days, but the editor had dispatched his reporter immediately upon hearing the news of the catch, convinced that interest would not have waned by then, even though it seemed the entire island had already heard the news. Besides, the reporter had said, this was a story that needed to be recorded for Tarpon's history.

"Hey, I didn't have anything to do with either event," Jackson defended himself, lamely. "George is the one who knows Buffett, and he was driving the boat that caught the fish. I just happened to be holding the pole – rod, I mean."

"Oh, come on. I bet you willed that fish on to your line to avoid having to talk to your idol. You told me just two days ago that you would never tell him how much he means to you." She paused and then asked, seriously, "So, did you?"

"Well," Jackson hesitated before adding, "sort of." He finished with a shrug.

"What do you mean, sort of?" Maggie asked, sitting on the bed, trying to show a willingness to listen, and hoping to coax the story out of him.

"I got started, and then we got interrupted," Jackson volunteered, grudgingly.

"So, you were actually having the discussion of your dreams when you caught the tarpon?

"No. He was talking to George when I caught the tarpon – or it caught itself, I mean. We had talked a little before that, about how much I love his music, but we sort of got sidetracked when I quoted Habakkuk."

"No!" Maggie jumped up from the bed. "Don't tell me you preached to him?" Maggie said with a widening grin. Jackson shook his head and looked down, realizing that he was going to have to explain the entire sequence of events. Before he could start, Maggie added, "I would never have thought of that, but now, it doesn't surprise me, the way you've been lately." Jackson smiled sheepishly.

"When the time finally came, it seemed the only thing to do – to try to introduce my idol to my God."

"Yes! I knew it would come to you," Maggie said, putting her arms around him in a congratulatory hug. "That's what this is all about, isn't it – who are you going to follow?" Maggie was truly excited now, but she released him and stepped back to continue the discussion. Jackson was frowning, however.

"No, I don't think so," he said, lowering his voice to catch her attention. It worked. Maggie immediately stepped closer and looked directly at him, willing him to continue. "You asked earlier this week if this was actually about me, and I thought it was, then; but today, I realized we were both wrong. It isn't about who *I'm* going to follow, it's about who *he's* going to follow." He paused, and waited for her response. Maggie looked back at him blankly at first, but then nodded her head as she responded in an almost reverent tone.

"Heaven help you."

XXXII

"Not bad, George," Bette said. "You caught a tarpon and a rock star, and fulfilled someone's lifelong dream all on one morning fishing trip, and you didn't even go offshore." George was washing down his boat, as Bette sat on the step of the pier extending from the dock, beside the boat. "You must be feeling pretty full of yourself, but then, when aren't you?" She exhaled cigarette smoke and waited for his response.

"Not a bad day at the office, I'd say," George smiled in return.

"You can't ever have had a bad day at the office. You would have to go to an office, first."

"Hey, you know we keep an office for the family business."

"The *family* keeps an office, is more accurate – the family does. I've never seen you there, and I'd bet they haven't, either. This is your office," she said, pointing to the boat.

"Well, I've spent several days at Jackson's office, and those were some bad days. Does that count?" George offered.

"I guess so. I know what a family business can be like, especially when the lawyers get involved, or if the family business is lawyering." She paused and flicked her ash into the water, and thought of Bob, before turning back to George. "You do seem to have taken a liking to Jackson, though."

"Oh, it's not Jackson's fault, of course. He's a good kid, and pretty sharp in meetings. That's why I invited him to go fishing."

"Well, I don't know what kind of lawyer he is, but Maggie acted like she was afraid he would get hurt out there fishing."

"She's a smart woman," George said, smiling again. "The fisherman's equivalent of the 'chicken or the egg' question remains unanswered."

"You mean, is it the fisherman or the guide?"

"Yep. You know, I felt in my bones that something interesting was going to happen when I brought Jackie and Jimmy together, but I never thought it would be a tarpon! I've seen Jimmy more recently than I've seen a tarpon. How can you explain that? And how can you explain that I *predicted* we would catch one? I was just trying to goad Jimmy, and break the ice between him and Jackie. Weird, really weird." He had finished washing down the boat, and had climbed out to sit next to her on the dock.

"Well, I certainly can't explain that, but I am curious why you didn't release the fish. They're so rare, it seems a shame to keep this one." Bette spoke, as if she was trying not to sound critical.

"Well, that's another thing. We didn't kill it. You know I support catch and release, but this fish didn't seem to want to be released," he started to explain. "I know it sounds silly, but just start with the fact that we hooked the thing in the first place - or Jackson did - and the way it happened. That's strange enough, but then it didn't really put up much of a fight. Sure, he ran for a bit - almost burned Jackie's hand before I got to him and steadied the rod – but there were no jumps and not really that much fight. In fact, when we got him up to the boat, he just sort of laid on his side and let out this little sigh."

"What?" Bette couldn't help but question his story.

"You know, when they release the air in the swim sack. It sounds like a sigh," George explained.

"No, I've never heard of that. I told you, I've only seen one tarpon in my life," Bette replied, still sounding skeptical.

"Well, you can look it up for a full explanation, but they have some kind of bladder that works almost like a lung. The experts think that this is what makes them jump, and perhaps helps them fight so hard, but anyway, this one didn't do either. He sort of just came up alongside of the boat, and gave up the ghost. We were all so excited we didn't actually realize it until we had him in the boat, and he didn't flop much. He just sort of laid there, letting us praise him. We did the measurement and took a picture, and I suggested we should let him go. It was Jimmy that noticed he didn't show much life. So, instead of pulling the hook and dropping him back in, we splashed a little water on him and then laid him back in the Gulf with the hook still on. It just hung there. Even when the water filled his gills and should have revived him, he just floated. It was almost like he gave up willingly, you know, like a sacrifice."

"Now, that's interesting," Bette said.

"More than interesting. It's *strange*. A few strange things happened out there today," George concluded. They were both now looking out to the port without focusing on anything. Bette noticed George's serious look.

"George," she said, mocking his serious tone, "most people would say that something strange happens whenever you are around, and certainly when you are in charge."

"Is that so?" he answered. "I'm glad not to have disappointed them today." He stood up to further break the mood he had created. "I hope I didn't disappoint Jackson. It can be a little bit of a letdown when you finally meet your idol, you know. He was probably more relieved than excited about catching the tarpon – it distracted us and lightened the conversation."

"So, what exactly did happen? Was he an adoring fan?"

"Oh, I'd say he played it pretty cool. I sprung it on him cold. Jimmy just appeared, well almost stumbled, out of the cabin like he was crawling out from under a rock – looked the part, too. Jackie must have been shocked, but he didn't let it show. In fact, he almost ignored Jimmy, until I really started needling them both. I think that loosened things up. Finally, Jackie did admit to being a fan, and started to describe what Jimmy's music means to him. It was getting a little deep for me, so I shut him up by saying we were going to move to another hole. Incredibly, he hooked the tarpon along the way."

"So, what did Jimmy do, just ignore him? Before the tarpon, I mean."

"Sort of, at first, but, I swear, I think he was pretty flattered by Jackie's comments, talking about what all of the songs mean to him. He certainly listened then. Even when Jackie quoted some guy I've never heard of – Habakkuk. The quote was something that Jimmy liked, and he was starting to explain it when I cut him off. I said they could talk about that later, and Jackson joked that it would give us time to figure out who Habakkuk is." He shrugged. "Beats me."

"You mean you really don't know?" Bette asked.

"You know I don't read much."

"In this case, maybe that is an acceptable excuse. Even for students of the Word, he is a pretty obscure author."

"You know who he is? How?" George asked, also sounding truly surprised.

"You know the schools I went to." She slapped her thigh as she rose to leave. I guess the Sisters were good for something." She shook her head, and smiled one last time as she turned. "I've got to have another long talk with Jackson."

XXXIII

The office at the Tarpon Inn was dark and apparently unattended as Jackson pushed open the French door and peeked inside. He paused, but then went in. He looked around at the familiar walls with a new sense of relationship, but still wondered at the strange surroundings. He wondered even more at being asked to meet Jimmy Buffett here, which added to the surreal nature of the entire day. Surely, he isn't staying here, Jackson thought, assuming that the faded glory of the office must reflect the state of the guest rooms. Then he remembered George saying he had rented a house down the island.

George had given him the message after Jimmy left the dock. They were to meet at the Inn at 9 p.m., for a celebration dinner. Maggie had practically accosted him when they returned to their condo, demanding a minute by minute retelling of the entire encounter with Buffett. Despite the realization of his life's dream, Jackson felt oddly depressed about the day. He had been surprised by George's trick, but he felt that he had recovered quickly and managed to regain a bit of his dignity by the end of the ordeal. Of course, he started by making a fool of himself with the fishing pole. Then he seemed to have intrigued Jimmy a bit with his comments about his music. Catching the tarpon certainly threw everyone off balance.

Jackson was still not sure whether he was happy or sad about catching the fish. Did it make him more important in Buffett's eyes, or did Jimmy just think of him as Lucky Jackie? Did the excitement of the catch take away his chance to really talk about Buffett's music? It certainly cut short the discussion, or at least George had. That was strange, since George had set the whole thing up. But would he be having dinner with Jimmy if he hadn't caught the fish and had kept on talking about his music? Who knows? He cleared his throat, and then coughed.

"Is someone there?" A voice called out, and Jackson looked around to see a stocky older woman enter the room from a doorway in a corner behind the counter. "Oh, sorry, I didn't hear you come in. I was doing my dinner dishes. Can I help you? Oh, wait, you're the guy that caught the tarpon!" Jackson smiled, amazed that the feat could be recognized so quickly, but then looked at the walls and realized that this was where it was most likely to be recognized.

"I saw you over at the dock earlier," the woman explained, "but I didn't know you were staying here."

"I'm not. I'm just meeting some friends for dinner." Jackson stopped, pleased that he had not revealed who he was meeting, and shocked at the thought that he had just referred to Jimmy Buffett as a friend. "I was supposed to meet them at 9," he added, looking at the clock on the wall, which read 9:12.

"Well, what's the name? I'll look them up," she said, as she moved down the glass counter and picked up a ledger. "Sorry I can't call them, but we don't have phones in the rooms." Jackson hesitated, and she continued. "I reckon you've got some celebrating to do. The only tarpon we see in Tarpon anymore are in this room." Now, she, too, looked at the walls. Jackson still hesitated, not knowing what to say, when George and Bette appeared outside the office door.

"There's the man!" George said, as he held the door open for Bette. "Sorry to keep you waiting. Where's Maggie?"

"She's on her way. Took a little longer in the shower."

"Too much excitement?" George smiled his bandito smile at Jackson. "I'm sure you had a lot of explaining to do."

"Well, we've got all week to make the fish story even bigger than it already is," Bette said. "I understand it's going to be front page news in the *Jetty*. An awkward silence followed, until George seemed to read Jackson's mind.

"Bubba's gonna meet us over in the restaurant," George said. He raised his eyebrows as if to signal the use of Jimmy's alias. "I guess we can go on over, unless you want to wait here for Maggie?"

"Are we eating here?" Jackson questioned.

"Not *right* here," George said. "The restaurant's out back in the courtyard; got the whole place to ourselves after 9, compliments of the owner – and Bubba, of course."

"Another long-lost friend of his?" Jackson asked.

"Nope. Another long-time friend of mine. Let's go on over, and I'll introduce you." George turned to the woman behind the counter. "Scottie here will send Maggie along, won't you Scottie?"

"Sure thing, George," she growled. "I'll also deny to anyone else that I've seen your ugly mug tonight." George laughed, and waved as they went out the French door into the dusk. As the three of them were walking around the corner of the Inn, Maggie called from across the street, under the town's lone stop light.

"Hey, wait up," she said as she let a car turn before she stepped into the street. Jackson thought she looked her best. Her renewed tan complemented her white cotton dress. As usual, she wore little make-up, but perhaps more than usual. (Seeing Jimmy Buffett was cause for some special preparation, she had said, sheepishly.) She had only pulled her hair into a ponytail, as she usually did, but still the overall effect was moving to Jackson, and made him feel proud – perhaps even to the point of shortening dinner, a dinner he had only dreamed he might one day attend. Then he thought perhaps he should work to prolong dinner to extend his satisfaction of causing other men to envy him.

"Hey," he said back to her, as she joined them on the sidewalk on their side of the street. They kissed a polite hello, and she moved on past him to greet George and Bette.

"Where's the party?" She asked as they continued down the sidewalk past the corner of the Inn.

"Right there," George pointed through a gate at the rear of the Inn, to a beach-like cottage in the courtyard. It was built on pilings and had a veranda about four feet above the ground. At the railing, like a sea captain on his ship, stood Jimmy Buffett dressed in white shorts, a Hawaiian shirt, and flip flops. Music was coming through the open doors behind him, kettle drum and six-string guitar. Maggie and Jackson gave each other the same look.

Is this for real?

"About time you got here," Buffett called, as they came up the steps. "I've had a hard time keeping a low profile." He grinned as he met up with Maggie. "Ah, I don't think we were properly introduced this afternoon." He extended his hand, but not fully, so that she had to move closer to him to shake it. "I'm Jimmy Buffett. I know you're Maggie. I want to tell you, I had one interesting day with your husband."

"Me, too," Maggie said.

"Way to go, Jackie," he said, and shook Jackson's hand. "Or do you prefer Jackson? I heard both out there today."

"Jackson," Jackson replied. "Only George and my mother call me Jackie."

"Leave it to George to try to fill a maternal role," Bette said. Jimmy smirked at George, who was now standing beside Jackson, with Bette beside him.

"He was actually doing some of that for me today when you caught the tarpon. Right, George?" Jimmy said.

"That's only for you to tell, of course," George shrugged.

"Maybe I will, before the night is over," Jimmy answered. "And you, my dear, must be Bette," he said, again extending his hand, but this time with his arm full length.

"Yes," she answered politely, and Jackson was certain that she blushed.

"I gather that you have known George for about as long as I have," Jimmy said, not questioning."

"Oh, longer, I'm sure," Bette found her usual voice, much to her pleasure. "We've been fishing together since my debutante days."

"Another debutante in your life!" Jimmy said, looking at George. "Either George has fallen from a previously undisclosed social standing, or Texas society has taken a decidedly quirky turn. Which is it, Bette?"

"The latter, of course," she smiled at George, who obligingly twisted his moustache.

"Another topic for us to explore tonight, for sure," Jimmy answered. "Now, get on in here so we can close the curtains and maintain some privacy."

Full dark had fallen, and the courtyard was lighted only by mosquito torches and the candlelight from the tables in the cottage. They went through the open French doors into a room with two tables pushed together at its center. Each was covered with white linen and set for formal dining. Several other tables against the outer walls of the room had been stripped bare, and clearly were not going to be used again that evening. A waiter closed the doors behind them and immediately drew long linen curtains that made the room feel soft and dreamlike. *This is a dream*, Jackson and Maggie said to each, other with a glance.

"Everyone take a seat," Jimmy directed. "I'll let you chose your own, but I insist on being your host this evening. George says this is one of the best restaurants in Texas. Where did you say the chef is from, Dallas?" He looked at George.

"No, San Antonio, and he's better than anyone you would find in Dallas. His name is Christopher and he'll be out to greet us shortly, I'm sure. He's selecting the menu himself."

"Sounds good to me. You know how I love to eat, especially seafood." He sat down at the head of the table next to Maggie, who had taken a corner seat to accommodate her left-handedness. Jackson was to her right, across from George. Bette was on Jimmy's left, across from Maggie. The end chair, opposite Jimmy, was empty.

"Where's Bob?" Jackson asked Bette, not sure that it was his place to inquire.

"Oh, he'd never go out to eat this late. I'm sure he's asleep by now. Besides, he doesn't care for Mr. Buffett's music, at least not as much as we do." She turned and grinned mischievously at Jimmy.

"We should have invited Will," Jackson said, with a slightly sarcastic look at Maggie.

"That would have livened up the conversation," Maggie replied, in the same tone. There was a brief moment of awkward silence until Jimmy replied to Bette, ignoring Jackson and Maggie's exchange.

"I don't know which is the bigger insult," Jimmy said, "her husband not liking my music, or her calling me 'Mr. Buffett.' I don't hear that too often – only from doctors and police officers."

"You still seeing both of them professionally?" George asked. "I thought you were telling me about how much you've changed."

"I was trying to, when Jackson so rudely interrupted me with his fish of the century." Jimmy focused seriously on Jackson for an instant, and then asked. "Do you realize what a big catch you made today?"

"Which one?" Jackson replied.

"Hmm," Jimmy said. "Let me think about that for a second. I may not be as quick as you." He paused, watching as the waiter poured a small amount of wine into his glass for approval. Jimmy took a sip, and nodded to the waiter, who then began to serve the others full glasses. "Okay, I think I got it," he smiled at Maggie, as she took her first sip. "I was asking about the tarpon."

"No, I don't think I do," Jackson answered, "at least I didn't at first. I'm beginning to get the picture, though."

"Let me and George, maybe Bette, too, explain it to you, then." He leaned forward and put his elbows on the table. "To sport fishermen, the tarpon is one of the most revered catches – a holy grail of sorts. It is the embodiment of our quest, a smart, strong adversary made even more worthy by an evolved wariness, and even more prized by its increasing rarity."

"Whoa!" George almost yelled. "When did you start writing for *National Geographic*?"

"Hey, I told you I was changing. I think about things more. I've got to. I'm a writer now. Maybe even a poet." He shot a quick look at Jackson.

"I see," George observed. "I thought it was just because you've been spending so much time alone." He stopped himself from laughing, immediately wondering whether it was possible to be unfair to Jimmy. Jimmy smiled at him, though, making George's face relax.

"Definitely part of it, too," Jimmy nodded, while taking a full drink from his now full glass. "Your little town here is a living example of what I'm saying. Obviously there were tarpon here once, right? So, why did Jackson just catch the first one in more than 20 years? Like any other precious jewel, sooner or later its shine is going to attract too much attention." He paused again, as each of them thought of the shimmering silver scales and the light glinting off them as the fish had come out of the water, and even later, on the dock. The shine was still electric as it lay on the dock, even with the life having gone out of the fish. They all knew that its power had been many megawatts stronger in the water. Blinking in the candlelight, Jimmy continued.

"A writer and fisherman named John Cole claims that the tarpon sparked what amounted to a full-scale recreational industry." Almost in a dramatic aside, he added "As a writer myself, I felt obligated to give proper credit for ideas." He paused again for effect.

"I've read *Tarpon Quest*," Jackson said, almost nervously, as if it was impolite to say so. He stopped there, trying mightily to keep from launching into his usual extended exposition. Jimmy paused long enough to let Jackson not speak, and resumed.

"Somehow, that does not surprise me," he said. "Anyway, I think the lure of fishing is similar to that of hunting. One goes out into the wilderness, or at least the unknown, and matches himself – or herself," he looked at Bette and Maggie as he continued, "against the prey." Of course, we've got more tools these days, particularly in hunting, but in fishing the technology has improved tremendously, as well. To catch something as powerful and imposing as a tarpon gives one a great sense of accomplishment. Fishermen wanted it, back when this place took its name from the tarpon, and they still want it today. Right, George?" Jimmy looked down the length of the table, and seemed to be offering the stage to George, but George didn't accept it, and Jimmy pushed forward. "Of course, guys like George proved ultimately to be too much even for something as magnificent as a tarpon. A triumph of men over beast, right George?" He tried again.

"Hey, don't ask me – or blame me," George finally shrugged. "*I've* never caught a tarpon. Better consult the expert." He held out his hand, palm up, toward Jackson.

"Sorry," Jackson said. "As impressed as I am with Jimmy's observations," he looked at Maggie, not at Jimmy, "I can't really comment. I'm not a hunter, or a fisherman. I don't get the urge he described – I never have, and doubt I ever will. Perhaps, I should apologize to the tarpon for not being worthy of him." Maggie sniffed, and rolled her eyes, but Jackson didn't let her speak. "That's what Ike McCaslin would say, right Jimmy?" He looked at his idol at the end of the table, as if he were stepping on his toes to see what they were made of. Without hesitation, Jimmy spoke back to him.

"You are right. No one you just described would be permitted to take a bear in his hunting camp. In fact, you might not even be allowed into the camp." He paused, and looked around the table for recognition in any of the other faces. Seeing none, Jimmy turned to Maggie and said: "It's from a Faulkner story, *The Bear*, but I don't care what Faulkner would think about this moment. I say this tarpon should feel honored." Jimmy raised his glass to Jackson, and the others joined him in a toast. Maggie was the first to put down her wine glass.

"Fish don't have feelings," Maggie made herself heard this time.

"Maybe not, but a tarpon actually breathes air," Jimmy responded. Maggie looked back at him blankly, not sure whether she understood the significance, so Jimmy explained. "You see, it has this internal sack that actually extracts oxygen from inhaled air like a lung. When it releases this sack, it emits a sound that is just like a human sigh, a sad one at that. I heard it from Jackson's tarpon. John Cole also said something like 'a fish that struggles to breathe as it senses its life is in danger stabs the conscience of your soul.'" Jimmy paused again, but with no response from his audience, he finally added, "I'm not sure if I would go quite that far, but feelings or no feelings, the tarpon definitely has spirit." Maggie began to nod her head, seemingly almost convinced, but then refused to concede.

"Sounds like Mr. Cole thinks about things as intently as Jackson does. Even so, Jackson can't be given much credit for just throwing his line in the water. What skill does that take?" Jackson looked down, knowing that she was simply repeating what he had said himself a few hours earlier, but somehow feeling diminished.

"Oh honey, be nice to your husband," Bette said.

"It's okay," Jackson spoke up, putting his arm around Maggie and leaning toward Jimmy. "We have agreed that we won't remind one another of our limitations, but we also encourage one another to remain humble. I accept her statement that I'm no fisherman." He touched Maggie's shoulder, and she smiled at Bette. "If anyone should be credited with this catch," Jackson concluded, "it's George. He was driving the boat; it was his rod; he was responsible for me even being there. Even more importantly, he *prophesied* that we would catch a tarpon. The fact that I was the one who reeled it in just makes his fish-guiding - and his prophecy - all the more impressive."

"I'll drink to that," Jimmy said, raising his wine glass, and the others followed.

"You'll drink to anything," George said to Jimmy, "but I will take credit for a fine day, and the start of what should be a pretty fun night." His bandito smile reappeared as all of them murmured "hear, hear," and toasted each other. The waiter appeared at just the right moment in the discussion to clear salad plates and serve the main course, blackened redfish, first to Maggie and Bette, and then to the men.

"Well, this is my favorite dish! Did Jackson put you up to this?" Maggie looked at George.

"Actually," Jimmy broke in, "this is my favorite dish, too. I heard this chef of George's is famous for his Cajun spices. I guess you and I will be the judge of that, now!" He picked up his fork and prepared to take a bite of fish, but then turned to Jackson. "So, Jackson, are you going to reveal the mystery, or just keep us in suspense?" His sincere tone surprised Jackson.

"What mystery? About the Cajun spices?"

"No, from this afternoon," Jimmy said.

"What mystery?" Jackson asked again. "I was just holding the pole – rod, I mean. You see. I can't hide the fact that it was dumb luck." He shrugged.

"Not the *fish*, man," Jimmy explained. "I *know* that was luck. I was there. I'm talking about this Habakkuk guy you were quoting."

Jackson looked at Maggie quickly, and they both seemed to ask for the second time that night, *is this real?* Jimmy didn't seem to notice. "I liked what you said he said." Jackson paused before answering, considering carefully whether he should accept Jimmy's invitation.

"Nah," he said, finally. "You don't really want to hear about that." He stopped, wondering if he should add 'Do you?' when George cut in.

"Come on, Jackie. You owe it to me. I don't know if Jimmy really wants to hear about it, but he would have anyway this afternoon if I hadn't cut you off. So, let him have it now." The whole table laughed as George threw his linen napkin down the table at Jimmy. Jackson looked at Maggie, who nodded her head as if to say 'you're on.' His mind raced, wondering again how he could have thought of this moment so many times without having actually thought of what to say when it finally came to pass.

"Haven't you guys figured it out?" He asked, to buy time.

"I haven't even thought about it," George shrugged.

"That's not true," Bette contradicted him. "You mentioned it to me this afternoon. I practically told you who Habakkuk was. Weren't you listening?" George looked puzzled. "*Parochial* school, remember?" Bette said. Still George stared blankly.

"Ah, I get that hint," Jimmy chimed in, sounding pleased with himself. "I thought the name sounded vaguely familiar. I went to Catholic schools myself, you know. Must be Old Testament," he said, cautiously.

"Correct," Bette said. "See, George, Jimmy is full of surprises just like you. How many people would expect him to identify a minor Old Testament prophet with only one hint?"

"Probably zero," Jimmy answered for himself. "I guess I haven't killed all the seeds the sisters planted in my brain."

"So, with that mystery resolved, what else can we talk about?" Jackson said, assuming with some relief that his opportunity had passed.

"Oh, I still want to hear about Habakkuk," Jimmy insisted, "and why you would associate me with him – or perhaps George – whichever you were thinking of." Again, Jackson looked at Maggie, and again she nodded. He then looked at Bette, who was smiling while smoking, and then finally at George, who looked back at him half-amused and half-amazed. Jimmy, at least, looked completely determined. "Well?" He insisted.

"If I must," Jackson sighed, and leaned forward to rest his elbows on the table. Dessert had been served, and he was the first to have finished the crème brulee. He pushed his plate toward the middle of the table as he began. "Habakkuk was a prophet of Israel in the 8th century B.C. Not much is known about him, personally, except that his name probably means "embraced by God." He is one of the so-called 'minor' prophets whose writings are part of the Jewish scriptures and the Christian Old Testament." He paused as he realized the rest of the table – the entire room – had grown very quiet.

"Go on," Jimmy said, seemingly aware that he was responsible for this discourse. "I'm following you. I just don't know where you're going." Jackson smiled slightly, and took a drink of water before continuing.

"This afternoon I told you how important your writing is to me. I gave you just a few examples. There are many more, but you're not the only writer I value."

"Really?" Jimmy said, mocking himself. Jackson put up his hand as if to say, 'but wait!'

"That's one of the things I love about your work – it is very self-confident." Everyone laughed, including Jimmy. "Anyway, if you are measuring yourself by my standards, you *would* be confident because I put you in my top three personal influences: one is my marriage (he put his arm around Maggie, and she lowered her head suppressing a smile. One is Scripture (that's where Habakkuk comes in), the other is literature, and that's where you and Faulkner come in.

"I've been dying to hear this," Bette exhaled. Jimmy, too, looked pleased.

"Hard for me to stop you now," he said. "Bette and I both want to hear it."

"Well, I've already told you about my comparison of your work with Faulkner's, and how I felt totally vindicated when "Somewhere Over China" came out. As you might expect, I didn't get a lot of agreement from others about the seriousness of your work – even if my English professor loved the idea, but there is the quote from *Mosquitoes*, right there on the album cover." Jimmy nodded. "And I got even more support from "No one speaks to the Captain." I recognized that title as a reference to Marquez even before I read the liner notes. The fact that you were getting inspiration from guys like Faulkner and Marquez was an indication that you had some substance behind the partying facade. That you even wrote songs about them added more weight to my ideas." Jimmy shook his head again, but this time more as an acknowledgment than assent. Jackson continued before Jimmy could speak. "But those are just personal connections. It doesn't make you a great writer or even a deep thinker, just because you've read a few books that some other people think are great. No, you begin to distinguish yourself, in my opinion, in your writing about personal relationships." Jimmy smirked, and spoke before Jackson could continue this time.

"I assume you're not talking about 'Why don't we get drunk."

"Of course, not," Jackson interrupted, "although there is a certain social reality about that song, if not actual Calvinism." Everyone laughed, more out of a desire to ease the mood than the merit of his humor, Jackson thought, but he refused to be distracted. "No, I'm talking about songs that – and forgive me if I get too personal here, or if I'm actually wrong - I'm talking about the songs that express your pain and longing for your relationship with your wife." Jackson paused only for a second as Jimmy looked quickly at George.

"Don't look at me," George said, raising both hands in front of him. "He's coming up with this all on his own."

"Absolutely," Jackson started up again. "I have not discussed this with George. You don't think he would actually sit and listen to it if you weren't here insisting on it?" Jimmy looked at George, as Jackson continued. "No, these opinions do not represent the views of my host, my wife or my new friend," he said, as he looked around the table.

"Or anyone else on the planet, most likely," George added,

but he gave Jackson his best smile and held out his hand as if to say, 'after you.' Jackson was not offended, and pressed on.

"Whether they're about your own personal life is not important, at least to us, at first. What is important at first is to recognize your ability to write about relationships, and the struggle we all have to make them work, and to learn from our mistakes. You understand that aspect of the human condition, and you convey it powerfully in some of these songs. Earlier this week I explained to Maggie how much I love *Riddles in the Sand*. Again, it's not important whether it's really about you; but you depict perfectly the struggles that many couples have had, and how hard it is to pull out of a downward spiral in a relationship once its begun. But you go even farther. You actually show that you can, and how to do it!

Of all the bridges I've ever crossed
High and lonesome and wild and lost
I feel this time we'll take it to the end
We don't care what the people may say
If there's a price it's the price we'll pay
And we'll burn that bridge when we come to it

Jackson actually tried to sing the words, but stopped midway through, and recited the rest after George started laughing.

"Yeah, I know, I'll never get Jimmy's job, but you can only laugh at my singing. You can't laugh at these words." Jackson kept his focus on Jimmy. "I love the line 'of all the bridges I've ever crossed, high and lonesome and wild and lost.' He could be talking about a place, but I think it is a metaphor for the situation, the trial they are facing, or he could even be describing the girl herself – probably is. What man hasn't known a girl like that – high, lonesome, wild and lost. For some reason we think we want someone like that." Maggie shifted in her chair, unable to avoid the suggestion that she was either like that, or not actually the woman Jackson wanted. "It's okay, sweetheart. I used to think that's what I wanted until I met you. You're definitely the bridge I needed, and you know I realized it immediately." Maggie seemed satisfied.

"This isn't about us, anyway, it's about him, right?" She pointed to Jimmy.

"It's at least about his art," Jackson said. When Jimmy remained silent, Jackson continued. "And then there is the conclusion that they'll 'burn that bridge when they come to it.' That's a great twist on a good take-off. He mixes the wisdom of not worrying about a chasm until you face it, and the mistake of burning metaphorical bridges that you may need some other time, to come up with a strategy, a resolve to burn through whatever future trial they have. It is a picture of extraordinary will to save this relationship." Jackson paused, not intending to stop, but sensing that it would probably be a good time to. Before he could actually decide to follow his intuition, Bette reached for another cigarette and spoke to Jimmy while performing her lighting motif.

"Mr. Buffett, I believe you've truly reached the big time," Bette said, as she struck her lighter and raised her hand, holding the flame before her face. "You've gotten serious critical attention." Jimmy leaned forward and managed a slight smile.

"Serious is right, but I don't think the real critics will agree," he said, in a serious tone.

"Real?" Bette scoffed. "You're telling me this isn't a real critical analysis?"

"Hey," Jackson interrupted yet again, "I don't need defending. I know I'm obsessive, and I agree with Jimmy. I can't be a real critic until I publish my views. Maybe I will someday, now that I've been able to tell you all about them. I thought I couldn't do it." He looked at Maggie and they exchanged smiles, then he added, "but it probably wouldn't count, because I'm obviously not objective."

"Objective or not, I'm impressed," Bette said, "even if Jimmy isn't."

"Hey, I didn't say that," Jimmy answered quickly. "I like what he's saying, it's just not what the reviewers usually comment about. I'd like to hear it more often."

"I think there are others who feel like I do," Jackson said, "but I can't point you to anything in writing. Of course, I could say more, if you can stand it." He looked anxiously at Jimmy.

"I think the question is if *they* can stand it." He waved at Bette, George and Maggie. Maggie and Bette both started to speak, but then both looked at George.

"Hey," George shrugged, "this is all my fault to begin with. How can I break up the party now?" Jackson smiled and leaned forward to begin again.

"And I really do owe you, George, but probably not as much as you owe Jimmy for subjecting him to this." He looked at Jimmy who shrugged, too. "Ok, I could talk all night. You've got, what, twenty albums out?" Jimmy nodded, but still didn't answer. "Anyway, staying with my focus on your beautiful songs that deal powerfully with pain in personal relationships, I have to talk about *Island*. A slight smile crossed Jimmy's face, but still he didn't speak, and Jackson continued. "If people would just listen to that one song and absorb the words, I wouldn't have any trouble convincing folks that you're a poet. I know you give credit to a co-writer, and I have no idea how these things come together or get credited, but even half-credit in this type of writing would merit notice. Obviously, it's based on John Donne's Meditation XVII." He stopped and looked around the table.

There were no looks of recognition. "'No man is an island unto himself'?" Jackson stated with a question-mark. Heads nodded. "I thought you'd recognize that. You'd also recognize another phrase that appears in this devotion – it was written as a church sermon, you know." Again he was met with blank stares around the table, until his eyes met Jimmy.

"'Ask not for whom the bell tolls,'" Jimmy said quietly. "I've always wanted to write a song about that, but it's just too associated with Hemingway. And, as you've noted, I'm more of a Faulkner guy anyway."

"That's funny," Jackson said, "I've never thought about it until now, but you would think, with your persona, you would be more drawn to Hemingway than Faulkner. I'll have to think about that some more."

"That's just what you need to do," Maggie said.

"Ok, I said I only wanted to mention this one other song," Jackson defended himself. "Jimmy starts from a known truth – that we can't live our lives separately from everyone and everything else – and then proceeds to establish that a woman exists, someone he loves, who has done just that, at least when it comes to their relationship." He glanced over at Jimmy, whose expression had not changed. "Maybe I'm wrong about that – there is no mention of the island being a woman – but it sure makes sense to me, and you dedicated it to your wife in the liner notes. I think back to 'high and lonesome and wild and lost,' and assume you have to be talking about the same thing, or same person." This time Jimmy couldn't contain a smile.

"You can make that connection if you want," he said.

"I want," Jackson said, looking at Maggie, "but even if it wasn't a woman you were writing about, the idea is profound. Whatever it is you're trying to obtain, you've been frustrated and stopped.

I tried to book passage, but you have no ports
And I tried to sail in but your wind and waters have
Torn my sails and broken my oars.

Island, I see you in the moonlight
Silhouettes of ships in the night
Just make me want that much more

"Sure, this could be written about any desire or goal that a person has," Jackson said, "but I think the chorus gives us the real context."

When the need for love, heart and soul accompaniment,
no longer make me different from you.

Comparing his personal need for love to an inanimate object's absence of need makes sense, but commenting that a person he is longing for has no such need, as if she is an inanimate object, is more powerful. Consider that she has no ports and that her winds and waters have torn his sails and broken his oars, and you've got a perfect picture of a broken relationship that can't be healed. Add the image of 'silhouettes of ships in the night' – obviously passing, not meeting or even colliding – and you've got a traditionally powerful metaphor for a relationship that can't work."

Jackson stopped and looked down at the table, allowing his eyes to glaze. "It's just a beautiful song, a poem really, and devastating in its treatment of the subject – whatever or whoever she might be. It certainly leaves me with sympathy for the speaker. He has a deep longing for her that he's trying to fulfill, and it's not happening. Of course, maybe you all would observe that he should just stop beating his head against the rock, so to speak."

"That idea crossed my mind," George said. Bette punched him.

"Hush up, and let the man finish," she insisted. "You admitted that this was your idea."

"Thanks," Jackson said, "but I probably shouldn't go down that path after all we've covered already.

"Oh, why not?" Bette protested. "I'm loving this, and not just because I know George is hating it," she punched him again. "I don't know what Jimmy and Maggie are thinking." She noticed Jimmy and Maggie exchange looks, before Maggie spoke.

"I'm hearing it all for the first time, just like you guys." Maggie said. "I always learn more about my husband when he's talking to other people." Jackson rolled his eyes, but shrugged at the same time, expressing guilt and dissatisfaction. Finally, Jimmy spoke, quietly without inflection.

"So, what should the speaker in this song do, if not stop beating his head against the rocks?" He asked. Jackson looked at Maggie and despite her previous rebuke, she gave him a smile that said 'answer the man.' Jackson followed orders.

"I think the answer is in Donne's meditation. I can't quote it exactly, but he says something like 'tribulation is a treasure, whether it is another's or our own.' He thinks it causes us to reflect on the source of our deliverance, and this part I can quote – 'secure myself by making my recourse to my God, who is our only security.'" He paused and again no one responded or even flinched. Jackson pressed on, more emphatically than before. "That is the one element of your work that I had not seen – one that I was not looking for at first, but which recently I have become very interested in finding." He looked at Maggie and paused. For the fourth time she nodded, encouraging him. Before he could continue, Jimmy turned to her and spoke.

"Do you know what he's talking about?"

"This time, yes," she answered immediately.

"Do tell," Bette quipped, as she lit yet another cigarette,

then pushed her dessert plate toward the center of the table. As she exhaled, Jackson noticed the smoke reflecting the candlelight, smelled the sweet tobacco scent, and thought of what an appropriate setting this was for this discussion.

"I'm talking about a sense of spirituality – not just depth of thought and meaning. Obviously, I think you've got depth. You've written these and many other beautiful, powerful songs – poems. Poet. That's what I think you are, and maybe I've convinced this audience, at least." Jimmy smiled broadly this time, actually appearing to be embarrassed, but Jackson continued. "But I just can't stop there. There are many writers in this world who are thoughtful and profound. What I want to see, though, is whether they can tackle the biggest riddle. Does their writing reflect any curiosity about God, or their relationship with Him?"

Jimmy leaned back in his chair, separating himself from Jackson, but still Jackson did not stop. "You may flinch and be uncomfortable – you may even disagree with me - but I'm certain that I've found God in your writing – from the very first song you released, right through to the latest album." Jimmy started to speak, and Jackson knew he had to let him, but he decided to direct him. "Tell them the name of the first song on your first album."

"The Christian," Jimmy admitted reluctantly, adding quickly, "but it's not what you think."

"I know," Jackson interrupted, "it is a cynical attack on religion as it was shown to you growing up and – maybe – as you have observed as an adult. But my question to you – and to anyone I get to have this conversation with - famous or not – is whether your conclusions about Christianity come from an investigation *of your own?* As a lawyer, I would ask if you have actual knowledge, or whether you have adequate qualifications to support your expert conclusion?" He paused again, but knew that Jimmy didn't want to answer this question, and he decided not to make him. "That's why I quoted Habakkuk."

"I was wondering when we were ever going to get around to him," George interrupted.

"I told you where this was coming from," Bette joined in. "and you asked him to go ahead. We just took an extended detour through Jimmy's life work – or life's work to this point. Go on, Jackson." She spoke with an authoritative tone, that was punctuated as she leaned forward and smashed out her cigarette in her dessert plate. Jackson hesitated, but Jimmy agreed.

"Oh yeah, I can take it if they still can," Jimmy said. Only Maggie acted as if she wanted to offer encouragement, but then didn't.

"Okay," Jackson began again. "Out there today George kept talking about us catching a tarpon. It was just talk, of course, but considering the miracle of the circumstances – that I was fishing with Jimmy Buffett – the *idea* of catching a tarpon didn't seem so outrageous. Of course, I hardly knew what a tarpon was, and have just learned that it is so rare and coveted, even in a place that bears its name. Anyway, this combination of events, and the need to think of some way to engage you in conversation beyond just saying that I am an obsessed groupie, somehow brought me to Habakkuk." Jackson paused again, but still sensing and hearing no objection to his commentary, quickly continued. "As I said, he was a Jewish prophet who wrote one of the books of the Bible that practically no one reads – even those who study Scripture regularly - he glanced at Maggie - but he said some amazing things, both prophetically and poetically, about the Jews and God's plan for them as a people. I think his words can still be applied today, to the Jews, to us and, yes, even to you, Jimmy. The passage I quoted is in Chapter 1, verse 5, where the prophet declares on behalf of God: 'Look at the nations and watch, and be utterly amazed. For I am going to do something in your days that you would not believe even if you were told.' That's the NIV translation – New International Version – translated from the original Hebrew." He directed the explanation to George and then looked back at Jimmy. "You said this sounded like something you might have said to some people in Nashville." Jimmy nodded and almost smiled, but instead smirked. He didn't speak, so Jackson continued. "I'm guessing that you were thinking of some record producers who told you that you would never make it in their business – or who maybe didn't even take the time to tell you that, but just ignored you completely."

"You guessed right," Jimmy said.

"That would be an appropriate use of the quote," Jackson continued, "as a response to someone who has wronged you. In fact, that is sort of the usage God had in mind, but in a slightly weightier context. He was referring to the fact that He was going to use the Chaldeans to attack and almost destroy the Jews – not just let the heathen army conquer His chosen people, but *cause* them to do it, because of the Jews' disobedience. Do you know who the Chaldeans were?" Jimmy stared blankly.

"Babylonians," Bette said quietly.

"Very good!" Jackson complimented Bette. "And do you know who was the Babylonian king at this time?"

"Nebuchadnezzar," Bette answered again, followed by a long exhale of smoke.

"Excellent! We really need to offer a toast to your Sisters, but before we do here's the bonus question: "Who thinks he's Nebuchadnezzar today?"

"Saddam Hussein," Bette said, as she aggressively stamped out yet another cigarette, visually expressing disgust at the person.

"Obviously, it's not just your parochial education we should toast. You have stayed up on current affairs. Well, done! George, you certainly hang around with some fascinating folks." George nodded his head in a mock bow.

"Anyway," Jackson continued yet again, "think about that information for a minute, in a modern context: God affirmatively stating that he is going to use someone like Saddam Hussein to discipline the Jews. Does that sound incredible? Then think about the fact that someone predicts such a thing and it actually happens! The Babylonians did, in fact, attack Judah, the southern kingdom in Israel, first in 605 B. C. and then again in 586 B.C., destroying the temple and most of Jerusalem. Now, apart from wanting to kill the messenger who predicted this, you would also not want to believe that this was what God intended, right? There are many principles that can be derived from that one statement, but the main one is that God is at work in the world, whether or not he affirmatively announces His intentions. He sometimes - if not *always* - uses means that we would not expect. Consequently, we don't think to look for God in most events – certainly not unpleasant ones like the sacking of Jerusalem and the exile of the Jews. Oh, some will ask 'where was God?' But most will not accept the notion that He was present – Heaven forbid that he could have directed the scene – no pun intended. I've been trying to understand this for some time now – trying to remember to look for God everywhere, particularly where *I* want to be. I *want* to listen to Jimmy's music, just like I want to read Faulkner, and watch baseball. In fact, Maggie will tell you I have a *compulsion* to do these things, at least baseball and Jimmy." This time Maggie smirked, but she nodded her head in confirmation, and Jackson explained further. "If I feel compelled to do these things, then I must find something good in them, right? It only makes sense that I would want God to be present in them. That would mean that my desire is okay – approved by Him." He recognized a plaintive tone in this last statement, and decided it was time to take a break. His extended pause caused the others to shift in their seats, until Jimmy finally spoke.

"I think I follow you," he said cautiously, as if he really didn't want to. "You like my music, but you want it to be okay with God that you do, so you are looking for some kind of redeeming value. Sounds like a rationalization to me. I can see the good in Faulkner, of course. I share your affection for him. Baseball's okay, too, but I'm not an idealist about it. Of course, I could share your affection for Maggie, but that would be impolite." Maggie grinned, but didn't speak. "But, as to my stuff, I think I'm losing you there. You mentioned my first song, 'The Christian.' Sure, that's the title, but like you said, it ain't a hymn." He paused, not wanting to explain, but also not sure he should yield the floor back to Jackson. "Have you really listened to it?" He asked in his own plaintive tone.

"Of course, I have," Jackson said. "I know you are being cynical and critical of the behavior of Christians, but that doesn't require the conclusion that Christianity is worthless. Did you quit the music industry just because it was being run by a bunch of…" Jackson stopped before using a term he did not usually employ. The circumstances could have justified it, but he caught himself, not wanting to go outside of his character, or to undercut his observation about religion. Jimmy said the word, and then continued.

"We all know what they are, even if you're too good to say it. But you've got a point. I didn't quit."

George, Maggie and Bette again shifted in their seats, noting that Jackson had just scored points in the debate, if it was a debate. Regardless, the three of them seemed to decide collectively to remain spectators.

"Okay," Jackson began again. "Consider that fact while I

go back to Habakkuk. He heard from God that He was going to use the Jews' enemy – a pagan enemy, even – to practically destroy them. What should he do with that information? Get mad? Be bitter? Try to get the Jews to change?"

"All of the above?" Jimmy offered.

"I think so," Jackson replied emphatically. "In your first song you criticize others by saying 'You've been acting like Jesus owes you a favor, but he's too smart for you to fool.' If you think Jesus is too smart for others to fool, I assume you would agree that the same applies to you?" Jackson paused yet again, trying to determine if the realization had ever hit Jimmy before. If so, he did not show it, so Jackson pressed on. "Did you give them (or yourself) an alternative? You can't just do nothing since you feel something, and that's just what Habakkuk did. He argued with God about whether this was the best strategy for reaching the Jews, but eventually he accepted it. And that's what this quote is about – the sovereignty of God. He is present in all things, and His will *will* be accomplished. Later, Habakkuk concludes that 'The earth will be filled with the knowledge of God, as the waters cover the sea.' - a poetic promise that, believe it or not, brings me back to your music. I said today that the message I hear in your music is not just a search for a deeper meaning, but a longing for and an expectation of fulfillment. All your fans feel that they can have fun listening to you, but I believe I can have a better life, that there is a joy – a satisfaction –," he looked at George and smiled, "I can get from life if I just chose to do so. Whether you realize it or not, that is a very hopeful message. "'Mother, Mother, ocean, I have heard you call,'" is a really *Christian* message.

"Hmm." Jimmy leaned forward and appeared flustered. "You're telling me I'm a Gospel singer? Now you're going from rationalization to blasphemy."

"No, I'm not saying you are - yet. I'm suggesting that

there is an element of spirituality in your music. We haven't even begun to talk about the Gospel." Jimmy sank back in his chair. "Jimmy, people like your music for essentially one reason – it gives them an escape from their burdens. As I said this afternoon, most people experience this by getting drunk and dancing around with thousands of other like-minded people."

"Like parrots," George finally spoke, but Jackson ignored him.

"Some of us, and I bet there are more than you think, achieve this sense of peace just listening to your songs. The melodies are fun, and the phrases are like poetry, but most importantly, the *feeling* they evoke together is profound. We've talked about only a couple of the songs you've written. There are dozens more; and I'm not talking about the party songs. I'm talking about your serious ones. Every fan knows 'Come Monday' and 'A Pirate Looks at Forty' and 'He Went to Paris.' Most know 'The Captain and the Kid' and 'Havana Daydreamin.' Some know 'Son of a Son of Sailor' and 'One Particular Harbor.' But what about 'Cowboy in the Jungle' or 'Distantly in Love' or 'Wonder why we ever go Home' or 'That's what Living is to me', or 'If the Phone Doesn't Ring;' or 'Biloxi;' or 'Death of an Unpopular Poet.' That one goes way back to your beginning. These are great songs, poems actually, with messages worthy of Yeats or Frost, not just Faulkner or Marquez. 'I can't help but be ruled by inconsistency, not unique, just distantly in love.' 'Years grow shorter, not longer, the more you've been on your own. Feelings for movin' grow stronger, so you wonder why you ever go home.' 'The stories from my favorite books still take on many different looks, and I'm gone again, home again.' That's Chatwin's "Songlines." Some humans only feel at home on the road, but the reality is that all humans are on the road, whether they know it or not. That's what your music conveys. I could name lots more songs and lines where you prove that. They sound like Scripture to me, and they have the same effect. They provoke me to reflection, they inspire me to action. They make me want to live better than I do. All of this is the function of Scripture, wouldn't you say?"

Jimmy didn't respond, but only continued the blank stare that had formed shortly after Jackson had launched his final assault. "Well," Jackson continued, "whether you want to admit it or not, you are an instrument in the hands of God. The question to me is whether you are going to be Nebuchadnezzar, destroying God's people, or are you going to be someone like John the Baptist, a voice crying in the wilderness, which, of course, brings me to the New Testament.

"Waiter!" George called, breaking the stunned silence. "Can we get some espresso? Better make it doubles. This is obviously going to take a while longer." Undeterred, Jackson continued.

"Habakkuk's very words come up again about seven hundred years later. Think about that, too. Wouldn't you like for someone to be singing your songs seven hundred years from now? And here we are still talking about him two thousand years after that! If words survive for 2,700 years, I'm guessing we are supposed to pay attention to them. Anyway, in the 1st century A.D., another prophet, at least I would call him a prophet, says these same words to the Jews again." Jackson stopped and looked at Bette.

"You've got me this time," she conceded.

"It's Paul. You know, the former Pharisee Saul who became the apostle to the Gentiles, and took all the missionary journeys. On his second one, he crossed over from Asia into Europe where there were more Jews to oppose him. By then the enmity between Jews and Christians was building, and Paul was the focal point. After all, he used to be the chief persecutor of Christians on behalf of the Jews. I like to describe his conversion as if Madeline Murray O'Hare had become the president of the PTL Club. Anyway, Paul came to a place called Pisidian Antioch, where there was a large Jewish population. We know this because they actually had a synagogue there. He went to the synagogue and started preaching about Jesus. The Jews got angry because they didn't accept Jesus as the Jewish Messiah. They started to seize Paul and maybe stone him, when he quoted Habakkuk, only this is how it is translated this time: 'Look, you scoffers, wonder and perish, for I am going to do something in your days that you would never believe even if someone told you.' I love that slight paraphrase. Paul does that a lot, altering or splicing quotes to get his effect - a lot like songwriting, I'd bet," he added, as his own aside to Jimmy. "You've got two choices: either accept the truth of the Gospel Paul has revealed, or continue to wonder about it - meaning not accept it - and perish."

"Hey! That's the name of your law firm." George interjected, sounding skeptical, but also as if he wanted to change the subject.

"Yeah," Jackson said, "kind of a weird coincidence. Different spelling, of course, but maybe there's a connection. I haven't really thought about it before."

"That's hard to believe," George said, with a shake of his head. Jackson looked at him for a moment before he shrugged, then turned back to Jimmy and continued.

"Anyway, Paul is focusing here on the consequences of just wondering but never deciding – not the consequences of actively disobeying, like in Habakkuk's time. He's challenging the Jews to see what they are missing." Suddenly, George stood up and let out a short cry. Jackson stopped his explanation of the Gospel, realizing that George and the others could not listen while he was reacting to the espresso the waiter had just poured in his lap.

XXXIV

"Ouch," George added to his exclamation, but without as much conviction. Bette stood up, too, and started to wipe away the excess liquid, but stopped herself just before touching her napkin to the front of George's pants.

"Did it burn you?" She asked instead.

"No, but these are my favorite pants." He shook his legs, and then shimmied his whole body, his happy demeanor already starting to return. "Actually, these are my only pants," he added, finishing with a wide grin. "Of course, they would be white."

"Well, they're two-toned now," Jimmy chirped, his tone definitely lightened by George's mishap.

"I'm very sorry, sir," the waiter said. Just then, the owner came from the kitchen, finally making his previously announced appearance.

"Ah, George, that's not the way I wanted your meal to end. You must let me dry clean your pants. If it doesn't come out, I'll replace them, of course."

"Fair enough," George shrugged. "That's all we can do for now," he added, as he sat back down.

"Oh, George can afford a new pair of pants," Bette scowled. "You ought to make him buy them himself for ending our fine conversation, not to mention blaspheming the Lord's name." She mimed the sign of the cross. "Anyway, you must be Christopher," she said turning back to the owner.

"Yes, I am, thank you," the small man said, appearing relieved. "It seems too late to ask if you enjoyed your meal," he added, yet with a trace of hopefulness in his voice.

"Nonsense," Jimmy answered. "It was a fine meal. George wetting his pants can't dampen the enjoyment for us. It probably enhanced it." No one contradicted him. "Your fish was excellent, by the way. The spices were sharp, but overall the dish was light."

"Certainly lighter than the conversation," George observed, shifting in his chair, and adjusting the wet fabric in his lap.

"Well, I hope you enjoyed yourself, all of you, and that you will come again," Christopher said. "Oh, by the way George, there is a photographer in the office who would like to come over to take a picture."

"Hey, I thought we kept this a secret," Jimmy interrupted in complaint. "I didn't want any publicity." Christopher looked slightly embarrassed.

"You'll forgive me, Mr. Buffett, but I believe the photographer is looking for this gentleman," he gestured at Jackson, "the one who caught the important fish." Now Jimmy looked embarrassed.

"I guess you beat me again, Jackson," he admitted.

"What do you say, Jackie? Seems to me a front page picture showing me to be incontinent would be a fitting end to this day." George started to rise again.

"I guess I can stand in front of you," Jackson offered, as he, too, stood up.

"Fine with me," George said. "Let's go over there and leave Jimmy to ponder your preaching – I mean philosophizing – or whatever you were just doing." Jackson looked over at Maggie, who answered his unspoken question.

"You go ahead," she said. "Bette and I will stay here and keep Jimmy company, if that's alright with him."

"You're kidding, right?" Jimmy said with excitement. "Don't you mean if it's alright with him?" He pointed up at Jackson.

"We can handle you, don't worry," Maggie said, looking at Bette. "Besides, you probably need me and Bette to explain to you what Jackson just said." Jackson rolled his eyes slightly.

"In that case, I'm definitely going with Jackie," George said. He turned to Christopher. "This guy's in the office? How did he know we were here?"

"This *lady* is in the office," he corrected George, "and she said that she was at the dock for the weigh-in and a young man told her to look for you here."

"Ah. That would have been Eddie." He went over to the French door and opened it slightly. Without fully pulling back the curtain, he let Jackson slide past him through the door, and then looked back and pointed his finger at Jimmy.

"Don't you mess with my friend's wife," he said firmly, but softly, so that Jackson did not hear.

"George!" Maggie protested. "I can take care of myself."

"And aren't you worried about me?" Bette called in protest, as George pulled the door closed behind him. He could hear muffled laughter from behind the curtains as he walked across the veranda and down the steps to join Jackson, who stood alone in the courtyard. It was now quite dark, with all of the lights from the cottage blocked by the curtains, and only one light from the Inn still lit.

"That was some speech you made in there," he said to Jackson.

"He asked to hear it," Jackson replied, confidently George thought.

"You're right, but I'd be shocked if he understood it. No offense, but you're a bit deep for guys like me and him. I don't think that deeply about the Good Book, and I can't believe anyone thinks that deeply about Jimmy's music – even Jimmy." Jackson laughed, not offended at all.

"You may be right. When you've been thinking about these things for as long as I have, you can't help but be deep, but also not surprised if it sounds silly to others. Truthfully, I didn't even know what I was going to say. I just sort of made it up as I went along. Hope I didn't ruin the evening."

"No," George said, as he slapped Jackson's back. "Jimmy seemed to like it. Just don't let me forget to tip that waiter for spilling the espresso on me, ok?"

"Understood," Jackson answered, as they started across the courtyard to the back door of the office.

"This should be fun," George said, opening the screen door. "I hope she brought the weight. Can't believe you didn't want to stick around for that." George said.

"Why should I? I don't know what an impressive weight is. I have no context for it."

"There you go again. You keep talking like that, and I'm going to send you back to those Dallas judges." This time he patted Jackson on the backside, telling him with the slap that he was serious but not malicious. They both entered the office from the back door, and were surprised and startled by the brightly lit room. A movie-set spotlight had been set up in the corner, casting a very white glow across the faded furnishings, and reflecting off the glass case serving as the front desk. The shadows cast by the three dimensions of the scaling walls made Jackson feel even more uncomfortable than he had in his first encounter. The place now felt like the *inside* of a fish.

"Here he is," Scottie growled, as Jackson stopped in the middle of the room, "the fisherman of the week."

"Hey, this doesn't happen every week!" George called from behind him. A young woman came out from the corner where the light was clipped to a tripod, and held out her hand to Jackson.

"I'm Molly Fletcher, editor of the *Jetty Caller*. Normally my husband takes the pictures, but he's at a convention. He's going to be really mad that he missed this. I got some great shots of the tarpon at the dock." She paused, apparently waiting for Jackson to speak. When he didn't, she looked past him and added, "Hello, George. I might have known that you would have a hand in this." For the third time, George tried to wave off the accusation.

"I'm just a witness to history," he shrugged.

"That's for sure, considering how long it's been since we've seen a tarpon around here," Molly answered. "And the weight, well that's just amazing; but I guess as a journalist I shouldn't be surprised when history repeats itself." George and Jackson looked at each other uncertainly. George asked the question they were both thinking.

"What was the weight? It didn't look like a record fish to me, but I've not seen many tarpons, of course." Molly first looked at them blankly, and then her face brightened with excitement.

"You're not going to believe this." She walked over to the glass counter and gingerly picked up a tarpon scale. "It's a record of sorts, that's for sure," she added, as she held it out to George. He took it from her carefully, holding it between his thumb and forefinger like a laboratory slide. George held it up to the spotlight, and saw the expected writing on its underside. Jackson, too, could see the numbers through the scale, but his signature was not yet there, of course. He moved around behind George and read over his shoulder. 77 lbs., 8 oz. He and George looked at one another. Jackson had no context, so George spoke.

"A nice fish, but that's no record. I don't get it," he said. Molly chuckled.

"I guess I shouldn't have expected you to. You're no historian." She said, as she walked around behind the counter and reached in to remove a similar scale, but one encased in clear plastic, like a paperweight. "Look at this," she insisted, as she handed it to George in the same gingerly fashion as she had given him Jackson's. She took Jackson's back from him in the same manner, but still held it out so that Jackson and George could compare them. They repeated the act of reading the numbers, first through the plastic covering of a true historical archive of a U.S. President: *Franklin D. Roosevelt, 77 lbs.* 8 oz., and then at Jackson's scale held in the light by Molly.

"Habakkuk was right. I don't believe it," George said to Jackson.

"This is somebody's joke," Jackson said, as he turned back to Molly. "Either you're playing a joke on us, or someone's playing a joke on you."

"You're right to think so, but I was there for the weighing myself. I can verify your weight. It wasn't until I came over here looking for you that we discovered the coincidence. Scottie gets credit for that. She looked at your scale and realized it right away." Jackson looked at Scottie, waiting for her to admit that this was a prank. She shook her head.

"I guess working in this office and looking through the glass at that scale for ten years has finally come to something," she said, and beamed proudly, as if she had caught the fish or become a historian herself. "I recognized the number right away." Molly turned again to Jackson.

"I guess your name is going to be linked with Tarpon and President Roosevelt for a long time. Once you sign your name, Scottie wants to keep your scale in the case with the President's, if that's okay with you. I have the light set up so I can get a good shot of you autographing the scale on the glass counter, with the President's below." She set Jackson's scale on the counter for him to sign. Then, suddenly she asked him a surprising question, not like a reporter usually asked. "By the way, who *are* you?"

XXXV

Maggie and Bette looked at each other like high school girlfriends about to ask the same boy to the dance.

"Maybe I'm the one who needs protection," Jimmy had said to Maggie, as George had closed the door on them. "George always thinks the worst of me," he now added, directing the comment to Bette.

"I'm not sure he would consider it 'bad,' but I think it is interesting that you do," Bette said, lighting another cigarette. "Is that a guilty conscience reawakening in you?" Jimmy looked at them both before answering.

"Truthfully, it's never left me." He smiled sheepishly, and then added, "You won't tell anyone, will you? Especially your husband." He touched Maggie on her bare shoulder. She was startled.

"Why not?" She asked. "He'd be encouraged."

"That's why. He might come back with some more of his theology." There was no criticism in his voice, but Maggie still felt that she needed to defend Jackson.

"I don't think he was preaching, do you Bette?"

"No." Bette exhaled a smoke ring in Jimmy's direction. "Sounded to me like a divine critique of your life's work – and a favorable one."

"You could say that," Jimmy conceded. "Parts of it I liked. Some of it I even understood."

"Oh, I don't believe that," Maggie said. "You're the only one around the table other than Jackson who has read all that stuff he was talking about – except for Bette's Bible knowledge. But, he's not getting his observations about you from the Bible. He's making comments about the Scripture based on your writing! You understood that, and I think it scares you."

"Right," Bette said, this time without smiling, joining forces with Maggie. Jimmy leaned back in his chair again, as she continued. "I've been waiting to hear Jackson's testimonial about you, and now, I have to say, it was pretty convincing. I honestly didn't think he could make you a serious artist, but he just may have. Close enough, anyway." She cocked her head, blew smoke and winked at Maggie, not trying to hide it from Jimmy. After a pause, Jimmy leaned forward again.

"This is definitely not the kind of evening I was expecting – or am used to. I don't know whether you two are confused, or just me."

"If Jackson were here, I know what he would say." Maggie started singing the chorus of the title track of one of Buffett's most popular albums, and Bette finished with her.

"You turn my very words against me," Jimmy protested.

"You see what I mean! There you are quoting Dickens while trying to convince us that the conversation was over your head," Bette insisted.

"Literature I can handle. I'm just not comfortable with religious discussions, I'm afraid," Jimmy responded.

"I'm not sure you would want to be Ebenezer Scrooge, in either case," Bette observed. "But tell me, what was it about those Catholic schools that spooked you so much? You seem to have been hit pretty hard by the experience."

"You, too?" Jimmy asked. "I can't seem to get away from

religion with you guys around." Neither Maggie nor Bette laughed. Bette gave him a blank stare, and then turned up her hand, still cocked, with a cigarette between the middle and index fingers, saying 'So?' as emphatically as with any voice she could affect. Jimmy understood. "Alright, maybe I'm a little militant against the church, but you went through it; you know all about the guilt thing and the hypocrisy. Not the Sisters, though. I mean, they were strict disciplinarians, but at least they were sincere. It was the priests that I couldn't stand. They gave us all these lectures about how we had to live our lives, and you could tell that they didn't practice any of it themselves, or, at least, didn't believe much of it." He paused, and Bette exhaled smoke in his direction.

"Exactly what kind of lecture did they give you?" She asked. Jimmy looked at her respectfully, but did not answer immediately. She doubted that he would answer her at all, but after a moment he did.

"First, I would say the whole confession thing. I mean, didn't you feel stupid going into that booth and telling all your impure thoughts to a guy that you know had the same thoughts about your sister?" He paused, and then realized the gender difference, but Bette didn't wait for a correction.

"Having the thoughts was one thing, acting on them would be another," she said, and Jimmy laughed out loud.

"That's not what Jimmy Carter said, and I think he was quoting Jesus."

"True enough," Bette allowed, "but that doesn't seem to be what bothered you about the process."

"You're right, there. It wasn't even the principles, it was more the … process." Jimmy seemed to have just discovered the word. "Yes, that's a good word for it," he convinced himself. "We would go into this box and drop our sins like our parents used to go into an outhouse and drop their, well, you know what I mean." He looked down, actually starting to be embarrassed, Bette thought.

"Oh, I get the picture," Bette said, "and it's a pretty good analogy, but did you ever think about the fact that you really did need to be accountable for what you had done – perhaps even to a sanitation worker?" Jimmy looked at her intently for an instant, but didn't speak, so she continued. "You see, I had a lot of the same feelings you just expressed – in fact, I had exactly the same thought – that the whole thing was a bunch of, well, you know. But, as I've gotten older I've begun to rethink things. It started when I had my own kids, and Bob and I agreed that they should be exposed to religion. We weren't going to force them to believe it, but we didn't want them to be completely ignorant of it. I suggested the Catholic Church, of course, but Bob wouldn't have anything to do with it. He grew up Baptist, and you can just imagine what those preachers would have done if I had walked into their revival meeting." She paused and smiled a little, wishing that she had done just that. "Anyway," she continued, after checking that Jimmy was still listening, "we settled on the Episcopal Church. Have you ever been in one?" Jimmy shook his head. "Well, you should. I know it's got its issues, but it will be familiar to you. I-"

"Hey" Jimmy interrupted her, "I don't know how we got into this discussion, but I wasn't exactly looking for recommendations on where to go to church. I'm not likely to follow them even if you give me some." He said this without insult, Bette thought, so she wasn't discouraged from pressing him further.

"You don't have to take me up on it, I know. You don't even have to go to church. But, I think we got into this discussion because I heard some excessive criticism in your voice, and Jackson found it in your song. What was it Shakespeare said? – 'methinks you doth protest too much'?"

"Hamlet's mother says that, objecting to the actor playing a queen who has married her brother-in-law after he murdered his brother, her husband," Jimmy said. "Not exactly applicable to this topic, I would say."

"You see, you're still blowing your cover with all this literary knowledge. Jackson's right, you know, you are a serious artist – but you're either having too much fun as a pop star, or you're too scared to be open about wanting to be taken seriously. You've got to use another persona to protect the real you." Bette stopped quickly, unsure if she had gone too far. Jimmy smacked the table with his hand, but smiled again.

"That's it! This is really more than any rock star should have to endure - or pop or country – whatever kind of star I am. You guys are supposed to be in awe of me. Why are you giving me all this religious psychological stuff? I already paid my analyst thousands of dollars for that. I don't need any more of it – even for free – especially, not for free."

"Well," Bette said, "that's only true if what you're getting from your analyst is any good. I, for one, think we are giving you some pretty good stuff here – which brings me back to your earlier question. We are having this conversation because I think you should look at religion again. I even think you *want* to, and you *know* you should." She reached down under the table and pulled out her purse, but instead of her cigarette case, this time she withdrew a small black leather-bound book with gilt-edged pages. "Here," she said, "look at this." Jimmy gasped.

"Are you going to actually *read* Scripture to me? First Jackson quotes it, and now you pull out the actual book and hit me with it?"

"Now, stop it," Bette snapped. "This is not a Bible, it's a prayer book – The Book of Common Prayer – written in the 16th Century by the men who founded the Anglican Church.

You've probably heard that it was founded on Henry VIII's bed – that was the official teaching of the Catholic Church, as I recall – but there were actually some pretty devout men who guided the king in his break with the pope. One of them, Thomas Cranmer, wrote this prayer book to be used during services, and as a devotional." She began flipping through the thin, delicate pages. "He also wrote out the principles that the church founders believed. Sort of like a creed or doctrinal statement. They are called the 'Articles of Religion.'" She found the page she was searching for near the back of the little book, and laid it open on the table. The fine leather cover and soft binding let it rest open, reverently, before Jimmy. The type, though quite small, was in bold print, and Bette read aloud without having to bend near to the page:

'*There was never any thing by the wit of man so well devised, or so sure established, which in continuance of time hath not been corrupted....*'"

"What makes you associate that thought with me?" Jimmy asked, in a tone that suggested he already knew the answer.

"Because you're a smart man," Bette said firmly, knowing that this was not the answer Jimmy was anticipating. "You're a smart man, who I think is still interested in religion, but not the kind he got as a boy. I think if you study these Articles, you'll see that you were led astray when you were a kid. It's not about confession booths, beads or candles, or even priests and the Pope. It's about faith, and it's about destiny." Jimmy sat back, and Bette assumed he was shocked. "You see," she said, "you are looking for your destiny just like the rest of us. You're probably less sure that yours is as a rock-country-pop star than I am sure mine is as a housewife. It's worth a little more study, particularly now that you've admitted you're smart enough to understand it for yourself." Jimmy leaned forward, again shaking his head.

"That's slick. You get me to agree that I'm smart, and

then make me feel like I'm stupid if I don't want to make an informed decision about religion. Very slick."

"Inspired, I would say," Maggie finally interjected. Bette smiled back, but quickly returned her focus to Jimmy.

"Just remember that the people who taught you religion could have been just as wrong as the ones who said you would never make it in the music business," Bette continued. "Why shouldn't the same principle apply here? Better find out for yourself, before you become a truly tragic figure." She closed the little black book and handed it to him. To her surprise, he accepted it.

"Sometimes I feel like a tragic figure," Jimmy said, and then paused. Maggie thought he was waiting to see if the admission caused any laughter. It didn't. "I've had a lot of success, sure, but I've let it get in the way of some important things in my life." He paused again, and Maggie found herself wanting him to continue, but then hoping he wouldn't. "There is no way to say this without sounding cliché, or even pathetic, but being famous is not all it's cracked up to be."

"Yes, I'd say that is a cliché," Bette drawled, as she stamped out another cigarette.

"And I know pathetic when I hear it," Maggie said, "but I don't think either Bette or I are qualified to argue your exact point."

"I'm not looking for your sympathy," Jimmy responded first to Maggie and then looked to Bette. "I pay a shrink for that. I would just like for some people to understand that it is not all margaritas and sambas. There are downers that go along with the highs." He stopped again, looking this time as if he meant to.

"I'll accept that," Bette replied, "but remember that Scrooge changed. Although his name is still associated with 'Bah, Humbug!', the story actually ends with the news that no one kept Christmas in their heart all year round better than

Ebenezer Scrooge." Bette then stopped, as this time Maggie was staring at her. "What?" Bette asked her, "didn't your folks ever take you to see *"A Christmas Carol*?" Maggie shook her head, and spoke.

"No, but even if they had, I don't think I could have used the story in an argument like this. And you even recognized Jimmy quoting from it earlier?"

"Well," Bette grinned slightly, "I have to admit that I actually acted in it for two Christmas seasons in our community theatre. It was fun, and I really came to understand the true importance of the story. Scrooge *really* changed." She turned back to Jimmy. "He changed, and you said yourself that you have changed. The whole world is changing. Take a look at Eastern Europe. The Berlin Wall may even be coming down – next thing we hear, there may be no more Soviet Union. If entire societies and belief systems and world powers can rise and fall in our short lifetimes, don't you think it is possible for us to change individually during the same span of time?" Bette stopped with this question.

"I never really thought about it in those terms," Jimmy admitted.

"I can't say that I had, either, before now," Bette admitted herself, "but it seems logical, right?" Jimmy and Maggie both nodded, and Maggie spoke.

"Let me tell you what won't seem logical, but what I know Jackson has been thinking about and studying." She turned and spoke directly to Jimmy. "You may be doubting yourself so much because it's not your nature to change."

"What do you know about my nature?" Jimmy asked, but not in an agitated tone.

"Well, we really need to have Jackson here to explain it, but I think he would start by admitting that no one can truly know the thoughts of another person, and he would prefer that we talk in universal terms. He would say that it is not *our* nature to change," she motioned around the table. "I'm not ready to explain that, you'll have to ask him; but, I can comment about your tendencies, because I feel like I live with you. I absolutely live with your art, and I doubt that you would deny that it tells me something about your nature," Maggie said quietly. Jimmy did not argue with her. "Your songs almost always talk about the need for people to change, to adapt to their circumstances, but now you seem to be telling us that you can't. I think that's what Jackson was trying to say. He focused on what you do for him, but implicit in his commentary is a statement important to you – your art isn't just coming from you." She paused, and swallowed. "God is talking through you, and to you, and He is able to bring about the change you need."

"God?" Jimmy rolled his eyes, and pushed his chair back again. "Not you, too? What are you all up to? I thought you liked me. Why are you attacking me with God?"

"*We* aren't. Jackson is the thinker in our marriage. I'm just trying to interpret him a little for you. You seemed to want it, but I'm not trying to corner you."

"It crossed my mind to do that to you," he looked directly at her.

"Hey!" Bette spoke sharply.

"It's okay," Maggie waved her hand. "He's just being honest – I think, or just trying to change the subject." Jimmy nodded, and relaxed as he leaned back in to the table. "Either way, I'm flattered, but all that says is that you are thinking about things differently. I assume you haven't usually thought twice about such an action? You're married, right?" Instantly she felt naïve, acting as if the question was relevant to the discussion.

"Sort of," Jimmy answered truthfully. "We've been separated for years." Relieved that he had taken her question seriously, Maggie tried to reply seriously.

"I don't want to pry into that situation, but I would suggest that you take whatever energy that generated your comment to me and invest it in your marriage." Again, she was shocked at her assertiveness, only this time she was concerned about being condescending, rather than naïve.

"I have," Jimmy answered, "it just doesn't get me anywhere."

"Then I'd say you should just keep trying," Bette stepped in for Maggie. "You didn't get where you are today by giving up easily. I'm sure you made more than a few mistakes and compromises along the way, but that ought to just add to your resolve in this instance. You care. I can hear it in your voice, and see it in your face. I didn't need Jackson's higher criticism to prove that." They were all silent for more than a minute, but it did not seem awkward. They each had something to consider, carefully. Jimmy was nodding his head to himself conclusively, when Maggie spoke again.

"But you realize that Jackson wasn't talking about your marriage, right?" Jimmy looked at her, puzzled again. "No, and he wasn't really talking about your work, either." Now Jimmy leaned forward again, waiting for an explanation. "You know," Maggie digressed, "I read a quote from someone in your industry in *People* magazine this week." Bette laughed. "I know," Maggie admitted, "the source doesn't really stack up with the stuff you guys have been quoting all night, but I think the quote does. The musician was talking about finding some meaning to his life. He said something like 'I've got no family, no self-respect – I've put everything into the rock and roll business, and I don't think they're going to give me a crown for it in heaven.'"

Bette exhaled more smoke, and an audible "Hmm" came with it. Maggie kept her focus on Jimmy.

"Didn't you hear Jackson asking you that question? He said you are, we all are, instruments in the hands of God

– even Nebuchadnezzar, even he might not be an enemy of God? Of the Jews, yes, but not necessarily of God." Reacting to the surprised looks, she offered more. "I can't believe I remember Jackson telling me this, but in the Book of Daniel God calls Nebuchadnezzar his servant! If that is so, why can't you be?" Jimmy shifted back in his chair. "You dismiss it now," Maggie responded, "but have you really thought about it? You just said fame and fortune aren't what people think. Obviously, you want more. You *need* more." She paused just long enough to glance at Bette and make sure that she was still with her. Betted nodded encouragingly. "Look," she continued, "I don't know this stuff anywhere near as well as Jackson, or Bette. You may even have had more instruction in this than me with your schooling, but one concept Jackson has helped me understand – and which makes perfect sense to me - ought to hit home with you." Jimmy leaned forward again, ready to hear. "It's the simple question Jesus asked the rich man: 'what will it profit a man to gain the whole world, and lose his own soul?' You're getting the whole world Jimmy, but who's getting your soul? That's the question Jackson really wanted to ask you. That's what he's wanted to ask from the moment your music grabbed hold of him. I think he would have gotten around to it if the waiter hadn't stopped him. So, whatever you think of your wife, or your marriage or your manager or your friends or fans, or George or Bette or me or Jackson, all that matters ultimately, is what you think of Jesus. That's the question Jackson thinks you are asking in your music – not of him or any other fan – but of yourself. You may not have been acting like Jesus owes you a favor, but he's still too smart for you to fool."

Maggie stopped as the weight of her words pressed in upon them all. She could not imagine where they had come from, just like the words that had sprung forth the night she met Jackson. She fought the urge to retract them all, to apologize to Jimmy, or to simply run out of the room. She focused on Bette for stability, fearing that the room might start spinning, like her mind. Bette sat stoically smoking, not passing judgment on her, or Jimmy. Maggie wanted someone to answer her, but she couldn't bring herself to press Jimmy any further. She had said all that she could – more than she thought possible, or had ever even thought about, consciously, on these issues. In truth, the theory she had advanced was unimaginable to her just fifteen minutes before, and perhaps still even now. She couldn't stand the silence any longer, and resolved to speak again. She would not back down. She opened her mouth to say, in conclusion, that it was Jimmy's decision, not hers, but a decision that must be made. Indecision was a decision – wonder and perish - but before the words formed, the door to the cottage opened and George and Jackson entered, looking serious. Jackson held his arm out in front of him, palm upturned, with a thin object reverently presented between his thumb and ring finger. It looked to Maggie like a fragment of Scripture.

XXXVII

Well, Jimmy thought, is there really a Hell?

XXXVIII

"Why do you look so serious?" Bette asked, as George and Jackson reached the table.

"Oh, nothing much," George faked indifference, "just that Jackson's become a part of Tarpon history."

"U.S. history, you mean," Jackson corrected him, finally smiling at Maggie. George had been looking at Jimmy, and was puzzled by his blank stare.

"What have you all been up to?" He asked, then added, "Jimmy, you look like you've seen a ghost."

"A Holy Ghost, I would say," Bette interrupted. "Right, Maggie?" Maggie nodded. "But what's this about you being part of American history? And what are you holding?" Bette asked. Jackson presented the tarpon scale, still fingering it reverently. George answered for him.

"This scale proves that Jackson belongs to the great tradition of Tarpon, Texas, and U.S. Presidents." The others leaned forward to examine the scale, now resting on the tablecloth in front of Maggie. "As for Tarpon, we are told this is the biggest tarpon docked here in over thirty years, and the first in over twenty. As for the country, well, Jackson Riddle's fish miraculously weighed in at the same weight as the one Franklin Roosevelt caught here in *1937. 77lbs, 8 ounces!*" He finished with a flourish befitting a true historical account.

"Oh, come on! You're pulling my leg, for real, this time," Maggie protested. Bette let out a sigh with the exhale of her cigarette, and Jimmy remained quiet.

"Was I pulling your leg when I took Jackson fishing with Jimmy Buffett?" George asked. "You can see him for yourself." They all looked at Jimmy, and he finally managed a slight smile. George continued. "Now you can see this scale. That's what you would call documentary proof, right Jackie?" Jackson nodded. Maggie, Bette and even Jimmy looked down again, closer this time, and could see the numbers and Jackson's signature below them. Having read the testimony, they all looked back at George, who continued his recitation. "You can compare those numbers with the ones on the scale in Scottie's office, but I'm telling you they're the same. And the *Jetty Caller* is vouching for the accuracy of both. You aren't going to challenge the truthfulness of American journalism, are you?" He waited again, and could see that neither Maggie, Bette or Jimmy knew what to say. He turned to Jackson. "I think they're in shock, Mr. President."

"They sort of looked that way when we came in," Jackson observed. "Was it our return, or the tarpon's or something else?" He asked, looking first at Maggie and then letting his gaze drift to Bette, and finally to Jimmy. Again, all three hesitated. Finally, Bette spoke.

"Well, I think Maggie and I were doing a pretty good job shocking Jimmy here while you were gone. We touched on a few topics that might be as weighty as Jackson's fish, if not even matching his place in history." She managed to return to her usual confident tone, as she stamped out her cigarette. Still, Jimmy remained silent, and Maggie concentrated on the tarpon scale, as if waiting for it to speak. George could tell that the topic had not been fully explored, and went around the table to sit in his old seat.

"Don't tell me," he said, "that you two picked up where

Jackson left off." This brought a laugh from Maggie and Bette together, but no explanation. George exclaimed, "how could you even tell where he was, let alone where he might have stopped? We just went over the territory again while in the office, and I still don't know where we've been." He stopped, and finally Jimmy spoke.

"That's because you have no sense of irony, George. You introduce me to a group of your friends, and we both think they are really interesting, but then we discover that they are all fundamentalists." He said this emphatically, but without malice. "I thought they all died in the 60's," he added, and then he looked at Jackson. "What's this opinion you have about human nature? Maggie says you think I can't change?" Jackson looked at Maggie, and she again nodded her permission.

"Well," Jackson said, "if you really want to know." He took a deep breath, and then slowly descended into his seat between Maggie and George. "I guess I could start with Paul's assertion to the church in Corinth that, 'the message of the cross is foolishness to those who are perishing.' If that isn't fundamentalist enough for you, I can go deeper by talking about the depravity of man." He paused, expecting an objection or at least a derisive response, but surprisingly, no one spoke, not even Jimmy. "Ok," Jackson, said, and hesitated for another instant before continuing, "then, I really don't want to speak in terms of *your* nature personally, but I can give you my theology of human nature in general." Again, he paused, and took another deep breath. Finally, he concluded that it was the time to speak. "I believe it is against *our* nature to change. Left to our own devices, without any social support systems or civil restrictions, we would each go off in one direction – a bad one - and never look back."

"*Lord of the Flies*..." Jimmy suggested.

"Exactly." Jackson said. "That's an extreme example,

but a good one. History is full of cases where seemingly normal, decent people have done abnormal, horrible things – sometimes in remote isolation after a shipwreck, other times in the middle of main street America, and sometimes in entire industrialized, first-world countries. Haven't you ever wondered about that?"

"Of course I have," Jimmy responded, "but I think I concluded a long time ago that I would never understand it, and so I live – and write – my way around it."

Again, Maggie and Bette sang a line from one of Buffett's songs, only this time they started and finished together. Jimmy smiled at the women and at Jackson, who again took up his analysis.

"And change, or the need to accept change, either by attitude or latitude, is such a central theme in your music. It shows up over and over in your songs, not just that one. On your first album, there's a song called *Bend a Little*, where you say 'you've got to bend a little no matter which side you're on, or you'll soon be gone.' Then there's *Cowboy in the Jungle*, where you say 'you've got to roll with the punches', and *Somewhere Over China,* where you say you need 'to put a little distance between causes and effects.' Now, most people would simply describe your view as 'escapism.' I don't mean that as a criticism. It is, as you just said, the basis of your belief system, and one that has served you pretty well up to now. Obviously, a lot of other people buy into your approach."

"Assuming they really think about it," George interjected.

"But they don't have to, see," Jackson countered. "That's the amazing thing about Jimmy's music – it conveys this profound philosophical conclusion in a flippant, irreverent manner. So people can embrace it completely, without even thinking about it. Those of us who do think about it come to the same sense of acceptance, but only after following your tracks down many winding paths – 'songlines' I think you call them."

"Okay," Jimmy interrupted Jackson, "you mentioned that earlier. 'Songlines' have been a central theme of my writing for some time, but no one seems to have picked up on it."

"Oh, I think you are wrong again. I've read Chatwin. I think my songline is in Texas, but I'm not sure which part, yet. Anyway, you know what it means, don't you?" Jackson asked.

"Of course. It means that I feel this sense of being guided through my life – that I was supposed to be wherever I found myself at any given time." He stopped and looked around the room, as if to see if anyone was listening in. Seeing no one, he continued, now almost whispering. "It's my sense of destiny."

"Exactly," Jackson almost whispered back, but with emphasis, and then continued, gradually returning to his normal voice. "Why are you so hesitant to admit that? It's at the core of your philosophy, and it's probably in everything you've ever written. My question is not about your destiny, *yet,* but whether you understand where it comes from. Where do you get that feeling that you were meant to do this or that?"

"I haven't really spent much time on that one; I've been too busy following the feeling," Jimmy said.

"That's funny, because I've spent all my time just trying to figure out where it *comes* from. You should be thankful that you've had the clearer sense of what it is, rather than why it is," Jackson said.

"I honestly don't think I've ever doubted what I was supposed to do," Jimmy answered. "I may have been unsure exactly how it would work out, but I knew a long time ago how I wanted to go about it, and I've done that, without ever getting around to questioning whether it was my destiny."

"Well, actually, the apostle Paul – and John Calvin – would call it *pre*-destiny, and that's why I say it's not our nature to change, but really that's another discussion." He paused one more time, and took a deep breath, as if about to swim the length of the pool underwater. "So, how do you think you just know what to do?" Jackson asked Jimmy.

"You're going to tell me that it comes from above, aren't you?" Jimmy said, cautiously.

"You wouldn't feel like this if it wasn't coming from above," Jackson answered. "You should recognize that yourself, but since you asked, I can at least give you a little empirical evidence." George gave a cough and looked ready to break his long silence. "Hey, I am a lawyer, remember?" Jackson said, before George could speak. He glanced quickly at George, and then just as quickly looked back at Jimmy to continue. "Do you know how many times you mention God or Jesus, or refer to religion in your music?" Jimmy didn't answer, but Jackson didn't really wait for a response. "Much more than you talk about drinking or sex." Bette coughed this time, and Jackson snapped his head toward her. "It's true! He's got maybe two or three songs each about drinking and sex, and I have counted at least twenty where he mentions God prominently." He turned back to Jimmy. "Even one of your album titles is a reference to Jesus." Jimmy gave him a confused look. "Don't you know who actually wrote riddles in the sand?" Again, Jimmy remained silent.

"Is that where you got your album title from?" George asked him, suddenly interested in the connection.

"I don't think so," Jimmy mumbled softly.

"I would like to imagine that Jimmy chose that title knowingly, but we can give him a little grace on that score. I am referring to Jesus, and the story found in the Gospel of John. You all may not have picked up the reference, but you surely know the story of the woman caught in adultery," Jackson said.

"So that is where Jimmy got the name," George repeated his comment, but this time not as a question.

"Be serious, George," Jackson said, "because this story is very serious to me. I'm sure you know it, or at least the punchline - 'let he who is without sin cast the first stone' – but John also tells us that after Jesus said this to the Pharisees who were accusing the woman, he stooped down and wrote in the sand in front of them." Jackson looked again at Jimmy, who was now looking more apprehensive than confused, and then to Bette and Maggie, who were both shaking their heads in agreement, or wonder. Turning back to Jimmy, Jackson took another breath, and continued. "The text doesn't tell us what He wrote in the sand, but it says that as He was writing the men started to leave – the older men first, and then the younger ones – each leaving without saying anything and, of course, without throwing a stone. Tradition in the church teaches that what Jesus wrote was the sins of each of the men – or that they each recognized it as an account of their own sin, just as each had heard the Gospel in his own language on the day of Pentecost, causing them to be 'pierced to their heart.' I really like that, because it underscores who Jesus was – or what He is. He is the omniscient God. He knows each of us personally, and yet He still loves us, and forgives us. I also like to think that what Jesus was actually writing in the sand were the names of each of the woman's accusers, followed by a question mark. That would be the ultimate riddle in the sand: 'who do you say that Jesus is?'"

He leaned in closer toward Jimmy, and looked as intently as he could at his idol. "Maybe you did know there was a connection, Jimmy, when you chose your album title, because there's a song on it called "Bigger Than The Both of Us." In it, you sing, "I'm keeping heaven on my mind." I know you didn't write that line, but at least you were singing it. And why would you be thinking of Heaven at a time of apparent mutual infidelity, unless you knew it was where you will find forgiveness and redemption?" Jimmy didn't look confused now, but stunned.

Jackson decided it was time to give him a break, of sorts, and he addressed the others. "You heard our discussion earlier about his first album, and his song '*The Christian*.' Also on that record were a couple of songs that talk about hanging out with God's children, and saying that we'll understand things better when 'we finally reach His home and walk among the stars.' That song is ostensibly about why God doesn't own a car." He sent a sheepish look to Maggie, and then once again turned back to Jimmy. "In coming up with that idea, I'll bet you got inspiration from more than just the co-writer who is credited in the notes."

Jimmy's face now seemed incredulous, and Jackson pointed at him.

"That's the same way people have reacted to this realization throughout the ages, even from His own time on Earth. The Scriptures give us two perfect examples in the Samaritan woman at the well, who ran wildly through town telling all her friends that 'He told me everything I ever did,' and Nathaniel, who was awe-struck when Jesus told him He had seen him sitting under the fig tree even though Nathaniel knew that he had been many miles away at the time. They both were confronted with the daunting question of how to react when you become truly aware of the Lord of the Universe, and realize that he is aware of you. How will you react, Jimmy?

"That's what you all want to know?" Jimmy answered immediately, looking first at Jackson, and then to Bette and George and, finally, to Maggie.

"We do, but for your sake, not ours," Maggie said, and then turned to Jackson, who was smiling broadly at Jimmy.

"You wouldn't believe me, even if I told you," Jimmy said.

Lightning Source UK Ltd.
Milton Keynes UK
UKHW011857161220
375343UK00001B/78